CUNNINGHAM
SECURITY
DESPERATE

A.K. EVANS

Cover Artist
cover artwork © Sarah Hansen, Okay Creations
www.okaycreations.com

Formatting
Stacey Blake at Champagne Book Design
www.champagnebookdesign.com

Editing & Proofreading
Ellie McLove, My Brother's Editor
www.grayinkonline.com

DEDICATION

To anyone who has ever struggled in life. Because it sucks and you're not alone!

PROLOGUE

Ekko

THE CLOCK ON THE MICROWAVE INDICATED IT WAS JUST AFTER eleven-thirty at night. I had just crept down the hall to the kitchen to find something to eat. There was one can of chicken noodle soup left in my backpack, but I wouldn't be able to cook it without running the risk of waking my mom. I prayed I'd find something else in the house.

Opening the refrigerator, I saw it had nothing but beer and two-week-old leftover Chinese food inside of it. That food wasn't mine. It probably belonged to one of her men. I knew better than to take the food that didn't belong to me. The cabinets were bare, other than a few canned goods. My mother didn't keep the house stocked with food. Any money she had was spent on keeping her drunk and drugged up, which she apparently preferred over making sure she and her daughter were fed. When a man came over and they got their fix, sometimes he'd bring food. If there was enough, she'd eat.

I couldn't remember the last time she went to an actual grocery store. She might occasionally take a trip to the corner store to pick up a few things, but even those were rare.

So rare that I was in this predicament again.

Hungry.

No food in the house.

A mother who didn't care.

Sadly, I had grown used to the growling and the empty feeling I always felt in my belly these days and it looked like tonight would be another one of those nights I'd go to bed with nothing in my stomach. I hadn't had anything since lunchtime yesterday at school, which was mostly my own fault.

On that thought, I quietly made my way down the dark hallway back to my bedroom. If I hadn't spent the last two days after school at the library, I would have had enough time to come home and make the soup before my mom got home. I hated being here, so I stayed at the one place I had that gave me just a shred of peace and happiness.

The local library.

I guessed that most parents would have been worried sick if their child hadn't come home after school, but I learned quickly that the less my mother and I were around each other, the better. Wanting to avoid her after the encounter we had two nights ago, I figured it was best to just wait until I knew it was safe to come home. Thankfully, being able to sit down in a clean, comfortable chair at the library and spend hours reading never felt like a chore.

As soon as I arrived there, I quickly got any homework I had to do completed and then I spent the rest of my time reading. I consume books of nearly every genre, but my favorite is romance. I dream that one day I'll find a love like I read about in those books. That there will be a good man with whom to spend my days. That he'll stick around, unlike my own father, who walked out before I was even born. That he won't leer at young fifteen-year-old girls like the men who come around to see my mother do to me. That he'll love me, respect me, and protect me. I hope he'll make me feel like I am special. Most of all, I hope to be able to have a home with him that'll be unlike what I've lived in to this point.

That thought settled in me as I closed my bedroom door. Bedroom doesn't quite seem like the right word for it, though. There isn't even a real bed. Instead, I've got a small mattress thrown on the floor in the tiny room. There's a thin sheet covering the old mattress and a tattered, torn blanket for me to cover up with. Aside from that, I've got my backpack, a small dresser with some clothes, and a pair of worn-out sneakers.

With no other options and unable to ignore the rumbling in my stomach, I pulled the can of soup out of my backpack. I opened the front pouch that I put a plastic spoon in yesterday at school and lifted the tab on the soup can to remove the lid.

Cold soup.

It was better than nothing.

I sat in the middle of the mattress, struggling to eat slowly. It was difficult to control the urge to satisfy the hunger quickly. I forced myself not to hurry through it, though, realizing that if I could feel full on just half the can, I could save the rest for tomorrow.

As I sat there eating, my thoughts drifted to Ms. Grace. It was on nights like this when I missed her the most. Ms. Grace used to be our neighbor at the apartment building where we lived. She was an elderly, black woman who wore pretty dresses, gave incredible hugs, and treated me better than my own mother did. She didn't spend her days drunk or high on drugs. She was the kindest, most gentle soul I'd ever known. Sometimes, when my mother had one of her men over, I'd sneak out and knock on Ms. Grace's door.

"Oh, dear child," she said when she opened the door and saw me standing there for the first time. "Come inside."

I suspected she knew what was happening inside my own apartment, but she never made me feel bad about my situation. I was only seven years old the first time I knocked on her door. She allowed me to come inside, where we watched television together. We watched Jeopardy and Wheel of Fortune regularly from that point forward. And every night I managed to sneak out, she'd make sure I was fed. The first night, with me being an unexpected visitor, she made me a peanut butter and jelly sandwich. Every night after that, there was always a warm meal waiting to fill me up.

But she died six months ago.

And now I was eating cold soup, alone and in the dark.

I think she knew it was coming because two months before she passed away, she started giving me extra food to take with me.

"A snack for later," she'd insist, watching me intently until I put the food in my backpack.

Given that I was older, I didn't need to sneak out like I did when I was little. As the years went on, my mother became more and more dependent on her alcohol and drugs. She spent more time passed out than awake, so it was easy for me to make daily visits to Ms. Grace. I knew that she was the kind of person I aspired to be. She taught me what a real mother does, and it saddened me that she never had the opportunity to have children of her own.

"Wallace and I tried to have children, but it just wasn't in the cards for us," she admitted to me two years ago. "But we had each other and that was enough for us."

"Was he nice?" I asked.

She smiled, and it lit up her whole face. "He was the best man I'd ever known. In the fifty-five years we were married, there was never a single negative exchange. At least, not on his part. I had moments where I was moody as does happen to us women sometimes, and he always saw me through those times with love and tenderness. We had the occasional debate about things, but even in those discussions, he never denied me the right to my feelings. And he always made me laugh. That was the most important thing for me because what's life about if you can't laugh and be happy?"

I sighed, "I hope I can meet a man like Mr. Wallace one day."

"You will, my child. You just keep yourself focused on finishing up school and taking care of yourself. Don't get distracted by the things surrounding you. If you do what you've got to do to become the woman you want to be, he'll find you."

From that day forward, I knew I'd never forget the many lessons she imparted on me or the way she made me feel.

Now, as I sat here alone with the last can of soup I had from her, I fought the urge to break down. I missed her.

I missed her hugs.

Her kindness.

Her words.

Her company.

As much as I wanted to give in to that sadness, I didn't. I needed to stay strong and focused on what I had to do because I made a vow to myself and to her. The day I turned eighteen, I would walk away and never look back.

I wouldn't become my mother. I wouldn't choose drugs and alcohol and men over my child.

I was only a month away from turning sixteen. Then, I'd be able to get a job at the library and start saving. I'd only use what I had to just to feed myself and the rest of it would be saved. I had my plan. I only needed to wait a month to put it into action.

On that thought, halfway through my can of soup, I put

the resealable top back on and laid down to sleep.

Three days later, my plan was blown to smithereens.

The police barged in and arrested my mother along with her guy of the week.

I was put into foster care.

CHAPTER 1

Ekko
Almost Thirteen Years Later

"**G**O HOME EARLY, EKKO," MY BOSS, AND THE OWNER OF THE diner I worked at, ordered.

"It's okay, Jerry," I replied as I refilled the iced tea for one of my regulars, George. "I just need a second."

I topped off the glass, took in a deep breath willing the pain away, and walked back out to deliver the drink.

"Are you alright, dear?" George asked when I approached the booth.

I winced in pain, but tried to reassure him, "Yeah, I'm just not feeling the best today."

"You don't look well. Maybe you should head home early," he suggested.

"I'll be alright," I insisted.

After setting George's iced tea down, I went back into the kitchen. Placing my palms on the countertop, I looked down, closed my eyes, and took a few steadying breaths.

"You've been working double shifts for two weeks straight now," Jerry noted. "Take the rest of the night off."

I craned my neck and looked at him. "I need the money, Jerry."

And I did. I still had two and a half hours left before my

shift ended and I was so close to having enough money saved up.

"You can barely serve one table before you're back here doubled over in pain. You're dead on your feet. I don't know what's wrong with you, but I do know that you at least need to get some rest. Go home now. I don't want to see you back here until just before the dinner rush tomorrow."

I was supposed to work breakfast, lunch, and dinner tomorrow.

"But—" I managed to get out before I was cut off.

"It's not up for discussion, Ekko. I'll see to it that you're paid for working the full shift tonight. Cash out with Christie and come back to my office before you go. I'll have your pay-check ready."

I was so close to having enough. I couldn't leave now. "Jerry…please. I'm supposed to work all day tomorrow. I'll go tonight, but don't take more than half the day tomorrow away from me."

"Sorry, kiddo. You need a break. Cash out and come see me for your paycheck," he insisted before turning and walking away toward his office.

"Damn it," I hissed under my breath.

I did as Jerry instructed and ten minutes later, I was in my car on my way home. It's not exactly my home. It's actually my ex-boyfriend's apartment. Things have gone from bad to worse for me over the last couple of months and I ended up losing my apartment. Having no other options, I accepted Ryan's offer to move in with him.

Ryan is the only person with whom I have a long-standing connection. I have my co-workers, but the extent of my relationship with them doesn't go much past work. Ryan and I were in an on-again, off-again relationship for three and a half years. Recently, things between us have gotten to the point where I feel like he could live with or without me. For much longer than these last couple months, I've had that nagging feeling deep down that he's not 'the one' for me. So, while we weren't together anymore, I was staying with him. The longer I stay at his place without us being together, the more strained things become. I've come back from work and heard him with other women in his bedroom. Even though we aren't together and I don't want to be with him anymore, it would be tough for anyone to hear that.

Ultimately, Ryan was being decent to me and was willing to give me some time to sort things out, but I had until the end of this month to find new living arrangements. I only have four days left and have been working hard to get as much cash together as I can for a new place. I had already spoken with the landlord at a spot not far from where I worked. I needed eighteen hundred dollars to cover first and last month's rent along with one month's rent for a security deposit. I only had fifteen hundred. If I could have finished out my night tonight and worked my full day tomorrow, I am certain I would have made the extra money I needed. Now, I wasn't so sure.

I couldn't blame Jerry. His heart was in the right place. Unfortunately, him being a genuinely good person didn't help my financial situation. He knew I had lost my apartment, but he didn't know my current predicament. And sadly, unbearable stomach cramps, an indication that my period would be arriving sometime within the next week, had made things even more rotten.

My life hadn't been anything special to this point, and to be honest, I didn't think things could get any worse. Sure, I'd gotten used to it, but I wasn't sure how much bad stuff one person was supposed to shoulder.

After pulling into the parking spot at the apartment complex, I turned off my car, grabbed my bag, and walked to the door. I was going to take Jerry's advice and get some rest. Hopefully, I'd feel better in the morning.

But when I walked in, I realized I had been wrong. Things could get worse. I stood frozen for a minute as three sets of eyes stared back at me. One set belonged to Ryan, the other two were men that I didn't know. And it seemed my ex was in the middle of a drug deal.

"Ekko?" Ryan called, his surprise evident.

"You're doing drugs?" I snapped.

"Why are you back early?" he retorted.

I shook my head and walked to the spare bedroom. No way. I was not staying here. Aside from my bed and a small dresser, I didn't have much here, but what I did have was all that I had. So, I quickly grabbed my things that I could move and started packing them up. It couldn't have been more than three or four minutes when the door opened and Ryan walked in. I didn't make eye contact; I just kept packing.

"What are you doing?" he asked.

"Leaving," I returned.

"Where are you going to go?"

Without acknowledging him, I moved through the room and put the last of my things into my bag.

Gathering my bag up off the bed, I began walking toward the front door.

"Ekko?" Ryan attempted getting my attention again.

When I made it to the front door, he grabbed my wrist. I turned around, yanking my arm away, and seethed, "Don't ever touch me again!"

"Stop and talk to me first," he begged.

I shook my head. "Not a chance."

"I'm not doing drugs, Ekko. I only sell. You can't go to the cops."

I opened the door, stepped outside, and turned back to

look at him one last time. "Newsflash, Ryan! Selling drugs doesn't make you any better than the people that use them. And you *know* how I feel about drugs, which is precisely why I'm not staying here. I don't have a say over what you do, but I refuse to be anywhere where something like that is going on. This is it for me, Ryan. I am officially done with you. I'll be back in a few days to get my bed and the rest of my stuff."

At that, I took what I had in my hand and walked to my car. After tossing my bag in the back seat, I got in and drove off.

Forty minutes later, I was beyond exhausted, in heaps of pain, and had nowhere to go. I eventually settled on spending the night in my car. So, I drove to a place I hadn't been to in weeks. I was spending the night in the parking lot of the Windsor Public Library. While I could have gotten a hotel for the night, that would have required spending money that I really didn't want to part with. If I couldn't get all the money I needed together within the next day or two, I'd have to consider spending the money for a night at a hotel just so I could grab a shower.

On that thought, I lowered the back of my seat down and reached in the backseat for my fleece-lined sweatshirt. After wrapping it around myself, I did my best to ignore the pain in my belly and lingering nausea.

On the bright side, the pain in my stomach just barely overshadowed the loneliness in my heart. I couldn't believe the one person I'd grown attached to, the one person who knew what I grew up with, was hiding a secret so devastating from me. Maybe he didn't owe me any explanations since we weren't together anymore, but that didn't change the fact that it still hurt. I couldn't even begin to process how it all made me feel, so I gave in to the pain and exhaustion and closed my eyes.

The sun hadn't even begun to shine when I woke up, shivering. It was the middle of October, so the sun was coming up later and later and the overnight lows were in the mid-twenties. I turned the key one click in the ignition and waited while the digital clock lit up. It was just before six in the morning. I needed some heat, so I turned on the car. Idling away my gas wasn't a smart idea, so I figured I'd let the car run long enough to warm it up and then I'd shut it off again.

In three hours, the library would open and I'd at least be able to go in, use the bathroom, splash some water on my face, and stay warm. For now, I hoped I'd be able to heat the car up enough that I could get comfortable again and fall asleep for a few more hours.

It was just after ten thirty when I woke up again. I was grateful I was no longer frozen, but I needed to use the restroom. Once the seat was upright, I scooped up my handbag and got out.

After I handled my priority of relieving my bladder and making sure I looked half decent, I went out to my favorite spot in the library. Walking through the adult fiction section, I found one of my favorite romance authors and pulled out a book. I needed to get lost in a different world for a bit. If I gave myself the time to sit and think about the harsh reality of my current situation, I'd certainly have a nervous breakdown. I knew it'd be much better for me to get caught up in someone else's problems, even if they were fictional, than to focus on my own.

This had been my life for years. Continuously rehashing in my mind just how bad things have been for me since I was a kid wouldn't do me any good. With my mind made up, I grabbed a free cup of tea and a donut from the tray that was set out every morning and curled up in one of the cozy chairs to get lost. The warm tea certainly helped with the lingering, but thankfully much less severe, cramps.

Several hours later, I'd been through a gamut of emotions. There was a happy-ever-after ending and that's what mattered most for me. I had to believe in the fairytale. Knowing that there was still a possibility for a chance at happiness, despite any trials or tribulations, is what kept me going every day.

I noted the time was three o'clock, so I gathered my things and made my way back out to the car. I crawled into the back seat, where I changed into clean clothes before driving off to work.

When I walked in fifteen minutes before my shift was set to start, I held my breath as Jerry took in my appearance. I didn't want to get him or any of the staff involved in my problems and I hoped he wouldn't be able to tell that I'd spent the night in my car. Thankfully, he gave me a simple smile and a nod of his head before he got back to work. I took off to the back office, where I put my purse away and got ready to start.

It was a busy shift, which I wasn't sure I'd ever been more grateful for. Even with the dinner rush, I still didn't have enough money for an apartment, but I was certainly much closer.

Thirty minutes before my shift ended, I put in my order for a triple-decker turkey club sandwich. It came with a side of fries, so I figured I'd be able to eat those tonight while they were warm, but that the sandwich would hold up well until tomorrow. Of course, I had enough money to buy myself the meal and eat it all tonight, but if I wasn't smart about rationing the food I did purchase, it would just take longer to get into my own place. I was working a double shift tomorrow, so I knew if I could manage to tough it out for another night or two I'd have enough to be in my own place again.

After cashing out for the evening, I paid for my food and left. Before I drove to the library parking lot, I decided to make a quick stop at the drugstore just down the road. I was struggling to part with the cash, but considering I hadn't showered since before work the day before, I needed to do something. I had deodorant in my bag in the car and figured I could use some baby wipes to freshen up a bit. My hair didn't require a daily washing to look decent, so I lucked out there, but I couldn't go more than another two days without it needing a good wash. I prayed I'd have enough money for the apartment saved up before then.

Once I made my purchase, I drove to the spot I parked in the night before. I ate my fries slowly, knowing I could possibly save some for the next day if I could eat only just enough to take away the empty feeling in my stomach. I managed to have a quarter of them left by the time I closed the container and shrugged on my heavy sweatshirt before slipping my arms through the sleeves of my jacket.

While my mind was in survival mode, keeping me going from one day to the next, as I tried to find sleep I couldn't help but allow the hollow feeling in my heart to take over. It was starting to hit me just how horribly I'd failed at life. I hated to think how disappointed Ms. Grace would have been with me for not finding a way to follow my dreams.

All I wanted, all I still hoped for, was a real career as a librarian. A career and, dare I say, a family. I wanted to be part of something. I wanted to feel like I belonged somewhere and that I was loved by someone. Someone who'd want to raise a family with me one day. And maybe just a friend or two to be there when I needed a good laugh or a shoulder to cry on. But I could barely afford to feed myself, so my dreams had to take a back seat. At the rate things were going, though, I didn't think I'd ever get to chase them.

As visions of unread books, a faceless husband, and tiny children danced through my mind, my tears soaked into the headrest and I fell asleep.

The next morning came quickly. I was beyond tired, especially because it had been significantly colder on night two of sleeping in my car. My shift at work started at eleven and it was only quarter past nine. That would give me enough time to go in and use the bathroom at the library, grab a free coffee and donut, and then read a few chapters of a book. I decided today, though, that I'd actually borrow a few books from the library. I didn't have a whole lot of free time, but if I could manage to read instead of thinking about how miserable I'd been feeling, it was worth it.

Before I knew it, I was back at the diner and my day was flying by. It wasn't overly busy, but it had been steady. Just after the lunch rush, I took my break and had my club sandwich from the night before. Then, just under an hour before my shift was set to end, Jerry walked back into the kitchen and said, "Ekko, you've got someone at table four."

"On it," I replied as I walked back out into the dining area.

I hadn't taken more than seven or eight steps toward the direction of table four when I saw who it was. I'd only ever seen him once before, but it was a face I knew I never forget.

The man who saved my life a few months ago.

Dom.

I didn't know his last name or anything else about him other than he worked for a private investigation company—I didn't even know which one. I also knew he was one of the most breathtaking men I'd ever seen. He was tall, which I knew wasn't saying much since I was five foot two and nearly everybody was taller than me, but he was easily six foot two or three. He had been wearing a baseball cap the night he saved my life and tonight he had on a beanie. He had what looked like a neatly groomed four or five days of dark scruff on his face. Dark-brown eyes, olive-toned skin, and a gorgeous smile.

It was all beautiful, but nothing came close to those dimples.

Ugh. I envied the woman that got to see those dimples daily. At least I could look at them now. Because he was here. And I was here because of what he did for me.

It was a few months ago, before I lost my apartment, when a man showed up at the diner. I'd been having my usual stroke of bad luck and the man offered an ear. He also offered me a job opportunity. I stupidly accepted his business card and agreed to meet him at a local tavern. When I showed up there and he didn't, I added it to my ever-growing list of disappointments. But when I left, things got worse. I drove back to my apartment, angry that I'd wasted not only my time but also my gas. When I got out of the car, I was almost abducted. Thankfully, before I was taken, Dom and another guy he worked with showed up.

I'll never forget what he did for me that night. Aside from rescuing me, stopping the abduction, and keeping me out of being thrown into a sex-trafficking ring, he showed so much concern for my physical and emotional well-being. He took me to the police station to give a statement and then saw me safely back to my apartment. I've held on to that memory for months and have always been upset that I didn't find out more about him so that I could have thanked him properly. At least now I'd have that opportunity.

"Dom," I greeted when I approached his table.

Something came over his face before he responded, "Ekko."

"You remember me?"

"Sugar, a face like yours isn't one that's easily forgotten."

He called me sugar. I couldn't deny the way that made me feel.

I offered him a friendly smile and shared, "Well, I'm happy you stopped in. I've been hoping I'd run into you."

His eyebrows shot up, silently questioning me.

"I've been meaning to thank you for what you did for me that night, but first, can I get you something to drink?"

He ordered a water and the grilled chicken over jasmine rice with steamed veggies. I guessed that was part of the reason he was in such excellent shape. He ate well.

After giving his order to the cook, I returned to his table with his water.

"So how are you doing?" he asked.

How embarrassing it would be if I told him the truth. "I'm here," I answered, hoping that'd satisfy his curiosity.

He was not the least bit content with my response and replied, "That's not saying much."

I shrugged my shoulders and countered, "It could always be worse, right?"

I'm not sure he liked that answer either, but it's all I was going to give him. I would have been mortified if he knew my situation. I suddenly felt very self-conscious.

"I'm going to go clean up a few tables. I'll be back shortly with your food," I said, excusing myself from the conversation.

I cleaned up the few tables from other patrons who had already left and went back to the kitchen. The night was winding down so I only had him and one other table that had already gotten their food and paid their bill. They were merely hanging out having a good time at this point.

I took Dom's food out to him, set it down, and asked, "Is there anything else I can get you?"

"I'm good for now," he replied.

I gave him a nod and offered, "Let me know if you need anything."

At that, I turned and walked away while he ate. Ten minutes later, my other customers had gotten up and left. I cleaned their table and mentally calculated how close I was to having enough for the apartment. I was still a hundred and twenty-five dollars shy of what I needed and considering I didn't work a double shift tomorrow, where I'd be certain to make up that money and then some, it looked like I'd have two more nights out in the cold.

Shaking off the thought, I went back to check on Dom. I was surprised to see that he had finished.

"I'm so sorry I didn't get back here sooner. I assume everything was alright with your order?"

He nodded.

"Can I get you any dessert or coffee?" I asked.

He thought a moment and shot back, "Will you join me for dessert?"

Dessert. I hadn't had dessert in…I couldn't even remember when I'd had dessert.

"Um, I'm not sure that's allowed," I replied.

"The man wants to have dessert with you, Ekko," Jerry startled me as he walked by. "There's nobody else in the diner and we're closing soon. You should have dessert with him."

I wanted the ground to swallow me up right there. Dom was way out of my league. I couldn't possibly have dessert with him.

"So, Ekko…what do you recommend we share for dessert?" Dom asked, his eyes twinkling and the dimples popping out.

I had no idea. I hadn't had any of the desserts. Desserts were a luxury I couldn't afford.

"Well, the most popular choices are either the brownie sundae or the chocolate peanut butter pie."

"Oh, tough choice. Let's do one of each and find out which is better."

I thought I might die. Two desserts. With the man who

saved my life.

Trying my hardest to hide my excitement, I agreed, "Okay." Then I moved quickly to get a brownie sundae and a piece of chocolate peanut butter pie.

It really wouldn't matter to me which tasted better.

CHAPTER 2

Dom

"**W**HAT DO YOU THINK?" I ASKED HER AFTER WE'D BOTH taken a bite of each dessert.

She scrunched up her nose in decision. "The brownie sundae. It's the perfect mix of hot and cold."

I couldn't help but smile at her. I'd been watching Ekko for months now. She had no idea that I'd been keeping an eye on her, though. After the night she was nearly kidnapped and thrown into a sex-trafficking ring, I vowed to look out for her. It was evident from the discussion I'd had with her that night that she didn't have anyone else around for her. She mentioned an on-again, off-again boyfriend, but that was it.

No family.

No friends.

I wasn't the kind of guy that would ever put myself in the position to come between people who were committed to each other. That said, I had no issues moving in when I knew things ended. And it was evident to me that things ended when I saw what I saw last night.

She always worked late. In fact, not only was she always working late, she was always just working. It angered me to see how much time she spent at the diner, especially over the last two weeks. Double shifts every day for two whole weeks.

As beautiful as she was, you would have had to have been blind to not be able to see how much of a toll the work was taking on her.

As a private investigator, I still had my own work that kept me busy daily. Even still, I always made it a priority to check in on Ekko. If anyone knew, if she knew, I might be labeled a stalker. But there was something about her. Something that continued to pull me toward her. She was always on my mind and I couldn't relax not knowing if she was safe.

When I arrived at the diner two nights ago, I was surprised to see her car was already gone. Wanting to make sure she had gotten back to her apartment safely, I drove there.

I knew it wasn't her apartment, but her boyfriend's instead. The night I was there to stop her abduction, she told me she was in a bad situation and was going to lose her apartment if she didn't get something figured out. I remembered her saying she had a boyfriend, but she also made it evident that she didn't want to have to resort to moving in with him. It gutted me to see her need to do that not long afterward when she needed a place to live. It was even worse when I saw where he lived. It wasn't a good area and it was littered with drug dealers.

When I made it to his place that night, her car wasn't there. I drove around town taking every possible route between the apartment and the diner trying to find her, but I didn't have any luck. It was difficult for me to find sleep that night. I didn't know her all that well, but for some reason, it bothered me not knowing if she was okay. The next day, I arrived at the diner much earlier than usual and saw her car there. I waited in the parking lot until I saw her inside. Over the last few weeks, her demeanor had changed. It was the worst I'd ever seen her. Other than being exhausted, there was a look of hopelessness and despair. I waited until the end of her shift and followed her when she left.

After making a stop at the drug store, she drove to the library. I knew she liked going to the library because prior to the last two weeks of working double shifts, she always made weekly trips there. She'd spend hours there sometimes. It was the only time I ever saw her smiling. But I couldn't understand why she was at the library so late at night, well after it had closed. She parked her car toward the back of the lot, where it wasn't as visible from the road. I waited to see where she was going to go, but she never got out. Two hours later, she still hadn't left her vehicle. I decided to take a chance and walk over. I'll never forget what I saw when I looked inside.

The most beautiful and heartbreaking sight I'd ever seen. Ekko was asleep in her car in the parking lot of the library. Sitting on the passenger's seat was a takeout container with a plastic lid through which I could see there was an uneaten sandwich and a handful of fries in it. But the worst thing I saw was her tear-stained cheeks. It took everything in me to not wake her up and take her home with me. I decided right then and there that I had to do something—I was not going to let this woman continue to live out of her car. I'd do whatever I could to help her get through this rough patch. That's precisely why I was here now eating desserts at close to eleven o'clock at night.

And I learned that Ekko liked the brownie sundae best.

"Then it's yours," I offered the rest of the dessert to her.

She looked back down at the dessert like it was the greatest thing she'd ever been offered before her wide eyes came up to look at me. Then, she looked down at the chocolate peanut butter pie with those same eyes. I had a feeling if she was living out of her car, she probably wasn't eating well either.

"I've got to tell you," I began, sitting back in my seat. "Dinner filled me up and I hadn't planned on dessert. I only agreed to it because I wanted to talk to you. This pie is good and it'd be a shame if it went to waste."

"You aren't going to have it?" she asked, her shock evident.

I shook my head and admitted, "Maybe only a bite or two more. Have you had dinner? I'm sure it gets busy here."

She looked down at her lap and answered, "Yeah, it was pretty busy tonight, so I didn't have an opportunity to eat any dinner yet."

"Sounds like you should have the sundae for dinner and the pie for dessert then," I offered.

"Sundae for dinner only if you share the pie for dessert," she retorted.

"Deal."

As she took a few bites, I simply watched her. She ate slowly; I'd never seen someone eat so slow before. I didn't mind, though, because I was just going to get to spend that much more time with her.

"So I think I remember hearing something about the women in Windsor sex-trafficking ring being found," she started. "Were you behind that?"

"Not just me, but I was on the team that was mostly responsible for it. One of the women who was taken acted quickly and is a big part of the reason we found them when we did."

"That's incredible. I'm happy they were found," she said.

I remembered that day vividly. Seeing the terror on the faces of the women that had been taken was difficult to witness. I was happy that Ekko hadn't been one of them. I gave her what information I could about the case, which was mostly everything that had been in the news already.

As I spoke, I struggled to remain unaffected by her innocent and effortless sexiness. I couldn't get over the way she ate. It was like she was savoring every single morsel she put in her mouth before taunting me by bringing her pretty pink tongue out to lick her lips. And it seemed as though she was doing it in slow motion with each bite.

Ekko is a natural beauty. She didn't have an ounce of makeup on her face and even though she looked tired, she was still breathtaking. She's very petite, easily a foot shorter than me, with golden brown hair that falls to the middle of her back and a set of hazel eyes that have specks of gold and green in them.

"I can imagine how scary it must have been for those women. I don't know what I would have done if you hadn't been there for me that night," she shared as her eyes filled with tears.

I wanted to reach out and hold her hand in mine to offer her some comfort, but I didn't know how she'd feel about it. And even though I had a pretty good idea she was no longer with her boyfriend, I still hadn't confirmed it. I needed to know.

"I'm glad I was there," I assured her. "How have things been going for you since that night?"

Immediately, she looked uncomfortable. I didn't like seeing it, so I quickly added, "Hey, it's okay if you don't want to talk about it. I was just making conversation."

She shook her head and insisted, "No, it's fine. I ended up losing my apartment and had to move in with my boyfriend."

Damn it.

She didn't say ex.

And now she was glancing around the restaurant nervously.

I didn't want to be the one to cause her the kind of distress I saw in her face, so I cleared my throat and caught her attention. "I'm…I should get going so you can finish up and get home. Can you get me the check?"

She stood and shook her head.

Confused, I waited for her to offer clarification.

"I told you I wanted to thank you for what you did for me that night. The least I can do is buy dinner for you."

"That's not necessary, Ekko."

With a few quick nods of her head, she said softly, "It is. Thank you again for that and for asking me to join you for some dessert. It was nice to take a break."

I certainly knew she needed one after the way she'd been working.

I got up out of the booth and pulled out my wallet. After throwing some money down on the table, I admitted, "The pleasure was all mine, sugar."

The sultry look in Ekko's eyes burned into mine. She didn't say any words before I went on, "Take care of yourself."

Her eyes rounded briefly in surprise before she replied, "I'm trying. You too."

After I gave her a quick nod, I turned and walked out.

I made my way out to my truck that was parked discreetly in the corner of the lot. I was going to make sure that Ekko made it somewhere safe tonight. Sitting across from her for that short time, listening to her soft voice and watching her perfect mouth, I couldn't bear to think she'd be sleeping in her car again. That's why I threw two hundred and fifty dollars down on the table before I left. I figured if she was no longer living with her boyfriend, that money would easily get her a nice hotel for the night.

Once I was in my truck, I watched through the window of the diner as she cleaned the table we'd been sitting at. I saw the shock register when she saw the money and the utter relief in her face and body moments later when she held it up to her chest over her heart and closed her eyes. As good as it felt for me to know I'd done something to help her, it also bothered me that she felt that kind of relief over such a small amount of money.

Just over ten minutes later, she walked out of the diner and to her car. I waited for her to pull out and drive down the road a bit before I followed. Sure enough, when she stopped driving it was in the parking lot of the Windsor Public Library, which was already closed.

No way was I going to sit and watch while she slept in her car again in the cold. I waited about twenty minutes trying to figure out how I was going to do this. When I ultimately made my move, I still had no idea what I was going to do or how it would play out.

I pulled into the lot, turned off my truck, and got out. I walked up to the driver's side window of her car and, thanks to the light in the parking lot, I saw she had lowered the back of her seat and was lying on her side facing the passenger's side. Her eyes were closed, but there was a smile on her face.

I tapped lightly on the window. She was startled and shot up in the seat, panicked.

Opening her door and getting out, she called, "Dom?"

"What are you doing out here?" I asked, cutting to the chase.

She looked everywhere but my face. "I was tired," she finally replied.

"Okay. And you thought you'd sleep in your car?"

I watched as she pulled her bottom lip in between her teeth and blinked back her tears. "I don't have anywhere to go," she whispered. "Did you follow me?"

"Yeah, and it's a good thing I did. I thought you moved in with your boyfriend," I reminded her of her earlier admission.

"I did. And I was living with him until I left him two days ago. I didn't have a place lined up yet to move to, though."

She left him.

"You left him when you had no place to go?"

She nodded.

That didn't make any sense.

"Why?"

At my interrogation, her breathing grew quick and shallow. Fear.

"Ekko?" I called.

When she brought her beautiful eyes to mine, I asked gently, "Did he hurt you?"

She shook her head slowly as a tear fell down her cheek. "No, it's nothing like that. It's just…I walked into the apartment two nights ago and learned that he's a drug dealer. I refuse to be around that stuff, so I left."

"You have nowhere to go?" I pushed, already knowing the answer.

She swallowed hard and shared, "Thanks to you, I will soon."

"Me?"

"I feel awful about accepting it, but the money you left at the diner today gave me enough so that I can finally get my own place."

The relief on her face when she was at the diner was because she knew she'd have a home again.

"When can you get into your new place?"

She lifted her shoulders and guessed, "Not long, I hope. Maybe a few days, I'm assuming. I am going to call the landlord first thing in the morning."

"You can't sleep out here tonight."

"I'll be fine," she assured me.

"I won't."

"What?"

"Ekko, follow me and you can stay at my place as long as you need."

She shook her head and vehemently refused. "I can't do that. You've already been generous enough and you don't even know me."

I narrowed my eyes a bit before I teased, "I think I can protect myself if you try to harm me."

She let out a laugh but quickly stopped herself. "That's not what I meant."

I barely heard her words because I was so intrigued by the sound of her laughter. It was captivating.

"I know," I confessed. "I also know that you've fallen on some hard times and you need some help. There's nothing wrong with that. I can help you."

"Okay, but I don't really know you."

"I rescued you from an attempted abduction and we just had dessert together. You know I work for a private investigation company and that the local police know who I am because of the work I do. Do you really think I'd hurt you?"

She shook her head and responded, "No."

"So you'll stay with me then?"

"I don't think I should." She held firm in her decision.

"Fine," I declared. "Then let me get you a hotel room for a few nights while you get your living arrangements sorted. There's no deadline."

"You would do that?"

There was no denying the surprise in her voice.

"Yes."

"Why?"

I grinned at her before I answered honestly, "Because you need help right now and I've got the means to give you that help."

Her lips parted, and my eyes dropped to them.

"What's it going to be, sugar?"

"You've already given me so much," she argued. "I can't

accept any more money from you."

"Looks like you're staying at my place then," I noted as I crossed my arms over my chest and cocked an eyebrow. I couldn't miss the heat that flashed in her eyes.

A moment later when I thought she was going to give in, she said, "I'll get myself a hotel room."

I held my hand out to her car door and said, "Lead the way."

"What?"

"I'm going to make sure you have a safe, clean place to stay tonight."

She sighed and got in her car. Once she started it up, I got in my truck and followed her out of the lot. Not much later, I pulled in behind her at what had to be the dumpiest, most unsafe motel in the entire city.

I hopped out of the truck, marched up to her door, and opened it. "Not a chance in hell you're staying here," I warned her.

She looked at the motel and back at me. "Why not?"

"I'm not convinced they even have beds here. Besides, if you moved out of your boyfriend's place because you don't want to be around drugs, then you shouldn't be staying here."

"Dom, this is all I can afford," she croaked.

"Let. Me. Help. You."

I enunciated each word so she'd understand just how serious I was.

"I can't."

"Why not?"

"Because you're you."

"Yes, I am me. That's not really a good reason."

"I have no business being anywhere near someone like you."

What the fuck did that mean?

"Someone like me?"

"You're going to make me say it out loud?" she worried.

Even though I had a feeling I knew what she was getting at, I returned, "Ekko, I have no idea what you are talking about. If you don't want to tell me what that means then tell me that you'll come with me back to my place where I'll give you a safe, clean, comfortable place to stay for a few days while you get your stuff sorted."

She closed her eyes and let out a sigh.

Finally, she gave in. "Alright, it's not like my luck could possibly get any worse. If you kill me, you'll really just be helping me out of a very difficult situation."

I didn't like hearing her say that.

"Nobody is killing you," I asserted.

"I'm just saying…it wouldn't be the worst thing that's happened."

I shook my head and demanded, "Follow me. My place isn't too far."

"Okay."

At that, Ekko followed me back to my place. The entire way there I tried to figure out how I was going to get her to see that she deserved to have someone who'd be there for her.

CHAPTER 3

Ekko

THIS COULDN'T POSSIBLY BE HAPPENING TO ME.

Though, I shouldn't be surprised because this was just the kind of luck that I had. I was about to experience the most mortifying moment of my life.

As if having to reveal the truth about my housing and financial situation to Dom last night wasn't embarrassing enough, now there was this.

After our standoff outside the motel, Dom insisted I come back to his place with him. I couldn't say I wasn't grateful for his hospitality. I was. Other than Ms. Grace, nobody else had ever shown me the kindness that Dom did.

We arrived back at his home last night when it was dark out. I didn't really have an opportunity to take in the neighborhood, but I knew we were in an actual neighborhood. He had his own house, not an apartment. I moved to grab my bag out of the back seat when he came up behind me and took it from me.

"Got anything else in the trunk?" he asked.

"That's it," I responded.

I felt ashamed by my lack of possessions, but Dom never made me feel like he was judging me.

"Okay," he replied. And for the first time since the night

he rescued me months ago, he touched me. He put his hand on the small of my back and began guiding me toward the front door. Feeling his hand on me sent shivers up and down my spine.

When we got inside, he turned on the lights and I was pleasantly surprised to see it was almost fully furnished. There were blankets thrown over the back of his massive sectional in the family room and a huge television mounted to the wall. He had hardwood floors throughout the entire first floor, a decently-sized kitchen with modern, stainless-steel appliances, and a cute, cozy breakfast nook off the kitchen. He had a formal dining room, but it wasn't yet furnished beyond the massive table occupying most of the room.

"Did you want anything to eat or drink?" he asked.

Food that I didn't have to pay for or ration? I wanted to take him up on it just because I had the opportunity, but the truth was that I was still full from the desserts we shared earlier.

"No, I'm good."

"Come on," he urged, as he put his hand at the small of my back again and directed me out of the kitchen. "Let me show you where you'll be sleeping."

We walked upstairs and down the hall to the open door at the end of it. When I stepped through the door, I realized we were in Dom's bedroom.

"Is this your room?" I wondered.

He gave me a nod.

I immediately tensed up as I suddenly figured out the real reason he was willing to help me out. It looked like I would be heading back to my car.

"Relax, Ekko. You'll sleep in here; I'm taking the couch," he explained, calming part of my fears. Even with the explanation, I still wasn't completely at ease.

"You can't give up your bed for me," I argued.

He merely dazzled me with his dimples. "Don't try to change my mind. You're getting the bed, I'm good with the couch."

"Dom," I started before he cut me off again.

"Did you see my couch when you walked in?"

I gave him a nod.

"Good. Then you know it's huge and comfortable. I have fallen asleep there many times before now. I'll be fine there. I want you here, where I can give you what I promised…a safe, comfortable place to sleep."

He was such a good man.

"Thank you," I squeaked, fighting not to break down.

"You're welcome. The bathroom is just through that door over there. Help yourself to anything you need."

I perked up. "Would you mind if I took a shower?"

His face softened. "Not at all."

I couldn't wait to take a nice, hot shower. I'd be quick about it, but I was going to enjoy every second of it.

"If you need anything else, just let me know."

"Thank you."

"I'm serious, Ekko," he warned. "Anything at all and I'm right downstairs. Promise you'll let me know."

"I promise."

And making that promise was the worst thing I could have done. Because now I was here, it was just after eight in the morning, and I was in a bit of a pickle.

Dom's bed was the definition of comfort. It was so magical I was certain that if I hadn't woken up with excruciating stomach pain, I'd still be sleeping.

I rolled out of the bed and went straight into the bathroom. That's when I realized I'd gotten my period. It was bad. It's been bad just about every month for the last eleven months, and I'd hoped every month that it would get better. At this precise moment, though, I would have agreed to a lifetime of excruciatingly painful, heavy periods to avoid this situation.

I was at Dom's place with no tampons and I'd gotten my period, which leaked through my panties and my grey sweatpants. I had a feeling I was going to walk back out to his bedroom and find that I'd leaked through to his bedsheets.

I quickly cleaned myself up and tried to come up with a game plan. Walking back out into the bedroom, I found that my suspicions were true. I needed to strip his bed, wash his sheets, and get them back on before he noticed. Of course, I also knew this was going to be an impossible feat.

Why did this have to be my life? Why couldn't I have just one thing that went right for me? As I pondered these questions, I crumbled to the floor next to Dom's bed. I pulled my knees up to my chest, breathing slowly through the pain.

Then, things got worse.

There was a light tap on the door before I heard, "Ekko?"

When I didn't answer, hoping my silence would make him think I was still asleep, the door opened. My eyes traveled up his body, which was covered only in a pair of lounge pants and a t-shirt, to his face. For the first time, I was seeing him without a hat. He had a perfectly-shaped bald head. I couldn't even fully appreciate him because I was distraught and in pain.

Dom wasted no time in coming over and squatting down next to me. "Are you okay?"

I shook my head.

"What's wrong?"

"This is so humiliating," I quietly cried.

"What? Ekko, you're just staying here for a few days until you can move into your new place. There's nothing for you to be ashamed of."

"That's not it, Dom."

He just stared at me with such concern, waiting for my explanation.

"I...do you have a washing machine?" I asked.

Dom didn't hesitate to answer, "Yeah. Do you need to wash your clothes?"

"Well...yeah, some of them. But more importantly, I need to wash your bedsheets," I explained.

"After sleeping in them for one night?"

I nodded and grimaced as I pressed my forearm a little further into my abdomen, trying to relieve the pain. Dom's eyes went to my stomach and then to his bed. Realization dawned in his features. He brought his gentle gaze to me, where he held my eyes briefly before he stood and walked into the bathroom. After I heard the water run for a few seconds, Dom came back to the bedroom.

He held his hand out to me and said, "Come here."

I hesitated a minute, but finally put my hand in his. He helped me up from the floor and led me into the bathroom, where I found the water I heard running was coming from his soaking tub.

"Get undressed and get in the bath," he instructed. "The water is warm and should help with the pain you're feeling. I'll take care of the bedsheets."

I was completely caught off guard at how much he knew about periods and how comfortable he was talking about it like it was no big deal.

Unfortunately, I didn't share any of this information with him. Instead, I lamented, "I'm so sorry."

"There's nothing to apologize for, sugar. Just relax for a while. I'll come back in a little bit to check on you."

At that, Dom excused himself and closed the door as he walked out of the bathroom. I stripped out of my clothes and got in the tub. The warm water felt great; I closed my eyes and took some deep breaths. I was still in an incredible amount of pain but felt some relief relaxing in the bath.

I'm not sure how much time passed, but when the water started to feel cold, I figured it was time to get out. I opened the drain, cleaned out the tub, and hopped in the shower to quickly rinse myself off. Then, I wrapped a towel around me just in time to hear a knock at the door.

"Ekko?" Dom called.

"Yeah?" I answered.

"Is it okay to come in?" he asked.

Glancing in the mirror, I confirmed I was completely covered. I walked over and opened the door.

Dom's eyes dropped briefly to the top of the towel but quickly came back up to my face. "How are you feeling?" he wondered.

"Miserable."

He held out two plastic grocery bags and said, "I wasn't sure exactly what you'd need so I got a bunch. I figured it was a good idea to have a variety."

I took the bags from him and looked inside. My heart swelled when I realized what he had done. "You bought me tampons?" I asked in disbelief.

He shrugged his shoulders and explained, "You only had your bag with your clothes in it last night. There's a drug store five minutes away, so I took a quick trip there while you were in the bath."

I couldn't help myself. I reached my hand out and touched his cheek. "I must have done something good at some point in my life," I said softly.

Dom looked confused by my statement, but I didn't explain it to him. I just went on, "Thank you."

He smiled at me before backing out of the bathroom. I

dumped out the bags and found that Dom had, in fact, picked up a variety. He had purchased every absorbency available. I took care of my business and threw on a comfortable pair of yoga pants, a camisole, and an open front cardigan. I was so grateful for the fact that I didn't need to go to work until just before the dinner rush.

Coming out of the bathroom, I found Dom had removed the bedsheets I slept in and put a fresh set on. In the middle of the bed, there were several other bags. Before I had the chance to see what was inside, Dom walked back into the room with a glass of water.

"Here you go," he said as he handed me the glass. "I got you some painkillers. They're in those bags along with a few other items."

I looked in the bags and saw that Dom had purchased not only several different painkillers but also a ton of goodies, including a bunch of salty snacks and an abundance of chocolate. He even picked up a couple boxes of tea.

I had to be dreaming. There was no way this was really happening. My curiosity got the best of me and I just had to ask, "How did you know to purchase all of this stuff?"

He let out a laugh and confessed, "I've had a couple girlfriends over the years."

I shook my head in disbelief. "Why did they ever let you get away?"

He didn't respond to my question. He simply changed topics. "I think you need some breakfast before you take any of that medicine, though. Do you like egg sandwiches?"

"I'm not picky," I answered honestly, mostly overjoyed that I was going to have a home-cooked meal for breakfast.

"I picked up the tea because I've heard some women say it makes them feel better, but I also have coffee if you'd prefer that."

"I'll stick with the tea."

He grinned at me, clearly proud of himself for purchasing it, and ordered, "Get in bed. I'll be right back up with breakfast."

"I can come down and help," I offered, even though the pain was radiating through my belly and lower back.

"That's alright. I've got it."

With that, he turned and walked out of the room. I moved to the bed, climbed in, and dug through the bags searching for the pain medication. It was while I was doing that when I tried to look at this situation as something other than another stroke of bad luck. I was in a warm house in a warm bed that belonged to a gorgeous man. A gorgeous man who had gone out and bought me tampons, chocolate, salty snacks, tea, and painkillers because I'd gotten my period. I had been embarrassed about it, but he never made me feel any shame. Once I found the pain meds, I curled up in a ball on my side and laid there, thinking.

When I really took the time to think about it, it dawned on me that any time he'd been around me, I had experienced more fortune than I ever had in my life. And I didn't mean that with regards to money. It was all about the protectiveness and kindness he showed me. He wrapped me in his arms months ago after I was nearly abducted and made me feel safer than I'd ever felt. And what he was doing for me now went beyond what I could ever express with words. My own mother never took care of me like this. I couldn't understand why Dom was so willing to waste his time on someone like me.

Dom walked in the bedroom a few minutes later carrying a plate, a mug, and a gorgeous set of dimples. Those dimples could make all my pain and troubles disappear.

It felt a bit wrong lusting after a man like Dom for two very specific reasons. First, feeling any attraction to someone when I'd officially just left Ryan only a few days ago seemed quick. Of course, we hadn't been together for quite some time and he had clearly moved on from me, so it's not like I was feeling sad over the loss of him. Once I learned of the drug dealing, it sealed it for me. I'd never go back to him and I wasn't sorry about that decision. But the other reason that my attraction to Dom felt wrong was because I had a feeling I was setting myself up for some serious heartache. I didn't belong with someone like him. He was good, clean, focused, and successful; I was everything but.

"Are the tea choices okay? Is there one you think you'll like?"

"They're all perfect, Dom. I don't think I've ever had so many options before."

I struggled to get myself upright in the bed again. Quite frankly, all I wanted to do was spend my day sleeping in Dom's bed. Once I was finally seated, he handed me the plate with the breakfast sandwich, which I noted was made on a freshly-baked bagel and sliced in half. If I didn't know any better, I would have thought he made the bagel himself that morning.

"Do you mind if I join you in here for breakfast?" he asked.

I gave him a questioning look and declared, "It's your home. Why are you asking me if you can be in your own bedroom?"

"Because I told you last night that I'd give you a place that was safe, clean, and comfortable. If me being in my bedroom with you would make you uncomfortable, I'd respect that."

Could he be any more perfect?

"I'd love to have some company," I shared.

Once again, he dazzled me with his dimples before he replied, "I'll be right back then."

A few minutes later, Dom walked in carrying a second plate and a mug. He sat down next to me on the bed.

He smiled at me but didn't say anything.

"What's your last name?" I blurted my question. I was doing anything I could to distract myself from the pain I was in and, truthfully, I really wanted to know his name.

He laughed. "That's a bit out of left field."

"I'm in a bed with a man and I don't know his full name. I don't think that says much about the kind of girl I am," I pointed out.

"We're having breakfast in bed, Ekko. It's not like you allowed me to fuck you without you knowing my name."

Just hearing him say those words sent goosebumps all over my body. "I know," I assured him, quickly trying to cover up my reaction. "I was just trying to be funny."

He gave me a look that told me he might not necessarily like my brand of funny before he answered, "It's Moore. Yours?"

"You're talking to probably the only Ekko Rose you'll ever meet."

His dimples came out and he admitted, "I'm completely okay with that being the case. That's a badass name."

I could feel myself beginning to blush, so I dropped my gaze to the plate and picked up half of the egg sandwich. We ate in silence for a bit before he spoke.

"Do you work today?"

"Yeah, but only the evening shift thankfully."

"You work a lot," he stated.

I took in a deep breath and as I let it out, I said, "Yep."

"What do you like to do for fun?"

"Read."

He raised his eyebrows and questioned me, "You think reading is fun?"

"Yes," I replied immediately. "It's just about the only traveling I get to do. And with the romance novels, which are my favorite, I get to believe that the dream is possible."

"I'm so confused."

After swallowing the last bite of the first half of the sandwich, I explained, "I will read just about anything, but I adore romance. A lot of people view it negatively and think it's all about sex. Some people go so far as to call it porn. But it's not. Of all the different genres of books I've read, nothing makes me *feel* the way a romance does. And it almost always has nothing to do with the steamy scenes as people might assume."

Dom gave me a look that told me he hadn't considered reading, or possibly reading romance specifically, in that way. I felt like I had given him some new perspective.

Looking down at the second half of the tasty sandwich that I really wanted to finish eating, I decided against it. It would be better to save it for later.

I set the plate on the bedside table and grabbed the water and painkillers. I knew I'd have about twenty minutes before they kicked in; I couldn't wait for the relief. Years ago, when I was doing a bit better financially, I always had them on hand for this specific reason. But when things got bad, it seemed like it all got bad. My financial situation turned sour and my periods got worse. I'd never had medication throughout the entire time they'd been this excruciating.

After downing the pills, I picked up the hot tea and took a few small sips.

"I have a heating pad if that would help," Dom offered.

I thought I might cry.

"That's really kind of you, but I can tough it out. You've already gone above and beyond. I appreciate you not making me feel any worse than I already do about what happened to your bedsheets."

Putting the last bite of his sandwich up to his mouth with his legs outstretched and crossed at the ankles, he asked,

"Why do you feel bad about something that your body does naturally?"

I had no idea. It was just something that I always felt awkward about.

"Possibly staining your sheets because I bled through my clothes has got to be the definition of utter embarrassment."

He was serious when he argued, "It shouldn't be."

Dom was so nonchalant about it—like it was no big deal. I wished I could have had that same attitude, but I didn't. My period was always something I felt embarrassed about. It's not like I'd ever had anybody to tell me otherwise.

We continued to chat, and I found that I really enjoyed talking to Dom. It seemed as though we were both giving each other fresh perspective on a lot of things that morning.

He glanced over at the bedside table when I put the half-empty mug of tea down and asked, "You're not hungry or it wasn't good?"

I looked at the remainder of the sandwich and back at him. "I am hungry, and it was delicious. I just thought I'd save the rest for later."

"Eat," he ordered.

I held his gaze but didn't move to pick up the food.

"Ekko, eat. If you're hungry, eat. There's an abundance of food here. You don't need to stop yourself from enjoying any of it."

"I don't want you to think I'm taking advantage of your kindness," I admitted.

"I know you aren't. Eat, please."

Dom didn't seem like he was going to budge, so I grabbed the plate and brought the sandwich to my mouth.

As I ate, Dom asked, "What time are you planning to meet the landlord?"

"I don't know yet. I was hoping to meet him this morning,

but I need to call him. I need to head to the diner first, though, so I can call him."

"Why do you have to go to the diner to call him?"

"Because they have a phone."

"You don't have a phone?" he asked, incredulously.

I looked down at my lap, feeling disappointed with myself. I used to have a phone, but it was no longer an expense I could justify.

Dom made a sound that indicated he wasn't happy before he got up and walked out of the room. Not quite a minute later, he walked back in and held his phone out to me.

"You can use my phone to make the call."

"Thank you. I'll be quick."

I reached for my purse on the table and pulled out the piece of paper I had with the landlord's number on it. I called him and was overjoyed that he had some time to meet me in a few hours. I disconnected the call and returned Dom's phone.

"He can meet me at eleven-thirty this morning," I announced, noting it wasn't even ten yet.

"What time do you have to go to work?"

"I have to be there by four-thirty."

After a gorgeous smile spread across his face, he declared, "Great. You can take some time now to relax and let the meds kick in. Then, I'll take you to your meeting with the landlord. After, we're going to go get you a phone and go out for lunch."

"I can't get a phone, Dom."

"Why not?"

"I don't have the money for it right now. I got rid of all my unnecessary expenses a while back, so I could continue going to school. It didn't really matter because I ended up having to leave anyway."

"A phone is not an unnecessary expense," he lectured me. "You need to have one for your own safety."

"No. What I need is a place to live. Once I get that sorted, I can start saving for a phone and other luxuries."

"I'll get you the phone, Ekko."

"Stop, please," I begged.

"What's wrong?"

"I can't handle this. I don't know what's going on or why you're doing all of this, but it's too much. I'll never be able to dig myself out of the debt I owe you if you keep doing this."

"You don't owe me for anything. I'm doing this because I want to, not because I expect you to pay me back for any of it. I'm doing it because from the little that I do know about you, it seems like you've lived rough for the last few years and you need a fuckin' break. I've got the means to give you that break. All you've got to do is allow me to help you."

My voice was quiet when I replied, "I don't know how to do that."

"Then give me the opportunity to show you how."

With those words, I couldn't fight him. I was tired and in pain, so I gave him a small nod. When I did, he wrapped his hand around mine and gave it a squeeze. His hand on mine brought me more comfort than I'd felt in a really long time.

"Thank you, Dom."

"My pleasure, sugar. Get some rest. I'll wake you when it's time to go."

CHAPTER 4

Ekko

"WHAT DO YOU WANT TO BE WHEN YOU GROW UP?" DOM asked as he sat on the opposite end of the couch from me eating his lunch.

We met with the landlord this morning and he showed me the one-bedroom apartment he had available in the apartment complex near my job at the diner. He told me he could have everything ready for me to move in within the week. I agreed, and we set up a time to meet and complete paperwork one week from today. I'd get my keys then, too.

While I was overjoyed that I was finally going to have my own place again, I was worried about what the next week would bring. I knew Dom had offered to allow me to stay at his place until I could get my living arrangements sorted, but I had originally told him it'd probably only be a few days. I had to figure out how I was going to address this with him.

After Dom and I left that meeting, he took me to get a phone. I still had reservations about it, but he insisted upon it. I ultimately agreed on the condition that the second I was back on my feet financially, he would transfer the bill into my name. By the time we finished there, Dom was set to take me out to lunch, but I really wasn't feeling the best. He noticed this and instantly decided we'd get the food to go.

We arrived back at his place about ten minutes ago. I went upstairs to use the bathroom and get the pain medication while he set the food out for us in the family room. Now, we were seated, eating, and he had just asked me what I wanted to be when I grew up.

"I hate to break it to you, but I'm twenty-eight. My twenty-ninth birthday is on the fourteenth of next month. I'd say I'm already grown up."

"I sure hope you don't believe that, considering I just turned thirty-one and don't think I'm grown up yet."

He was only two years older than me, yet he already had so much to be proud of. He had his own place, a new truck, a great job, and his very own cell phone plan. I had been rationing food, living out of my car, and trying to figure out how I was going to get the rest of my things from my drug-dealing ex-boyfriend.

I remained quiet so long considering all of this that Dom spoke again. "Earlier today you said you were in school. What were you going to school for?"

"I was trying to get my undergraduate degree in English, so I could go on to apply to a school to get my master's in library science. For as long as I can remember, I've always wanted to be a librarian."

A devious and devilishly-handsome grin spread across his face, putting both dimples on display.

"I'm not sure I want to know what that look means."

He laughed and added, "That's probably best. How much school have you finished?"

"I managed to get my associate's degree in English already. Thankfully, I don't have any student loan debt from that since I worked while getting my degree. I transferred and was in the process of getting my bachelor's degree, but had to stop when I had only a semester left."

"How much more school will you have to go through to get your master's?"

"I found a program that will allow me to complete it in three years and I'll be able to do it online, too."

"That's not that bad," he reasoned.

I rolled my eyes and pointed out, "Yeah, as long as I'm not seventy before I can start it."

"You'll be back on your feet in no time," Dom declared, not the least bit concerned. In fact, he seemed overly confident.

"So what about you?" I asked, needing to change the subject.

"What about me?"

"Well, I know you work for a private investigation firm, obviously. Did you always want to do that?"

"Not really. As a kid, I had no idea what I wanted to do. The older I got, the more I realized I needed something that would challenge me, mentally and physically. I knew I wouldn't be able to work in a job that was the same, day in and day out."

"Do you work odd hours and weekends like I do?"

"Sometimes," he stated. "It depends on what our caseload looks like. Since the sex-trafficking case was solved, we've not had anything that intense. A few things here and there that required more hours over the last few months, but for the most part it's been pretty quiet, and I've enjoyed having a bit of free time."

Free time.

I longed for the day I'd be able to get back to having a full day off to myself that I could actually enjoy. Lately, I didn't have very many days off, but the few that I did weren't very relaxing. I hoped I'd get some time to do that once I moved into my new apartment.

"What do you like to do with your free time?" I wondered.

"If the weather's nice, I'll go out on my bike."

"Oh, are there good trails to ride on around here?" I asked, pausing a moment before I went on to explain away my ignorance. "I've never really had much time to do anything outdoorsy."

Dom laughed. "I didn't mean a bicycle, Ekko. I meant I go out riding my motorcycle when it's nice out."

My eyes widened. "You have a motorcycle, too?"

"I actually have two of them," he clarified. "Have you ever ridden on one?"

I shook my head.

"When's your next day off?"

"Thursday," I answered.

"If you let me take you out on a date, we can go for a ride."

I stared at him for quite some time in complete shock. When I finally spoke, I stammered, "A...a date?"

Dom nodded.

"*You* want to go out on a date with *me*?"

"Yes."

"Why?"

"Because I like you and I want to spend some time getting to know you better. Isn't that why people go out on dates?"

"Yeah, but—" I started before he cut me off.

"But what?"

Even though I should have told him the truth, I didn't want to admit it. The truth that someone like him didn't belong with someone like me. That he deserved someone whose life wasn't in shambles. And I couldn't do it because I really wanted something good, even if I could only experience it for one night.

"Nothing," I finally responded. "I'd love to go out on a date."

Dom broke out into a huge grin, not even trying to hide how he felt about my agreement to go on a date with him.

I tried not to let the excitement I saw in his face affect me, but it was hard. The guy was gorgeous and seeing him like that, happy at the prospect of spending time with me, made my heart beat just a little bit faster. I needed some time to think.

"I don't mean to be rude, but would you mind if I napped for a bit before I have to go into work tonight?" I asked.

"Not at all. Go on up and get in bed. I can wake you before you have to go," he offered.

"Thank you, Dom. I really appreciate everything you've done for me," I replied.

Dom's face softened before he insisted, "You're welcome, Ekko."

At that, after Dom refused to let me help clean up from our lunch, I went upstairs. I quickly used the bathroom before climbing into his bed. As much as I could have really used the time to think, I couldn't. The stress and worry from the last couple of days mixed with long days of work caught up with me and it was merely a matter of a minute or two before I was asleep.

I only felt marginally refreshed when I woke to the touch of a hand on my shoulder and the sound of a voice calling, "Ekko?"

I rolled toward the voice. Once I was on my back with my head turned slightly to the side, my eyes fluttered open and I was staring into Dom's adoring gaze. It took me a few seconds to fight the pull inside me to not sit up and wrap my arms around him.

"Hey," I finally said, turning my head toward the clock on the nightstand.

"It's just after three-thirty," Dom shared. "You've got less than an hour before your shift starts."

All I wanted was to stay in Dom's bed. I'd never had the opportunity to sleep in something so wonderful in all my life. I didn't know if it was because he'd been so good to me over the last several hours, but I blurted, "You've got an amazing bed. If I didn't have to go to work, I could easily stay here all day. With your permission, of course."

Laughter bubbled up out of him. As wonderful as the sound was, I tried to distract myself. He was so carefree, and his dimples were out. I would have given anything to latch onto that. Unfortunately, I failed, and things were made even worse for me when Dom got serious again. "Works for me," he shared. Then, he added, "I'll tell you what…if we go out on that date on Thursday and find that we both want to keep learning about each other and see this go in another direction, I'll see to it that we spend an entire day together in my bed sometime."

If I wouldn't have looked like a complete fool, I would have started fanning myself right then and there. It would have been difficult to miss the intent or promise in Dom's tone. Part of me wished I had done that instead of what I ended up doing. For some reason, which probably had a lot to do with the fact that I hadn't yet embarrassed myself enough in front of him, I begged, "Please don't say things like that."

While the tone of Dom's voice before held nothing but promise, mine now held nothing but hunger. Dom heard it and knew it. He cocked an eyebrow and gave me a questioning look.

Instead of answering that look, I announced, "I really should get ready."

I saw the disappointment flash in his face briefly before he shut it down and stood so I could get off the bed. Dom left me to get ready.

I had no idea how I was going to last another week being in such close proximity to him knowing that I didn't belong here. To top it off, I didn't want to think about what Dom must have thought of me. I mean, I had just moved out of my ex-boyfriend's apartment. Sure, we hadn't actually been together in months, but Dom didn't know that. And now I was here lusting after him. I knew he didn't miss it and it made me cringe to think how that made him see me.

But it had been a while. A very long while since I'd felt wanted. I was craving intimacy and a connection to someone and I desperately wanted to relieve that ache.

Pushing those thoughts to the back of my mind, I finished getting myself ready for work and walked downstairs.

"Hey, I'm going to get going," I told Dom when I found him in the family room sprawled out on his couch.

"I can take you now and pick you up when you're done if you'd like," he offered.

Giving him a friendly smile, I declined, "No, that's okay. I appreciate the offer, though."

Dom sat up, stood, and walked over toward me. He stopped just a few feet in front of me and, with his voice low, confirmed, "You are going to come back, right?"

After hearing his voice like that, I couldn't find my own so I simply nodded.

"Be safe, Ekko."

"I will."

I turned and walked to the front door, instantly feeling Dom close behind me. I tried not to let it affect me and just kept moving. When I got to the door, Dom reached around me and opened it before he walked me out to my car. Once he closed my car door and I backed out of the driveway, I was finally able to think straight.

As I drove, I realized that I never felt more relieved to be going to work. I needed the time away from Dom. I needed something to occupy my mind and distract me from all the thoughts I had about this unfamiliar territory.

Unfortunately, while the busy night at work was proving to be a benefit to my financial situation, it offered little distraction from Dom. My mind kept wandering to all the sweet things he had said or done for me over the course of the last day. And it seemed that no sooner had I arrived at work when my shift ended and I was on my way back to his place, where I was sure he would be sweet and I'd fall further in lust with him.

When I arrived back at Dom's house, I rang the doorbell. He was at the door seconds later, letting me in.

"Hey, fun size. How was work?" he asked as I stepped inside.

I raised my eyebrows and repeated, "Fun size?"

He shrugged his shoulders and explained, "You're so little. And you're cute."

I had no reply to that, so I answered his question. "Work was good. Busy, but good."

"I take it that busy means that you didn't eat dinner?"

I shook my head and felt, for the third time, Dom's hand at the small of my back guiding me toward the kitchen.

"I figured. That's why I made food for us. I hope you like Asian dishes because I made sesame noodles with chicken and broccoli."

He waited until I was seated at the island before he set the food in front of me.

Perhaps I should have prepared myself for it, but I didn't, and I was caught off guard. He made food for me. For weeks now I had been worried about when I was going to have my next meal, but today I'd had breakfast, lunch, and dinner because of the man in front of me. Dom set a second plate down and sat next to me.

I was still staring at the feast before me when Dom's hand squeezed my leg, just above my knee. "Ekko?"

My head turned toward him.

"Are you okay?"

I couldn't fight it. I was so overwhelmed by his kindness and generosity toward me that I completely broke down into tears and buried my face in my hands.

Suddenly, I felt Dom's arms around me hugging me into his chest, where I only cried harder.

"Ekko, sugar, talk to me."

The concern in his voice and the hold he had on me only made me cry harder. Several minutes passed, with Dom comforting me before I pulled my face back from his chest and said, "You made me dinner."

"Yes, I made dinner for the both of us. Why is that upsetting you?"

"Nearly every day for almost eight years, I had one good person in my life who made dinner for me. That stopped about six months after my fifteenth birthday. Ever since, nobody has ever made me dinner. Most of my days for the last thirteen years have been filled with me worrying if I was even going to be able to eat, especially over the last year."

Dom's face went soft as he lifted a hand to the side of my head and brushed my hair back.

"It was never my intention to upset you, Ekko."

"I know."

"But I'd be lying to you if I didn't say that I already knew you had it rough. I see the way you eat. You savor every single bite like you might not have the opportunity to taste food again. I knew for certain this morning when you told me you were hungry but wanted to save part of your breakfast for later."

Feeling embarrassed, I dropped my head.

Dom put a finger under my chin and lifted my head. "You don't have to do that here, sugar. If you're hungry, you eat. There's always food here and you are welcome to help yourself to any of it."

I didn't know what I'd done to deserve having someone like Dom in my life.

"Why don't we eat while you tell me all about that one good person who was in your life?"

I gave him a nod and that's what we did. We ate Dom's sesame noodles with chicken and broccoli, which were amazing, and I told him all about Ms. Grace. That night, tucked in the warmth of his bed, I had a lot of thoughts running through my mind. But the one that stuck out was how I couldn't help but wish that Dom might just be that man that Ms. Grace told me would find me one day.

CHAPTER 5

Ekko

I T WAS QUARTER TO FIVE IN THE EVENING ON WEDNESDAY AND I
was dead on my feet. The past two and a half days had been
brutal. On Monday and Tuesday, I worked all day, from
the time the diner opened until closing. Today, I only worked
the breakfast and lunch shift, which meant that considering
tomorrow was my day off, it was more like a day and a half
break.

I had just pulled into the driveway at Dom's place. After
parking, grabbing my bag, and the grocery bags from the car,
I walked up to the front door and pushed the key into the
lock.

Yes.

I now had a key to Dom's place.

Before I left for work on Monday morning, Dom stopped
me and handed me a key.

"What's this for?" I asked.

"I've got to go to work today. I expect I'll be home before
you get back, but I still want to make sure you can get in, just
in case something comes up."

"You aren't worried about me being in your home alone?"

"Are you going to steal from me?"

My head jerked back. "I would never do that," I replied

quietly, hurt that he felt the need to ask such a question.

"I know that, Ekko. Do you think I'd be giving you a key if I had any doubts about the kind of person you are?"

"I guess not."

I had to admit that morning that it felt good to know he trusted me the way he did. There was no reason for him to do what he was doing for me, yet somehow, it seemed simply effortless.

I used this opportunity to bring up what I needed to discuss with him. "I'd like to think that you loaning me your key is an indication of how you feel, but I wanted to ask anyway to be sure."

"Ask what?"

"Well, when you first invited me here to spend the night, I told you I might only need a couple days, but you obviously know that the apartment won't be ready for a week. I honestly didn't expect it would take that long based on the conversations I had with the landlord previously. I wanted to be certain you don't mind me staying with you until it's ready?"

"Not at all."

"Are you sure? I mean, you've given up your bed for me."

"I'm sure I don't mind you staying here with me." He took two steps closer to me. "I also don't mind giving up my bed for you. Now, if you want to invite me to join you there, I certainly won't turn you down."

I felt the heat spread through my body. Dom had to know what he was doing to me because I was certain my neck and cheeks were tinged pink. I dropped my gaze from Dom's a moment. When I looked back at him, it took everything in me not to give in and tell him I wanted him there with me that night. All I needed was companionship and someone to hold me. I wanted someone to talk to.

Instead of telling him what I wanted, though, I chickened

out, said goodbye, and left for work. Needless to say, by the time I made it back to his house Monday night, Dom was already there. And he had, once again, cooked dinner. Thankfully, he didn't make it awkward.

Tuesday was the same, minus the key situation and the bed conversation.

Today was the first day that I was actually getting the opportunity to use the key because I had arrived before Dom. When I left work, I made a quick stop at the grocery store. Having worked so much over the last couple days, I had made a lot of money in tips. I knew I needed to be mindful of what I was spending my money on since I was going to be moving soon, but I wanted to do something nice for Dom to show my appreciation for everything he'd done for me.

I didn't have a lot to spare, but that was nothing new. Over the years, I had perfected the art of cooking on a budget. So, I picked up all the fixings for stuffed pepper soup. I would have loved to have splurged and made it with ground beef, but instead opted for the cheaper ground turkey. It hurt to know that I couldn't properly thank him by giving him what I believed he deserved.

When I stepped inside, I locked the door behind me and made my way to the kitchen. Dom mentioned earlier that morning that he'd probably be back closer to six-thirty, so I had plenty of time left to get everything done. While the rice cooked in a separate pot and the meat browned, I chopped up the onions and peppers. Once the meat was finished, I took it out of the pot and set it aside so I could cook the vegetables. Then, I added the meat back in along with the spices, broth, diced tomatoes, and sauce. Setting the heat to low to allow it to simmer, I made my way upstairs so I could shower.

As I stood under the warm spray of the shower, I finally started to settle into the break that was before me. My plan for tonight was to spend my night reading the rest of my book from the library until Dom got home and we could have dinner together. I really enjoyed spending time with and talking to him, so I was looking forward to doing that tonight at a reasonable hour.

Tomorrow, Dom was taking me on an official date. I knew he'd have to work during the day, so I planned to make a trip to the library and to reach out to Ryan. I wanted to let him know that I had found a place and that I'd be getting my things out of his apartment within a few days. Part of my plans for the day also included figuring out what moving company I could hire to get my bed moved for the cheapest price.

After I finished in the shower, I got out and threw on a pair of shorts and a V-neck t-shirt. For the past couple nights, I'd woken up in the middle of the night to change out of pants and put on shorts. Dom's bed was just that warm and cozy.

Once I was dressed, I grabbed my book off Dom's nightstand and went back downstairs to check on the soup. It was perfect, so I kept it on low to keep it warm and set the rice aside. I didn't want to add that until Dom got home; otherwise, it would be nothing but mush. My belly was growling, so when I glanced up at the clock on the microwave, I was thankful it was quarter after six.

Curling up on the couch, I opened my book and dove in. I was so caught up in my book that I never noticed how much time had passed. I only realized it when I finished the last page. I went back out into the kitchen and noted it was just after eight-thirty. Frowning, I turned off the stove and went back to the couch. Minutes later, I was asleep.

My eyes shot open when I felt my body being moved. That's when I realized I was in Dom's arms and he was carrying me up the stairs.

His voice was low and sweet when he spoke, "Hey, sugar. I saw you made dinner. Sorry I missed it and you had to eat alone."

Still slightly disoriented, I shook my head.

Dom curled my body tighter into his. If I wasn't so tired, I would have fought to have him put me down. Instead, I enjoyed how great it felt being pressed against him. I especially loved the feel of his hands on my bare legs.

When we reached the bedroom, Dom walked over to the bed, looked down at me with a heart-warming gaze, and gave me a gentle squeeze before he lowered me to the mattress. His hands left my body and I immediately wanted them back.

"Good night, Ekko," he said softly.

I didn't want him to leave.

"Dom?" I called, my voice raspy with sleep, as I reached out and wrapped my hand around his forearm.

"Yeah?"

"Will you stay with me tonight?"

Dom held my eyes in silence for a long while seemingly battling thoughts he was having. I watched as the muscle in his jaw twitched.

Finally, he answered, "I had a long day; I've got to shower first."

"Okay," I replied, my eyelids growing heavy.

"Go back to sleep."

At his request, I rolled to my side and closed my eyes. I listened as I heard the door to the bathroom open and close. I tried to wait to fall back asleep until after Dom was finished and got in bed, but once I heard the water running in the shower, it quickly lulled me to sleep. It was a good thing it had because otherwise I would have known that after taking his shower, Dom decided against staying in bed with me and preferred taking the couch instead.

Dom

Walking out of my bedroom last night and leaving Ekko there alone in my bed to sleep after she'd asked me to stay with her was the hardest thing I'd ever done in my life. Having had the opportunity to get to know her over the last few days, I felt myself growing more and more attracted to her.

The need in her voice and the hunger in her eyes when she asked me to stay had rocked me a bit. I wanted nothing more than to climb in the bed and curl up behind her, but I decided against it. Ekko deserved more than she allowed herself to believe. She was at a point in her life where she was vulnerable, and I didn't think it was fair to take advantage of that the way I could have with her invitation.

I had been looking forward to coming home from work and spending time with Ekko. She spent all day Monday and Tuesday working. The only time I got to see her was first thing early in the morning or when she got home late at night, exhausted and overworked. While I loved the drive she had to work hard so she could give herself more in life, I hated seeing how much of a toll it was taking on her. She was beyond tired and, given how much she worked, she never seemed to have any time for herself. Other than the library, she never did anything fun.

That's part of why I was excited to get home from work to spend time with her last night. I wanted to come home, make dinner, and watch a movie. We were going out on a date tonight and I had been planning on taking her out to dinner and to do something fun, so last night was really just about being close to her. All I wanted was to have her next to me on the couch while we watched a movie.

But my plans were shot to shit because of work. Levi, my boss and the owner of Cunningham Security, got into a situation on a case he was working on. He needed back up and I was available. As much as I wanted to get home to Ekko, Levi needed me, and I'd never let any of the guys on my team down. Aside from that, Levi was going to be getting married in a few weeks and I was certain his fiancée, Elle, would have lost her mind if something happened to him.

In the end, Levi and I got done what we needed to get done and I eventually made my way home. Unfortunately, it was a lot later than I had anticipated.

And if it wasn't torturous enough to know that Ekko was getting some time off from work and I couldn't spend it with her, I had to walk into the house and see everything that I did. To start, she was on my couch, asleep, looking like an angel. She had on a pair of tiny shorts that showed off her gorgeous legs. It was the first time I had seen her bare legs and I couldn't take my eyes away from them.

It was as I stood there staring at her that I noticed the aroma filling the house. Reluctantly, I tore my eyes from Ekko's legs and walked out into the kitchen to find that she had made dinner. It made me feel awful that she had gone through the trouble and I wasn't here to share it with her.

I left the kitchen and went back to Ekko. I slipped one arm under her back and the other under her soft, sexy legs before I lifted her up. Just holding her close to me with my hand on her leg, the scent of her consuming me, I felt my cock jerk.

I closed my eyes and took a deep breath, hoping to rein in the sexual frustration. After rescuing Ekko that night months ago, nobody else piqued my interest long enough for me to care about having even just a one-night stand. It had been a couple of months since I'd been with anyone and I was well past the point of being over pleasuring myself. But every time I did, it was always with thoughts of her filling my mind.

Climbing the stairs, I kept my eyes on Ekko's face. She looked so peaceful until her eyes fluttered open. I quickly apologized to her for not being there to have dinner with her. She didn't respond, and it made me feel even worse. That was, I felt awful until I put her down in the bed and she reached out to touch my arm.

Will you stay with me tonight?

I wanted to.

But I couldn't.

It wasn't how I wanted things to go with her.

So I gave her an excuse about needing a shower and told her to go back to sleep. Thankfully, by the time I got out of the shower she had fallen back asleep. I crept out of the room and made my way downstairs again. After putting some of the food Ekko made into a bowl and heating it in the microwave, I put the rest into containers and put it in the fridge. Before I fell asleep, I savored every bite of the delicious dinner she made.

Now, I was here on the couch, it was early in the morning, and I knew she was awake because I'd heard the toilet flush. I suspected she'd be walking down the stairs at any moment and I tried to prepare myself for the possibility of seeing her legs in those shorts again.

When too much time had passed and Ekko hadn't come downstairs, I decided to go up. I knocked on the door and waited.

"Come in," I heard.

I opened the door and saw Ekko sitting on the edge of the bed, her bare legs and feet dangling over the side. She looked sad.

"Are you alright?" I asked.

"Yeah," she replied, but I could tell she didn't mean it.

I walked over and sat on the edge of the bed next to her. The urge to touch her was overwhelming, but I resisted.

"Is something wrong?" I pushed for the truth.

She hesitated a moment before explaining, "No, I'm just thinking about everything I have to get done today."

"You don't work today, right?"

She shook her head but didn't offer anything else.

I decided to take a different approach. "Sorry about last night," I lamented.

The minute the words were out of my mouth, Ekko's body tensed beside me. My instincts kicked in and my hand immediately went to her thigh. She tensed further, and I watched her as her eyes stayed glued to my hand. Slowly, her stare left my hand and traveled up my arm, to my shoulder, and finally, my face. I wanted her to tell me what was wrong, so I waited.

"I guess it's safe to assume we aren't going to be going on a date tonight anymore," she stated so matter-of-factly.

My head jerked, and I questioned, "What? Why not?"

Confusion washed over her face. "I assumed you didn't want to."

"What could possibly make you think that?"

Her voice was just a touch over a whisper when she answered, "I asked you to stay with me last night." Once she got the words out, her eyes went to the floor.

I watched in complete shock as her breathing grew quick and shallow. I could tell she was struggling to remain calm. And then I felt the wetness on the top of my hand.

A tear.

She was crying.

"Ekko, look at me."

She didn't.

My hand left her thigh and came up to the side of her head. I ran my fingers through the hair there and used my other hand to turn her face toward me.

It was a good thing I was sitting because the anguish in her face would have brought me to my knees.

With my hands framing her face, I asked, "Sugar, why are you crying?"

She didn't respond immediately, but eventually spoke and completely gutted me. "It's not your fault, Dom. I've been on my own for as long as I can remember. And it's completely fine; I'm used to it. But I just wanted one night where I wouldn't have to feel so lonely."

I hated myself and could do nothing other than stroke my thumb over her cheekbone.

Even if I had wanted to, I couldn't even respond to her because she went on, "I'm sorry. It's just that you've shown me such kindness and generosity. I haven't had that since Ms. Grace gave it to me. I'm so confused about everything I feel when I'm around you. The only thing I know for certain is that for the first time in my life, it feels good."

I moved quick.

Keeping my hands on the side of her face, I brought my mouth to hers. The second my lips touched Ekko's, her hands went to my wrists and squeezed. A second later, she pushed past the shock and gave into what was happening. As we kissed, one of my hands dropped to her waist as the other slid into her hair and held her at the back of her head. My fingertips at her waist dug in while my tongue dipped in her mouth to taste her. The desperate sounds of Ekko's moans filled my ears as her hands found their way up my arms to my chest. I fell to my back in the bed, taking Ekko with me. She straddled my hips and my hands went to her thighs. Ekko and I continued to kiss as she began rocking her hips over me and my hands roamed over her body.

When I thought I might die from the torture of having her sweet, little body writhing over mine, I wrapped my arms around her and rolled her to her back. Disconnecting my mouth from hers, I kissed along her jaw and down her neck. I moved back up her throat, over her jaw, and to her mouth again before I pulled back to look at her. There was nothing but pure lust and desire in Ekko's eyes. I'd never seen her looking sexier than she did in that moment.

"Never, Ekko. As long as I'm around, you'll never be alone. I promise you."

"You feel so good, Dom," she croaked. "Everything about you just feels good and I don't want to lose that."

"You won't," I assured her.

The truth was, I didn't know where things would lead between the two of us, but I knew that I wouldn't just abandon Ekko. There was something about her that I was drawn to, and even if things didn't work out between us on a romantic level, I was certain I didn't have it in me to ever turn my back on her.

There was something innately good about her, and I knew it was something I wanted in my life.

"So then we are still going out on a date tonight?" she asked, hopeful.

"Fun size, you just proved to me exactly how much of a good time you can be. We are definitely going on a date tonight because I want more of everything you've got."

A smile formed on her face briefly, but it was quickly replaced with a frown.

"What's the matter?"

"What should I wear?"

It was evident she was genuinely curious, but there was a touch of worry in her voice at her question. I knew exactly where it was coming from, too.

"Keep it casual," I advised. "Tonight is all about having fun. Jeans, sneakers, and whatever top you want to wear. Ultimately, you'll need something long-sleeved, but a light jacket will suffice if you aren't wearing long sleeves otherwise."

Relief swept through her.

I knew it. She had been worried that I was going to take her somewhere fancy and she wouldn't have anything nice enough to wear. I expected I'd want to have her all dolled up for me at some point, but I wasn't ready for that yet. Tonight, I wanted her to let loose and enjoy her night off.

"Are you hungry for breakfast?" I asked.

She jerked her head up and down quickly. "I haven't eaten anything since yesterday morning," she shared.

"What?"

"I was waiting for you to come back from work last night so we could eat together, but I fell asleep before you got here."

"I thought you ate."

I was so angry with myself for not confirming it with her last night.

She shook her head.

"I'm sorry," I apologized. "Let me make it up to you this morning."

She grinned and agreed.

With that, I slid my arms under her body, behind her back, and instructed, "Keep your legs wrapped around me. I'll carry you down."

Maybe I was a sucker for punishment, but having Ekko's legs wrapped around me with her little body pressed against mine was worth it. I took her downstairs, where I made breakfast for her. I spent the entire time struggling to keep thoughts of how hot she was that morning from clouding my brain.

I was unsuccessful in that venture.

CHAPTER 6

Ekko

"I'LL BE BACK HERE NO LATER THAN FIVE-FIFTEEN," DOM informed me as we stood at the front door.

"Okay," I replied. "I'm going to run some errands today, but I'll be here way before you get back from work."

Dom smiled at me, took two steps toward me, and used his thumb and forefinger to hold my chin. Then, he lowered his mouth to mine. He kissed me, but his kiss was much different than the one from this morning. There was no tongue involved, yet Dom somehow made it just as hot as if there had been. This kiss was soft, sweet, and deliciously slow.

When he pulled his mouth from mine, Dom grinned and promised, "I'm looking forward to more of that tonight."

"Me too," I said softly.

Without another word, Dom turned and walked out.

Even though I had a few things I needed to get done today, I went over and collapsed on the couch. Then, I allowed myself to take the next twenty minutes to relive my morning with Dom.

It was crazy. I never suspected that Dom wouldn't have joined me after I asked, but when I woke this morning and he wasn't there, I had to admit just how much it hurt. I had been utterly devastated about how things had happened last night.

I had been sitting there on the edge of his bed contemplating how I'd gotten everything so mixed up. With everything he said to and did for me over the course of the last few days combined with the words we spoke and the looks we gave one another, I had gotten the impression that there was a bit more between us. When I woke up alone, I realized I had been wrong.

But then he walked into the bedroom this morning and knew something was upsetting me. It was never my intention to tell him the truth about what was bothering me, but I figured one more embarrassment wouldn't matter. And the moment I finished telling him what was bothering me, he kissed me.

And my entire world changed.

It was the most incredible kiss of my life. I had kissed guys before, Ryan being the most recent, but nothing compared to kissing Dom. If I hadn't been so turned on, I'm certain I would have cried at the feeling that swept through me. Dom kissed me with such passion and need, the evidence that he was just as turned on as me was pressed right up against me. I grew hungrier for him and he effortlessly rolled me to my back.

Being here on his couch now remembering the feeling of his mouth on my skin as it traveled down my throat, I failed to suppress a moan. The physical attraction to Dom was beyond anything I'd ever experienced before and that didn't even come close to the attraction I felt to him on a level that had nothing to do with how he looked.

Hearing him make that promise to me that I'd never be alone, that I'd never lose him in my life, had my heart bursting with emotions. I had wanted to latch onto the feeling of excitement about how things might develop between us, but I was worried. Life had taught me to be cautious and the uncertainty of the situation with Dom caused a bit of anxiety.

It had been less than a week and I was already finding myself growing attached to Dom. The problem with this was that I had a feeling that getting close to someone like him only to have it end would be the kind of thing that could destroy a woman like me.

A feeling of sadness washed over me.

No.

I wasn't going to allow that to happen. It wasn't very often I experienced happiness, so I needed to soak it up while I had it. Today started off great and I was sure Dom was going to see to it that it ended the same.

Picking myself up off the couch, I went upstairs to get dressed so I could run my errands. Twenty minutes later, I was on my way to the library. When I arrived, I grabbed my stack of books and went inside.

Once inside, the sadness I felt not quite an hour ago had completely vanished. I was in a place that brought me such peace, something I so often craved. On that thought, I decided I'd hang out and read for a while.

I quickly returned the books I had borrowed and finished and went in search of some new titles. I hadn't done a search in a while, so I figured I'd use the computer and check to see if any of my favorite authors had released any new titles.

Today must have been my lucky day because I scored two new titles plus one that I'd been dying to read that was always checked out when I was there. I found a good spot to sit and dove in.

Before I knew it, I had gotten three-quarters of the way through one of the books and it was approaching two o'clock. Since I still had to run to Ryan's to grab some of my clothes, I needed to leave the library now. I checked out my books and left.

Given that I hadn't returned Ryan's key, I knew I'd be able

to get in. I only hoped he wouldn't be around so that I could go in, get what was mine, and get out. Pulling into the parking lot at the apartment complex, I found I wasn't so lucky as I spotted Ryan's car parked in its usual spot.

I let out an audible sigh and wrestled with whether I should wait until he wasn't around before I attempted to do this. If I didn't have a date with Dom tonight, I would have waited. Unfortunately, in my haste to leave Ryan's nearly a week ago, I hadn't taken all my clothes with me. Some of my nicer things were still here and I wanted to make sure I put in the effort to look good for my first official date with Dom. I knew he said to stay casual, but I still wanted to look nice.

Mustering up enough courage to do what I had to do, I got out of the car and walked toward Ryan's door. Since he was there and I had no idea what I could walk in to, I chose to knock instead of using the key I had to allow myself in.

It might have been twenty seconds later when the door finally opened.

"Ekko? What are you doing here?" Ryan asked as he stepped back and allowed me to come in.

"I wanted to come by so I could not only get a few things but also to let you know that I should have the rest of it out of here this weekend," I answered.

He stared at me a moment and pressed, "Where are you staying?"

"That's really none of your business."

"You don't need to be a bitch, Ekko."

What did I ever see in him?

"I'm not being a bitch, Ryan. You and I are no longer together, and we haven't been for a long time. I thought we were at least going to be able to keep things friendly between us, but then I found out that you're a drug dealer. I'm not going to be around that, and you know why," I shared, even though it was all information that he already knew.

"So, let me get this straight. We're not together and we're no longer friends," he repeated. "Do I have that right?"

"Yes."

He smirked and said, "Then I guess you can get your things out of here when you pay me your share of the rent for all the months you were here."

"You can't be serious."

"I am. Your half of the rent would be three hundred dollars a month for…how many months was it? I'll be nice and say four, even though it was a little longer than that."

He was crazy.

Though, considering I dated him on and off for three years, I wasn't sure what that said about me.

"I don't have twelve hundred dollars to give you right now."

"That's okay," he started. "I'm not going anywhere. You can come back when you have it and then you can get your things."

I was desperate for those clothes and I had an extra seventy-five dollars on me. I didn't want to give it all away to him, so I tried to reason with him. "I've got fifty dollars on me. If I give you that, can I please go get some of my clothing?"

"Payment in full before anything leaves."

He knew how desperate I was and what my situation was like. He was making this difficult on purpose, knowing that he'd have a way to keep me tied to him if he played this game. Refusing to let him win and wanting to get what was mine, I took two steps in the direction of the room I had been staying in, but Ryan blocked me from going any farther.

"Why are you being such a jerk about this?"

"I'm not," he tried to defend himself. "I'm not going to do something for someone out of the goodness of my heart when I'm getting nothing in return."

"I'll pay you, Ryan. But I don't have that kind of money on me right now and I need to get some of my clothes."

He moved toward me and was inches away when he put his hand in my hair. "I'm willing to negotiate. Do you have anything else of value you can offer?"

How could I have not known how much of an asshole he was? Was I so desperate for a connection to anyone, to feel like I belonged somewhere, when I was with him that I couldn't see just what kind of person he was?

"I have *nothing* to offer you," I clipped.

"That's a shame. It would have been such a nice way to say goodbye," he proclaimed. "I guess you'll have to come back when you have my money then."

I had one final option. I reached into my bag and pulled out the phone Dom had gotten me. The screen lit up and I could see he sent texts earlier when I was at the library. I never knew it because I had silenced the phone before I went inside. Unlocking the phone, I looked up at Ryan and threatened, "I could call the police so they can see to it that I get what's mine. If you're nice about it, I won't tell them about the business you're running."

Ryan's eyes narrowed on the phone before they came back to me. "I think someone's been holding out on me," he began. "How does someone like you who was in such a hopeless situation end up with the latest and greatest smartphone?"

Shit.

I knew this phone was a bad idea. I tried dissuading Dom from purchasing this one and begged him to just get the cheapest phone there when he insisted on getting me one, but he refused to listen. Now, it was coming back to bite me.

"That's none of your business either."

At that moment, my phone rang, and Ryan snatched it

out of my hand. Nobody but Dom knew the number.

I tried to get the phone back from him, but Ryan was so much bigger than me. He held one arm out while he slid his finger across the screen and answered.

"Hello?"

I continued to try to get the phone but failed. Ryan's arms were so much longer than mine.

"Who am I? Well, I think the better question is who are you?" Ryan said into the phone.

There was silence while Dom replied.

"Ekko's right here. She's fine. Actually, she's not completely fine. She's being a bitch for no reason at all."

"Ryan, give me my phone," I demanded as I pushed my way closer to him, reaching out for it.

Ryan pushed back harder against me and I lost my footing. I fell backward and hit my face on the sharp edge of the coffee table. I cried out as pain seared through the side of my face and I felt the warm liquid dripping down my cheek.

"Oh, now she's gone and injured herself and is making a mess of my floor," Ryan taunted Dom on the phone. "I've got to go and get her out of here before she ruins my carpet."

I held my hand up to the side of my face and guessed I was cut somewhere pretty close to my eye, just on the edge of my eyebrow.

"Let's go, Ekko. You've got to go now," Ryan said from above me.

I looked up at him in disgust and tried to ignore the pain in my head. "I'm not leaving without my phone and my clothes."

"I hate to tell you that you're wrong. You are leaving, and you aren't taking anything with you. When I get my money for giving your ass a place to stay, you can have your stuff back."

The blood continued to stream down my face. I took a

few minutes to wipe at it with the sleeve and hem of my shirt, but it continued to flow steadily. This was not good. I needed to get something to hold against the cut.

Suddenly, there was a knock at the door.

Great, he probably had some clients coming over to buy drugs. I needed to get out of there before any of that went down, so I started moving to stand up. Ryan had already walked away from me toward the door.

My back was to the door as I used the coffee table to steady myself. That's when I heard Ryan ask, "Who the fuck are you?"

I turned around quickly, worried about who I might see. The eyes of a man I didn't recognize left Ryan and came to me. Then, his gaze turned murderous as he looked back at Ryan. When the man looked back at me, he asked, "Are you Ekko?"

My eyes rounded.

How did he know who I was?

"Yes," I squeaked.

The man, who easily had a good four or five inches and a significant amount more muscle than Ryan, looked back at Ryan and pushed his way past him. His eyes were fixed on me as he approached. My body grew more and more tense. This man was seriously intimidating. He was about the same height as Dom but didn't have as much muscle mass. That didn't mean he wasn't scary.

"I'm Levi," he said as he came to a stop in front of me.

Of course, this didn't tell me anything and I remained frozen on the spot, fearful.

"I own Cunningham Security. Dom works for me."

Relief swept through me at the same time I was wondering what Levi was doing here.

"Dom should be here any minute now. I was in the area

on a case when he called and said you were in trouble."

"Do you mind getting out of my apartment?" Ryan shouted.

"I want my phone back, Ryan," I shot back.

With his arm wrapped around my shoulders, Levi asked, "Do you have something that belongs to her?"

"She owes me money. When she pays me what she owes me, she can have what's hers. I'm keeping it as collateral."

"Ryan? Is that your name?" Levi wondered. It was evident from the tone of his voice that he didn't have much patience for the man standing in front of him.

I had a feeling Ryan knew it because he didn't answer. He simply jerked his chin in response to Levi's question.

"Let me tell you something. I'm good friends with many members of the local police department. Maybe you've heard of Detective Jackson Baines. I work closely with him on a lot of cases. Anyway, I've got him programmed into my phone and with the push of one button, I can have the WPD swarming this place. Do you think they might find anything of interest here?"

I lifted my hand that wasn't covered in blood and tapped Levi's shoulder. When he looked down at me, I asked, "Does Detective Baines like drug dealers?"

Levi's eyes sparkled, and he let out a chuckle. "No, sweetheart. He has a real distaste for drug dealers."

I pretended to think a minute by tapping on my chin and added, "Well, my ex-boyfriend here was kind enough to allow me to stay with him for a few months while I tried to get back on my feet. Unfortunately, I walked into this place about a week ago and found out that he's a drug dealer. I bet he's got something here that the police would love to find."

"I'm inclined to agree with you," Levi replied.

"Ekko?" Dom's panicked voice came from the doorway.

My eyes left Levi and went to Dom. He took one look at me and immediately directed his attention to Ryan. Instead of coming to me, Dom took slow, deliberate steps toward Ryan. My body grew tense. Levi must have noticed because he squeezed my shoulder a little tighter. A few more men, who had to have been with Dom, appeared in the doorway, but I couldn't pay attention to them.

Dom was closing in on Ryan, who continued to walk backward until his back was up against the wall. Dom's hand shot out and gripped Ryan around the throat.

"Why is there blood on her face?" Dom seethed.

"It…it was her own fault," Ryan stammered.

Dom's fingers squeezed a little tighter. "I'm sorry, did I just hear you say it was her fault?"

Ryan's eyes grew wide.

One of the guys in the doorway, who bared a resemblance to Levi, but had longer hair that was somewhere between blonde and brown, warned, "Dom's a crazy motherfucker, man. You might want to consider how you answer that question."

I recognized the guy from the night I was nearly kidnapped. He had been there with Dom that night, but I couldn't remember his name.

Another guy, with shorter dark hair and a body that was just as nice as the rest of them, added, "Yeah. I remember what he did years ago to the guy who thought beating and sexually assaulting Levi and Cruz's sister-in-law was acceptable. Dom had no personal attachment to that girl and her ex was begging for mercy when Dom was through with him. I can't imagine what he'd do to someone who hurt a woman who was special to him."

I gasped while Ryan's eyes shifted back and forth.

"She was reaching for her phone and pushed me," Ryan

explained. "I pushed her away from me and she fell."

Now Dom's gaze looked a lot like Levi's did when he first arrived…lethal.

"You pushed her?"

"She pushed me first!" Ryan tried to reason.

Keeping his hand at Ryan's throat, Dom stepped to the side and looked over at me. "Do you see her?"

Ryan didn't answer.

"*I asked you a question!*" Dom roared.

"Yes, I see her." Ryan's voice was small.

"So, that woman, who is maybe a hundred and ten pounds, moved toward you to get *her* phone that you had, and *you* pushed *her*? I don't like seeing my woman with blood on her face and, lucky for you, I need to see to her right now, so you're going to give me her phone without another minute of delay."

Ryan quickly pulled the phone out of his pocket and handed it to Dom.

Not taking his eyes off Ryan, Dom called, "Ekko, come here."

I was still stuck on Dom calling me *his* woman that I couldn't move.

Dom realized I hadn't moved and turned his head toward me. With his gaze laser-focused on me, he urged, "Ekko, come here."

Levi brought his hand to my lower back and gave me a nudge. I moved toward Dom.

When I was standing next to him, Dom asked, "Why did you come here?"

My lip quivered, and I dropped my gaze to the ground.

His voice went soft and he said, "Sugar, look at me."

When I looked at Dom, his voice, still gentle, asked, "What did you come here for?"

"I don't have a ton of nice clothes, but I had a few things here that I wanted to get before tonight. I wanted to look pretty for our date. But Ryan wouldn't let me get my things."

"Pierce? Cruz?" Dom called out never taking his eyes from mine.

Cruz. That was his name.

"Yeah?" one of them replied.

"Do you mind hanging out with this lowlife piece of shit while I go with Ekko to get her things?"

"Not at all," they replied in unison. There was an edge of delight in their voices.

Dom loosened his grip on Ryan's throat and finally let him go.

"Where's your stuff?" he asked me.

"In the second bedroom, down the hall."

We walked down the hall to the spare bedroom. Once inside, Dom ordered, "Get everything that is yours. You're not coming back here ever again."

"I can't," I replied, still using my shirt to swipe at the cut on my face.

"You can't what?"

"I can't take everything that's mine."

"Why not?"

"The bed and the dresser are mine," I explained.

He thought a moment before he instructed, "Get everything else as quickly as you can. I'll be right back."

Dom walked out of the room and I pulled out the rest of my clothing. It wasn't much, but it was all I had to my name. I found my worn-out suitcase in the closet and tossed it on the bed. By the time Dom came back into the room, I had put the remainder of my things in the suitcase. The only items that remained were the mattress, bed frame, and the dresser.

"Is that everything?" Dom asked nodding to my suitcase.

"Yes."

He walked over, picked it up, and ushered me out of the room. When we made it to the front of the apartment, Dom spoke to Levi. "The bed and the dresser are hers."

I looked to Dom, confused at what he was doing.

"We'll take care of it. Get her to a doctor to get checked out," Levi remarked.

Dom nodded and looked back at me. "Where are your keys?"

"In my purse."

"Give them to Levi," he ordered.

"What?"

"The guys are going to get your things loaded in Levi and Cruz's trucks. Pierce will drive your car back for you. You're coming with me so I can get your head checked."

"Oh, that's okay. I can drive my car now," I insisted, not wanting to inconvenience them any further.

"You think so?" Dom asked disbelievingly. "You've got blood pouring down your face. You're not driving anywhere right now."

Other than when he was speaking to Ryan, I'd never seen Dom so angry. This situation was already tense and I really didn't want to make matters worse, so I pulled my keys out and handed them to Levi.

His face softened when he took them from me.

At that moment, Dom put his hand to the small of my back and started guiding me toward the front door.

Once we were out of the apartment, he tossed my suitcase into the backseat of his truck before he opened the door for me. I climbed in while Dom went to the backseat again. When he closed the back door, I looked out and saw he had a t-shirt in his hand that he was dumping water all over.

He moved back to my door and brought the shirt up to

my head. Feeling the sting, I winced. Dom didn't say anything as he cleaned up my face. A minute later, he held a clean, dry shirt up to the side of my face and stated, "Hold this here."

Then, he got in and drove away in silence.

CHAPTER 7

Ekko

OM AND I HAD BEEN DRIVING FOR ABOUT TEN MINUTES IN complete silence when I couldn't take it any longer. I finally had to say something.

"Dom?" I called when we stopped at a red traffic light.

He glanced over at me but said nothing.

"Where are you taking me?"

"The hospital," he muttered.

Now I had two dilemmas. Not only did I not like the way Dom was acting, but I also could not go to the hospital.

"Um, I don't think the hospital is necessary," I said, hoping he'd listen.

He raised his eyebrows, leaned over the center console, and pulled the shirt away from my head.

"You're still bleeding. I'm pretty sure you need a couple of stitches," he concluded before looking up at the still-red traffic light.

No.

I couldn't.

There was no way.

"Is there somewhere else you could take me? Maybe a free clinic instead," I suggested.

His eyes shot to mine. "For your face? You want me to

take you to a free clinic to treat a wound on your face that could permanently scar you if not taken care of properly by a plastic surgeon? Do you want a reminder of that asshole every time you look in the mirror for the rest of your life?"

I couldn't afford a hospital bill, let alone a plastic surgeon.

And Dom was so angry. I didn't like how it made me feel. I wasn't scared; I never was around Dom. But seeing him so angry made me sad, especially because I knew I was the reason for it.

The light changed, and Dom started driving again. Clearly, he was irritated with me, so I remained silent. I'd just have to find out what this was going to cost me before I allowed them to do anything.

A few minutes later, Dom pulled into the parking lot at the emergency room. We went inside, and I did my best to ignore the stares coming from other patients in the waiting room. I couldn't necessarily blame them for staring. I had to look a bit frightening with the blood all over my shirt. After walking up to the registration desk and explaining what happened, the woman behind the desk asked for my identification and insurance card.

"I don't have health insurance," I murmured.

"Oh, that's not a problem. If you need to apply for financial aid to help with the costs, I can give you the paperwork for that."

"What's the estimated cost?" Dom asked from behind me.

"It'll depend on how many stitches she needs, how severe the wound is, what supplies are used, and the medications administered. If you can hang tight a minute, I can try to get you an estimate of costs."

We waited while the woman walked off.

I looked up at Dom as he looked down at me. He didn't look as angry anymore, just frustrated.

"I'm sorry," I said after a few moments of silence. "I never expected this to happen. I feel like an idiot, but I guess I was blind to just how awful he was when we were together. I didn't have anyone else; maybe that's why I chose to ignore what I probably always saw there."

"Ekko, why—" He started before he was cut off.

"Okay, so I have an estimate for the cost here, but there are so many factors that could alter this," the woman interrupted us. "Here's an approximation of what you can expect to pay assuming you need stitches. Of course, the cost is dependent on the number of stitches needed."

She held out a piece of paper and, though I didn't understand everything that was on it, I gathered enough to know I couldn't afford this. "So, I'm looking at just over twenty-one hundred dollars as my best-case scenario?" I inquired.

She gave me a look that told me she realized it was a lot of money, but that there was nothing she could do about it.

I looked up at Dom. "I can't afford this. I need to go somewhere else."

"I'll cover it, Ekko."

"No."

I was firm in my decision. He'd already done too much and if he thought he was adding this to the list, he had another thing coming.

"You are not doing this, Dom. I've caved on a lot, but I'm not going to be alright with you paying thousands of dollars for my medical care. I'm asking you to please take me somewhere else."

He struggled with what I'd asked of him but ultimately agreed. Once we were back in his truck, he pulled out his phone and called someone.

"No, not yet. We were just at the hospital, but Ekko doesn't have insurance. She won't let me cover the costs, so I need another option. She's going to need stitches."

He waited for the person on the other end to respond.

A moment later, he said, "I appreciate it. Where should we meet him?"

Silence again.

"Right. Thanks, boss."

Dom disconnected the call and looked over at me.

"We're going to Levi's house. Both of his parents are doctors and, lucky for us, his dad is a surgeon. Levi is going to have him meet us there."

I let out a sigh of relief. I had to believe that Levi's dad, even though he was a surgeon, might be less than a hospital visit.

With that, Dom backed out of the parking spot and drove off.

Levi's home wasn't far from the hospital. When Dom pulled into the driveway, I stopped breathing. The home was massive and absolutely stunning. I'd only ever read about places like this.

After parking, Dom came around the truck to meet me at my door. We were then greeted at the front door by a beautiful blonde-haired woman.

"Hey, Dom," she beamed, giving him a hug. "Levi should be here shortly. David's already here. Come on in."

"Thanks, rockstar. This is Ekko," he introduced me. "Ekko, this is Elle, Levi's fiancée."

With one hand still holding the t-shirt to my head, I lifted the other and offered a wave. "Hey. It's nice to meet you."

"You too, love. I'm so sorry to hear what happened. Let me introduce you to Levi's father so he can get you all patched up."

I dropped my eyes to the ground. Not only did Dom, Levi, and several of their other co-workers know about my financial situation, but now Levi's fiancée did too. It was obvious that they were well off. I shuddered to think what they must have thought of me.

Dom and I followed behind Elle.

When we stepped into the kitchen, an older gentleman walked over to us and held his hand out to Dom.

"Dr. C," Dom said as he shook the man's hand. "Good to see you."

"You too, Dom. It's been a while," he replied before he turned his attention to me. "Who's this young lady?"

"This is Ekko. Ekko, this is Levi and Cruz's dad, Dr. David Cunningham."

"It's nice to meet you, Dr. Cunningham. I appreciate you coming here so quickly to help me."

He offered me a friendly smile and insisted, "It's no problem, dear. And please, call me David."

After giving him a slight nod, David reached his hand out to the t-shirt covering the side of my head and suggested, "How about you go lie down over on the couch and we can get this taken care of?"

I walked over to the couch, laid down, and David got to work. He talked to me throughout the process, sometimes letting me know what he was doing and other times telling me about his son's upcoming wedding. I preferred the wedding talk since it offered a nice distraction from the pain on the side of my face.

Just as David finished up, Dom, Levi, and Elle all came into the family room. I sat up and Dom walked over to me.

"Are you okay?"

He was so different now. His voice was soft and gentle. He was no longer angry or frustrated.

I was so shocked by the change, I only nodded.

David chimed in and gave instructions on how to care for

the stitches. When he finished, I repeated, "Thank you again for doing this for me."

"You're welcome."

"Um, this is a bit awkward, but how much did you want for this?" I nervously asked.

David let out a bit of laughter before he looked at Dom. "You'll be there in December, right?"

Dom nodded.

I had no idea what they were talking about.

"Is this your plus one?"

Dom replied, "I haven't asked her yet, but that's what I was hoping for."

"Good," David said before turning his attention to me. "Levi and Elle are getting married in December. If you come to the wedding with Dom, I'll need you to save a dance for me."

"I can do that," I assured him. "But are you sure?"

"A beautiful woman like you? I'm more than sure."

Elle jumped in and declared, "Great. Now that that's settled, Ekko why don't you come with me? We can get you a clean shirt before I show you the library. Dom told me you're an avid reader like me."

I instantly perked up, the pain in my head and the awkwardness of the situation completely gone. "You have a library?"

Her face lit up and she bubbled, "Filled with romance novels."

I turned to look at Dom and asked, "Do you mind?"

He shook his head.

"I promise I won't take too long."

"It's okay, sugar. Take your time," he insisted.

I watched him a moment trying to figure out what the sudden change was all about with him, but he gave no indication. Realizing it wasn't the time nor the place to bring up a discussion about it, I stood and followed Elle.

She took me up to her bedroom, where she held out a clean top for me to wear.

"I have a bunch of my clothes in the truck," I explained. "I can just run out and grab something."

"It's okay," she assured me. "Besides, I have partly selfish reasons for sneaking you away."

"Oh? What's up?" I wondered.

"Well, maybe they're more purely curious reasons instead of selfish," she admitted. "I didn't know Dom was seeing anyone. While David was stitching you up, I tried getting the details from him about what was going on between the two of you, but he wasn't very forthcoming."

I shrugged my shoulders and confessed, "I'm not sure there's a whole lot to tell."

"Really? He seems to be completely captivated by you, and I was really hoping he had found a good woman. After what he did for me, I would love to know that he's getting something good in his life."

Suddenly, I was intrigued. "What he did for you?"

She closed her eyes briefly and when they opened again, she shared, "He saved my life."

"What?" I worried. "What happened?"

Elle shook her head and waved her hand in the air as if she was dismissing the melancholy thoughts she was experiencing. "It was a while ago, but I was being stalked. When my stalker tried to kill me, Dom was there just in time to save me."

"Oh my goodness," I blurted. "Are you okay?"

"I'm perfect now," Elle declared. "I'm happy and I'm getting married to the man of my dreams, something that wouldn't have happened if Dom hadn't been here that day. I just wanted to be nosy and see if Dom was on his way to finding the same."

I sat there in shock. She seemed like she was such a good person, a good friend, and Dom was lucky to have that in his life. What I would have given to have someone like Elle in my life.

"I'm not really sure where things are headed with us," I answered honestly. "I know that I like him…a lot. And we were supposed to go out on our first date tonight, but I think I ruined that."

Elle's eyes widened, and she exclaimed, "You're going on your first date tonight?"

"Well, we were supposed to…before all this happened."

"What exactly happened?"

I didn't know Elle at all. I wasn't sure why I'd even said as much as I already did. She was, much like Dom, way out of my league. As badly as I wanted to have a friend, I had to be honest with myself. I had no business being friends with someone like Elle.

It was almost as though she was reading my mind because she came over to me and wrapped her arm around my shoulders and assured me, "I just told you that I had a stalker that nearly killed me. It was someone I knew; it was someone I was close to. We all have our own problems, Ekko. I'm not judging you."

I took in a deep breath and let it out. I told her all about my troubles. I explained why I had gone to Ryan's earlier that day and how I ended up needing three stitches on my face.

"I'm so sorry you've been through all of this recently," she lamented when I finished my story.

"That's life, I guess."

Thankfully, at that moment, Elle changed topics and asked, "So, where are you going on your date?"

"I don't know. Dom just told me it was all about having fun."

"Do you have an outfit picked out?"

"Not yet. I was just going to go through my stuff I got

when I went to Ryan's and figure something out. I didn't think all of this crazy nonsense would have happened and that I would have had more time to figure it out."

Elle put her hand on mine and stressed, "I've got a closet full of cute tops. You're tiny, but I'm sure we can find something that'll be perfect. What do you say? Care to go shopping in my closet?"

"Really? You would do that for me? You don't even know me."

She didn't waver. She simply claimed, "I think I know enough to know I like you. Come on. Let's find you an outfit."

So, Elle and I went into her massive closet where she let me try on a bunch of her clothes. I ended up finding something that looked incredible and she insisted I wear it.

Afterward, we went and checked out her library. It was the most amazing thing I'd ever seen, but I didn't have the time to truly appreciate all of it since it was getting late.

"You can come back anytime you want to check out my collection," Elle offered. "And if you've got any good recommendations, I'm always looking for something new to read and inspire me."

"Inspire you?"

She leaned in and practically sang, "I'm Elle Blackman, singer and songwriter."

"Oh my goodness," I declared. "I feel so stupid for not realizing. I've heard of you, but haven't ever heard you perform."

"I'm always performing at Big Lou's. Maybe you can come and watch the next time I'm performing."

"I'd love to. If you let me know early enough, I'll try to make sure I'm not scheduled to work."

"Sounds like a plan."

Elle and I exchanged numbers and she promised to let me know her schedule. With the wedding coming up, she wasn't going to be doing too many more shows, but there were a few. I only hoped I'd be able to go to one.

"Come on," she urged. "Let's go back out there with the boys, so Dom can get you out of here to get ready for your date."

We walked down the hall toward the family room, where we found Dom, Levi, and David were relaxing on the couches, talking. Of course, once we entered the room, all talking ceased. Dom's eyes came right to me.

Elle's voice filled the room. "You need to get Ekko out of here so she has enough time to get ready for your date tonight."

The guys all stood, but Dom was the only one to move. He walked over to me and put his arm around my waist, curling me into his side.

"Thanks again for coming here on such short notice, Dr. C," Dom declared.

David shook his head and insisted, "It was my pleasure." Then, he directed his attention to me and added, "I'm looking forward to that dance, Ekko."

Since I hadn't been officially invited to the wedding, I wasn't sure how to respond. I simply nodded and smiled at him.

After, I looked to both Elle and Levi. "Thank you for being so kind," I replied.

Minutes later, Dom and I had said goodbye to everyone and we were back in his truck on the way back to his place.

While this ride there was just as silent as the ones from earlier today, this one was different. It was different because even though it was quiet, Dom reached across the console and held my hand the entire time.

CHAPTER 8

Ekko

I CREPT QUIETLY DOWN THE STAIRS.

When Dom and I got back to his place, he told me he was going to shower in the spare bathroom and then he'd be ready to go. I wanted to talk to him about what happened today, but decided against doing it at that moment.

So, Dom carried my suitcase and the bag I brought from Elle and Levi's place with the top she loaned me to his bedroom. Then, he took off to the spare bathroom while I went into the master bathroom. I took my time in the shower, mostly because I had to be careful not to get the stitches wet. Even though David put gauze over them, I didn't want it getting doused in the shower.

When I finished, I got dressed and went to my suitcase. I didn't very often wear makeup, considering the extra cost and the fact that I never really went anywhere other than work or the library, so I still had some left from before things got really bad for me financially. Not knowing when I'd get the opportunity again, I decided I'd use some tonight. I applied some mascara and a touch of lip gloss and left it at that.

Then, I fixed my hair and used the next twenty minutes to prepare my mind for what the night would bring. The day started off fantastic, promising even. It turned ugly rather quickly and I was unsure of where Dom's thoughts were. Realizing I could sit and ponder it for hours and still not have an answer, I decided it was best to just go down and talk to him about everything.

When I reached the bottom of the stairs, I moved just enough so I could see into the family room. Dom was sitting on the couch with his head down, his elbows resting on his thighs and his hands clasped tightly together.

I hadn't made any noise, but he knew I was there. He looked up at me and his face softened.

Dom's eyes traveled the length of me before he stood and walked over to me. Once he was standing in front of me, he brushed his knuckles down my cheek and whispered, "You look beautiful."

Despite having so many questions I wanted to shout at him regarding his mood swings throughout the day, I refrained from doing so. And even though I had a bandage on the side of my face near my eye that made me seriously question just how beautiful I could possibly look, I simply accepted Dom's compliment and replied, "Thank you."

The truth is, I didn't know if I'd get this opportunity again. I wanted to enjoy tonight for everything that I hoped it would be. I still planned to talk to him about what happened, but I was going to give myself this first.

"This top is Elle's. She was kind enough to let me borrow it," I shared.

"I'm happy the two of you got along. She's a really sweet person and she'll be a great friend," he remarked.

While I didn't disagree that Elle was probably an incredible friend, I didn't want to admit that I was unsure I'd ever be able to offer anything of value to a friendship.

"I can certainly see that, but I knew I liked her the minute I heard she enjoyed reading. Oh man, what I wouldn't give to have someone to talk with about my favorite books," I sighed.

"I'm sure Elle would love that, too," Dom said as he reached for my hand and squeezed. "But you should know that I'll listen to you talk about them."

I rolled my eyes at him. "I don't picture you as the type to sit around discussing romance novels."

"I'm not, but I'd do it for you."

I shook my head. "It's not the same. While I appreciate your willingness to do so, it'd be so much more fun to talk to someone who has read the book. I'm not certain I can convince you to do that."

Dom laughed and indicated with a shake of his head that having him read the books was not something that was going to happen.

"Are you ready to go?" he asked.

"Yes."

"Tonight, we'll have to go in the truck. I had planned to take you out on the motorcycle tonight, but I think we'll have to do it another time. You'll need to wear a helmet and I imagine it's going to disturb the stitches. So, we'll just wait for you to heal and then I'll take you out on it."

My shoulders slumped. I had ruined the plans for tonight. Maybe we were still going out, but I'd ruined our first date.

Dom noticed my mood shift because he implored, "I really hope you're feeling upset because you aren't going to be getting a ride on the bike tonight and not because the idea of another date with me saddens you."

He couldn't be serious. Why would he ever think that I wouldn't want another date with him?

"I was looking forward to a ride on the bike with you," I admitted.

His face changed as he agreed, "Me too."

We stood there in silence a few moments until Dom held

his arm out indicating I could walk ahead of him toward the door. I grabbed my jacket, walked to the door, and we left.

Dom took me to an incredible restaurant that served authentic Mediterranean food. I hadn't ever had it before and was a bit overwhelmed with the options, so Dom suggested a few dishes and we split a couple appetizers. I knew I hadn't ever had so much food in one sitting and felt truly indulged.

As if the overabundance of food wasn't enough to make me feel spoiled, Dom proved to be the best date. He made me laugh and we had excellent conversation. I was surprised to learn that the guys he worked with were some of his best friends and that they all referred to him as the life of the party.

When I asked him why he'd gotten that title, he replied, "What's the point of being here if we aren't going to really live and enjoy life?"

It was the truth. Unfortunately, it just wasn't always that easy.

We finished dinner, Dom paid the bill, and we were now in his truck on the way to the second part of our date.

Dom pulled into a parking lot at a shopping complex and I was utterly confused. After he turned off the truck, he turned to look at me and asked, "When was the last time you went bowling?"

"I've never been bowling."

"What? Okay, this is going to be more fun than I thought it would be."

A few minutes later, we were inside the bowling alley. A little more than half of the lanes were already taken by groups of people wearing the same shirt. Dom explained that they were league bowlers who compete against each other through the course of the season. They competed for weekly and seasonal cash prizes and sometimes have a pool for strikes and spares. Mostly, he stressed that a lot of the bowlers did it for the good time with friends.

After reserving a lane for the two of us and renting our shoes, Dom helped me select a ball. While I put the bowling shoes on, Dom entered our names into the computer.

I had to be honest. I was so excited to learn how to bowl and it surprised me considering I'd never really thought about doing much outside of working and reading. Even if Dom hadn't promised me a second date, I knew this was something I'd never forget.

Dom was an amazing teacher. He taught me how to hold the ball and how to roll it. He explained how the arrows on the lane worked and how I could use them to improve my chances of knocking down pins.

My first ball was a gutter ball, but I knocked down eight pins on my second try. I was so proud of myself and it was clear that Dom was, too. Six frames later, I knocked down all the pins and had my first strike.

"Strike!!" I shouted, jumping up and down.

Dom came over and engulfed me in his arms. "Congratulations!"

A few minutes later, we had finished our first game. Dom had kicked my butt, but I didn't mind. I had just had the most fun experience of my life.

"Want to play another game?" he asked.

"Can we?" I returned, my voice hopeful.

Dom grinned at me and we started our second game. I did much better the second time around. I didn't get another strike, but I did manage to get three spares and I celebrated every single one of them. My score improved from our first game, even though Dom still won.

When we got back to his place, Dom told me to go change and get comfortable in warm clothes. He wanted to spend some time with me out on his deck and, since it was the beginning of November, it was starting to get pretty chilly. Thankfully, Dom had a fire pit, and by the time I joined him outside, it was already warming the space.

Just as I was about to sit down on the lounge chair next to the one he was sitting in, he held out his hand to me and called my name.

I placed my hand in his and he gently tugged me down into his lap. Dom wrapped one arm behind my back while the other rested on my outer thigh. My head fell into the crook of his neck. I loved how it felt being there with him.

"How did you like bowling?" Dom wondered.

"I've never had so much fun before in all my life," I admitted. "Thank you so much for giving me something real that is worth remembering."

His arms tightened around me.

"It meant a lot to me, too. I've been wanting to take you out for a long time...since that day you were nearly kidnapped."

I pulled my head back to look at him. "Are you serious?"

There was no hesitation when he responded, "Absolutely."

It warmed my heart to hear that our date was something that he had been looking forward to just as much as I had.

I cuddled back into him and we sat there in silence for a while. I took the time to consider just how lucky I was that Dom had come into my life. As worried as I was that this would come crashing down around me, I also had to admit that since he'd been around, my life had never felt better.

Even if I had only been rescued that night and never seen him again, I would have always remembered what he had done for me. But he came back into my life when he walked into the diner and I didn't want to waste the opportunity to grab hold of him. I struggled with it initially, but Dom's persistence and gentleness were hard to overlook. And over the course of the last week, I experienced luxuries I never imagined I would. I no longer went to bed hungry or worried about where my next meal would come from. I didn't have to sleep in a car, freezing and dirty. I had someone who would watch out for me and make sure that I wasn't taken advantage of like Ryan tried to do today.

On that thought, I suddenly froze.

"You okay?" Dom asked.

I used one hand to push away from his chest and sit up in his lap.

"How did you know where to go today when you found me at Ryan's apartment?"

Now it was Dom's turn to tense up. He closed his eyes and let out a breath. When he opened them again and looked at me, he warned, "I have a confession to make."

I swallowed hard at his words. Just as I thought my luck was turning around, he had to say those six words. I had no idea what to expect.

"Please don't get angry at me, Ekko," he begged.

I didn't like where this was headed. "Just tell me, Dom."

Dom took in another deep breath and admitted, "I've been watching out for you ever since the night of the attempted abduction."

"What? What exactly does that mean?"

"I knew when you lost your apartment and moved in with him. I already knew that you spent a lot of time at the library. I also knew that you were killing yourself working over the last three weeks or so. And the night before I came into the diner to eat, I sat in my truck in the parking lot of the library making sure nobody went near your car."

He had been following me all this time. I wasn't sure how to feel. On one hand, I knew I should have been grateful that I had someone looking out for me, but I had been through so much over the last few months. He had known about all of it. That's the part of me that wasn't sure if I should feel creeped out by it.

"I don't understand," I started as I stood up. "You've been following me? You know everything I've been through the last couple of months. You know all of that and I feel like I don't know anything about you."

"Ekko, it became clear to me over the last week that I don't know everything about you. If I did, what happened this afternoon would not have happened. And I'm an open book. I'm not hiding anything from you. If there's anything you want to know, all you've got to do is ask."

I felt myself getting choked up. He'd been so kind to me over the last week, but something wasn't sitting right with me. Since he deemed himself an open book, I decided to take advantage. "So you knew that I had been struggling for months and you waited until I was living out of my car to offer help? Obviously, you don't owe me anything, but I don't understand why you wouldn't have approached me sooner. Were you just waiting it out until I was so beat down, broken, and desperate that I'd take anything you were offering no matter what it cost me?"

"Is that what you think?" he countered as he sat up straighter on the lounger, his legs falling off to either side. Clearly, I had insulted him. "Ekko, I wanted to wrap you up in my arms and bring you home with me the night I met you. But you were involved with someone else. I watched out for you because I wasn't convinced the man you were with was doing his part to make sure you were safe. Obviously, I was right about him. And I fucking hated watching you go to work and kill yourself day in and day out. But no matter how much I hated seeing it, I refused to get involved when you were with someone else. The minute I realized you were no longer with him, I stepped in."

"I haven't been with Ryan for months," I whispered.

Dom's body went rigid.

I ignored it, started pacing, and added, "I haven't wanted to be with him for a long time, but I was so desperate that I lived there because I had nowhere else to go. It was awful. I would come home some nights and have to listen to him in the next room with another woman."

He winced.

"Ekko, I'm so sorry. I had no idea."

I could feel my emotions bubbling to the surface. "Of course you didn't. Because you chose to just watch me from afar instead of approaching me. You were the first good thing to walk into my life in years and I had no idea how to reach you. Even if I had researched and figured it out, I'm not sure I would have done anything with that. You're everything you are and I'm the complete opposite. Do you know that I thought about you every day for months?"

I paused, attempting to prepare to go another round, but I couldn't because a sob escaped me. I heard movement and the next thing I knew Dom's arms were around me. My hands fisted the sides of his shirt as I planted my face in the center of his chest. With one arm planted firmly in place around me, Dom used the other one to comfort me further by running his hand up and down my back. He pressed kisses to the top of my head.

In between the kisses, he croaked, "I wish I knew you weren't with him, Ekko. I'm sorry. I fucked up."

Dom held me a while as I settled myself down. Finally, I took a step back and looked up at him.

"It's not your fault," I murmured. "There was no way for you to know. I just wish you'd walked back into my life sooner than you did."

"Please tell me you know that I would not have ever left you in that situation if I knew that you were going through it alone."

I did. That's just the kind of person he was. Maybe I didn't know everything there was to know about him, but I knew that. "I know," I said softly.

One of Dom's hands came up to the side of my throat. His thumb stroked back and forth along the skin there. Quietly, he shared his frustration with himself and the situation, "I can't believe I could have had you in my life months ago."

I couldn't say that I didn't understand his frustration. I did. Completely. But I had also been through enough in my life to know that bad things happen. We can only do our best to accept those things as they come and then move past them. I didn't want either one of us to be consumed with regret.

"You have me here now, though."

He grinned and said, "Yeah, I do."

Then, he lowered his mouth to mine, as I pushed up on my toes, and kissed me. We stood outside on Dom's deck by the fire and kissed for a long time. Our tongues explored one another's mouth while our hands roamed each other's body. Dom's hands were at my hips, running up along my sides, down my back, and over the curve of my ass, where he squeezed and pulled me tighter to him. Feeling his erection pressing into me as we kissed and touched, I grew more and more turned on. My hands were just as greedy as his, running along his well-defined biceps and shoulders, down over his chest, and back up around his neck, where I held on tight, afraid he might let go.

He eventually tore his mouth from mine and rested his forehead against mine. Out of breath, he managed to plead with me, "Sugar, invite me to stay in my bed with you so I can hold you tonight."

I pressed a kiss to his lips, smiled against them, and demanded, "Stay with me tonight."

Dom returned the kiss, put out the fire, and followed me upstairs.

Then, he spent the rest of the night in his bed holding me close to him. Together, we spent a good portion of our night kissing and touching, but somehow, refrained from going any further. I had a feeling, though, that the next time the opportunity arose, it wouldn't be so easy to deny ourselves the pleasure.

CHAPTER 9

Ekko

IT WAS FINALLY SATURDAY.

This meant it was also moving day.

After everything that happened on Thursday between the showdown with Ryan and my incredible date with Dom, I didn't think it was possible to have any more excitement in my life. Apparently, I was wrong.

I woke up yesterday morning, wrapped up in Dom's arms and instantly knew it was a place I never wanted to leave. While the revelations from the evening before could have easily ruined our night, I was happy that they didn't. When I took the time to consider everything, I realized that Dom's heart was in the right place. Maybe he didn't go about it the right way, but he did it for the right reasons and I chose to see that instead of faulting him for his methods. I certainly wasn't perfect, and I knew if I'd made a mistake when I had good intentions, I'd want to be forgiven.

As I laid there in his arms, though, I realized I still had questions. They were questions to which I really hoped I'd get answers.

With my body pressed to his side, my head resting in the crook of his arm, and my arm draped over his abdomen, I was so comfortable and didn't want to move. I did as little as possible and tipped my head back so I could look up at him. I was surprised to see that Dom was awake, looking down at me. The second our eyes locked, his dimples came out in full force. It was quite a sight to see first thing in the morning and I had no doubt it was something I could easily get used to waking up to.

"Good morning," I greeted.

"Morning, sugar," he replied. "How'd you sleep?"

"Better than ever."

Dom moved his head so that he could lean down and press a kiss to my forehead. It was such a simple gesture, but it was so incredibly sweet.

"We need to talk," I blurted, killing the moment.

I watched as his brows lifted in question before he stated, "That doesn't sound good."

Pressing my hand to the middle of his abdomen, I lifted myself up beside him and confirmed, "It's not bad, but I have some things that have been bothering me that I'd like to talk to you about."

Dom placed his palms in the bed at his hips and sat up. He slid back so his back was against the headboard and encouraged me, "Okay, let's hear it."

"Alright, so I'm not sure if this is the right thing to say or do since I'm not a hundred percent sure just where this thing between us is going. That said, I've dealt with more heartache and disappointment in my life to know that I'm not willing to set myself up for failure again."

Dom's face remained impassive, and that frightened me a bit.

I cleared my throat and just came out with it. "What was with the light-switch mood yesterday?"

"Come again?"

Shaking my head back and forth, I pointed out, "I know

the idea of us is new and I hope I'm not incorrectly reading into things that have happened between us. There's attraction and chemistry and I'm pretty sure we both feel it."

He gave me a quick nod, indicating I was correct in my assessment of a mutual attraction.

"I like you, Dom. A lot. But I don't understand what happened yesterday. You were so angry with me over the whole debacle at Ryan's. You went from being short with me, to silent, to sweet."

Regret flashed in his eyes.

He let out a sigh and explained, "I was never angry with you, Ekko. The situation made me angry. I was upset that you didn't think twice about going there without mentioning it to me. If you had, I wouldn't have let you go alone."

"I'm not completely helpless," I returned.

"You think I don't know that?" he questioned. "There's a difference between being self-reliant and being smart so that you stay safe."

My head jerked back. "So now you think I'm foolish?"

"What I think is that you've endured so much bad shit in your life that you don't worry about having something else just as awful to happen to you. It's like you just expect it'll eventually come and then you deal with the fallout afterward."

"I had no idea Ryan was going to react the way he did yesterday," I defended.

"Maybe not, but you left his place and slept in your car because you learned he wasn't who you thought he was. Didn't you consider the possibility that perhaps there was more about him that you didn't know?"

Sadly, I had no rebuttal because Dom was right. "I guess I didn't," I answered, my voice glum.

My eyes dropped to my lap. Between being almost kidnapped a few months ago and now this latest situation, it wouldn't be unreasonable if Dom thought I was simply reckless. I never considered myself to be that way. In fact, I always thought I was cautious. But things in my life had gotten a bit out of my control and I was doing the absolute best that I could to rein it all in and fix what went wrong.

I watched as Dom's hand wrapped around mine. "I'm sorry." His voice was gentle and when I looked up at him, it was clear he felt remorse.

"What are you sorry for?"

"When I called your phone yesterday and the voice that answered wasn't yours, it did something to me. Hearing you in the background and then having him say that you were injured, I lost all sense of reason. But walking in and seeing the blood pouring down your face sent me over the edge. I'm sorry that I directed my anger at you and then went silent. I needed to calm down and I was afraid if I said something, it wouldn't have been good. During those moments, I was running on emotions and not logic."

"Emotions?" I repeated.

"It's been a lot of months that I've been wanting to get to know you, Ekko. Now that there's an opportunity for that to happen, I'm not alright with something that isn't my choice or yours coming along and putting an end to it," he shared. "I was worried about you yesterday...more than I've ever been worried about a woman."

My lips parted in shock.

"I'll try to manage my emotions better next time," he promised.

Relief swept through me.

"Wow," I whispered.

"What?"

Shaking my head back and forth, I spoke freely. "I didn't expect that. I'm so accustomed to being the one at fault. I'm not sure anyone before you has ever apologized to me for something that I caused."

"Ekko, I'm responsible for my own actions. Regardless of what you do, if I fuck up, I'll own up to it."

Dom was such a breath of fresh air that I inhaled deeply. When I let it out, I stated, "And I'm still left wondering why any of your previous girlfriends ever let you get away."

I was given a moment to appreciate the dimples that came out before he snaked an arm around my waist and pulled me toward him. "Kiss me so I can take you downstairs and feed you breakfast."

After I kissed him, he cradled me in his arms and carried me downstairs where he made us breakfast. Following breakfast, we both got ready and went to work. By the time I arrived back at his place, Dom was already there and had dinner ready. He spent the night in bed with me again, but aside from a few kisses, he made no move to do anything else.

This is precisely the reason why I was happy it was Saturday morning and, more importantly, that it was moving day.

I was still in Dom's bed with him and I really wished he had made a move to do something other than just kissing me last night. I no longer had my period, it had been months since I'd been with Ryan, and I was seriously overdue for some sexual gratification. If I had to spend one more night with him in his bed without any relief, it might unleash a monster inside me.

I had been on my back looking up at the ceiling and was in the middle of thinking about having sex with Dom when he interrupted my naughty thoughts.

"Today's the big day," he declared.

Turning my head to the side, I looked at his beautiful face. My body instinctively rolled toward him and I reached my hand out to the side of his head. The only time I ever got to touch the skin on his head was in this bed. He was always wearing a baseball cap or a beanie. Either way, he looked fantastic.

"Are you sure Levi won't mind helping out today?" I asked. "I'd really hate to inconvenience him."

Dom had enlisted Levi to help move my bed and dresser. After the showdown at Ryan's, Dom had his co-workers take my things back to Levi's house to keep them there until I moved.

The plan for today was simple. Dom and I were going to meet up with the landlord so that I could sign the paperwork, pay the rent, and get my keys. Once that was all squared away, we were going to head over to Levi's, load up my things, and move them into my new place.

"Not at all. He's my friend and that's what you do for your friends," Dom assured me.

My thumb stroked back and forth on Dom's cheek as I said, "I know that, but he's got a wedding coming up in a few weeks. I don't want him being pulled away from something else he could be doing for that."

Dom laughed.

"You obviously don't know Elle that well yet," he remarked. "She's probably the most laidback woman you'll ever meet. She'll be happy just knowing that she and Levi are getting married. And while I'm sure she has a few details that are important to her for the wedding, she's not going to be one to stress over them. She's got Lexi to do that for her."

"Lexi?"

"Cruz's woman. She has her own PR firm and handles all of Elle's events for her music. They've become really good friends and Lexi's good at handling that kind of stuff. She won't see it as the job that Elle will. Ultimately, it'll give Lexi practice for when it's her turn because I'm sure it's only a matter of time before Cruz proposes to her."

Wow. I hadn't met Lexi, but it sounded like she had it all together. Elle had been so nice to me, so I was happy she had a friend that would help her with the details of planning her wedding.

"They all sound wonderful," I sighed.

Dom squeezed my hip and confirmed, "They are."

A sense of longing washed over me. I wished I'd one day be fortunate enough to find myself constantly surrounded by people like Dom, Elle, Lexi, and Levi.

Before I had the opportunity to get too consumed by the ache I felt at not having that, Dom suggested we get up, have breakfast, and get ready so that we could take care of getting me settled in my new place.

Not much later, Dom and I were on our way to Levi's place. When we arrived, I grabbed Elle's top out of the backseat. Levi met us outside.

"Hey, Ekko. How's your face feeling?" he asked.

"Much better, Levi. Thank you," I answered.

"Why don't you head inside out of the cold while Dom and I get your things loaded up? Elle's in the library."

He didn't have to ask me twice. I gave him a quick nod and took off inside with Elle's shirt. Walking into the library, I found Elle curled up in an oversized reading chair playing her guitar in her lap with a journal beside her. She was lost in her music and I stood there in awe of her beautiful voice.

She stopped singing, jotted down some words in her journal, and when she looked up, she noticed me.

"Oh my goodness," she started. "I didn't see you there, Ekko."

"You have an incredible voice, Elle," I praised her.

She waved me over to come and sit by her.

Once I was seated, I apologized, "I didn't mean to interrupt you. Levi told me you were here and that I should come in."

"No worries at all."

I held her top out to her. "Thanks for letting me borrow this. I really appreciate it. I washed it at Dom's yesterday; I didn't want to return it to you without washing it."

"How was it?"

"How was what?"

"Your date," she stated.

I smiled as I thought back to that night. The way that my time with Dom put the events from earlier that day out of my mind was more than enough to make it wonderful. But he did so much more than that. He gave me the best night of my life. Even with the revelation I had learning he had been watching out for me for months, it was still the most incredible night.

"That look alone says enough," Elle broke into my thoughts, her tone joyful.

I shook my head trying to bring myself back to reality. "Sorry. I get so distracted thinking about it. Dom was absolutely wonderful and I had such a good time."

Her face lit up. "I am so happy to hear that. What did you guys do?"

"He took me out to dinner before we went bowling. I've never been before and I had so much fun."

"That's great. When are you going out on your next date?"

I shrugged my shoulders. "We didn't officially set up another date."

"But you are going to go on another one, right?" she pressed.

"I think so. Things went well on Thursday and he did say he was going to take me out on his bike some other time, so I'm guessing that means there's at least one more date with

Dom in my future."

Elle didn't respond. A look of contentment fell over her face as she sat back on the oversized chair. I decided to take the opportunity to change topics.

"I love this chair," I announced. "It's got to be the most perfect place to read. One day I'm going to have to get myself something like this."

"Thanks. It's one of my favorite spots in the house," she declared. "I actually—"

Elle was cut off when Levi and Dom walked in.

"Ready?" Dom asked.

I gave him a nod.

"Are you driving separately, Levi?" Elle wondered.

"Yeah. We split Ekko's things between our two trucks," he replied.

She stood and walked over to him. "I'll ride with you if you don't mind. I could use a break from the songwriting."

"Works for me, sunshine."

He called her sunshine. His name for her described her perfectly.

The four of us filed out of Elle's library and out to the trucks. An hour and a half later, Dom and I said goodbye to Elle and Levi. While they hadn't done anything to make me feel bad, I had to admit that I felt ashamed and embarrassed.

Neither Elle's nor Levi's demeanor changed when they walked into my apartment, but once my two pieces of furniture were brought in, I realized just how little I had compared to the rest of them. It made me uncomfortable to look around my new apartment that I'd worked extremely hard for and see just how empty it was.

Even still, I tried not to let my disappointment with myself show. They had all been so kind to me and I didn't want their pity; I was certain it would only make me feel worse.

Dom asked me to go out for a late lunch with him before I had to head into work. I took him up on it partly because I had no food in my house, but mostly because I enjoyed spending the time with him.

After we finished lunch, I thanked him again for all of his help getting me moved in. He shrugged it off as though it was no big deal. Then, Dom pulled me in for a hug and hesitated to let me go.

"What's wrong?" I asked, hugging him back.

Keeping one arm around my waist, he lifted the other one and used his fingers to brush my hair back from the side of my face. "Would you mind letting me know once you've made it home?" he questioned me, his voice soft. "You've got a warm place to put your head tonight and I know it's in a safe area, but I'm going to worry about you anyway."

I thought I might cry at the concern he showed for me.

I fought against the urge and agreed, "Of course. I can do that."

"Thanks, Ekko. Have a good day at work."

"I will."

At that, Dom and I parted ways. Over the course of the last week, I'd grown so accustomed to having him there when I finished work. It felt awkward leaving because I knew that when I got off work, I wouldn't be seeing him. As proud as I was for finding a way to get myself back on my feet, I couldn't deny how much I was going to miss him.

When I left the diner that night, I made a quick trip to the store to pick up necessities before I went home. After putting away the food and toiletries I purchased, I sent a text to Dom to let him know I was home and then took my first shower in my new place.

When I climbed into my bed that night, hours after I'd last seen him, that's when it hit me. After having Dom there to hold me close to him the previous two nights, it felt strange to be by myself.

I missed him.

I was alone again.

And I hated it.

Dom

My bed never felt so big before tonight.

I had been trying to distract myself with television for the last two hours, but I would have been lying if I claimed that it worked. My mind had been consumed with thoughts of Ekko.

My pint-sized fighter.

One week of having her in my home—in my bed—and I had already become so addicted to her. The last two nights, I held her in my arms while we slept and I knew I never wanted to let her go.

But today I did.

I let her go.

And I knew it was something she needed to do. I knew that after everything she'd been through that she needed the time to stand on her own and take care of herself. But that didn't mean I liked it.

I hated it.

I already knew how strong she was. Living on her own, struggling, wouldn't change any of that for me.

I tried convincing myself that I was so high-strung tonight because I wasn't out there watching out for her and I didn't know for sure that she was safe. That wasn't it, though. It was something so much more than that.

Twenty minutes ago, my phone vibrated on my nightstand.

I'm home.

She was safe.

I waited a minute to see if she would say anything else, but I got nothing.

Thanks for letting me know. Sleep well, sugar.

I wanted to tell her I missed her, but I didn't.

Ten minutes later, she replied.

You too! xo

And for the last ten minutes, I laid here in my bed craving her.

Wanting her.

Needing her.

Desperate for her.

The events from the last two nights played over in my head and that didn't make things any easier. I had had her tiny body writhing against mine as we kissed. It took everything in me not to take her and consume her. I wanted her so bad, but I didn't want to do anything before she was ready for it. I didn't have any doubts that her body was more than ready for me, but I wanted to be sure her mind and her heart were, too.

I needed to know that what she felt for me went beyond appreciation and thankfulness. Because I knew that once I had Ekko, I wasn't going to give her up.

CHAPTER 10

Ekko

IT WAS FINALLY FRIDAY AND I HAD BEEN IN MY NEW APARTMENT FOR just under a full week. Saying that I was in my apartment only referred to the fact that I had been sleeping here because my week had been incredibly busy.

Other than the stop I made at the grocery store Tuesday evening after work, I hadn't done anything but work at the diner from the time I woke up on Sunday. Work had been my life all week until Thursday, when I had the morning off. I used some of that time to sleep in, but had to make a stop at the library before going to get my stitches removed.

Today, I went into work for the breakfast and lunch shift. Before I left work at three o'clock, I had already decided that I would be spending the rest of my evening at home. I needed a break and since I didn't need to be back at work until tomorrow afternoon, I was planning to do nothing but relax.

Aside from my trip to the library yesterday morning, there was only one thing that brightened my week.

Dom.

While I didn't get to see him, we managed to talk to each other several times throughout the week. Sometimes, it was simply a quick text in the morning or the afternoon just to check in. Other times, it was me sending him a message after my long days at work to let him know I had made it home and to tell him that I hoped he had a good day.

The only times I had a chance to talk to him were on Tuesday night and Thursday morning. Sadly, those conversations were brief.

I felt awful. Dom was currently paying for my cell phone and I hadn't had more than a five-minute conversation with him.

And I really wanted to talk to him. I loved talking to him. Unfortunately, my schedule made it virtually impossible to do much else besides work.

Now that I'd just gotten home from my shift, taken a shower, and felt like I finally had a moment to breathe, visions of Dom filtered through my mind. I had truly missed him.

I grabbed a book and made my way out to the living room. One thing I'd been thankful for is a partially-furnished apartment. It not only had major appliances like a refrigerator, stove, washing machine, and a dryer, but also a sofa, armchair, and coffee table in the living room.

No sooner did I sit down on the couch when I heard my phone ringing in my bedroom. I jumped up off the couch and sprinted down the hall to get it before I missed the call.

"Hello?" I answered, out of breath.

"Are you okay?" Dom asked.

"Sorry. As small as my apartment is, I still feel like I just ran a marathon to get from my living room to my bedroom just to get my phone."

He let out a laugh and confirmed, "So you're home?"

"Yes."

"Any chance you want to put in a little more physical effort and open your door?"

He was here?

"Are you here?"

"I guess you'll have to open your door to find out," he teased.

I hurried out of the bedroom to the front door and fumbled over my own hands trying to get the lock open. I was so excited to see Dom.

Once I managed to get it unlocked, I swung the door open and felt a rush of air leave my lungs.

Seeing him for the first time in a week left me feeling nothing short of relief.

Apparently, Dom was feeling something similar because he didn't wait for me to invite him inside. He stepped in, slammed the door shut behind himself, and slipped an arm around my waist as he bent his head to bury his face in my neck. I pushed up on my toes, wrapped my arms around him, and squeezed.

"Missed you, Ekko," he breathed.

He missed me. It felt so good to hear him say those words.

"I've missed you, too."

When he pulled back, he lifted one arm and I noticed he had carried a bag in with him. "I brought dinner if you care to join me."

Giving him a huge grin, I said, "I'd love to join you."

We walked into the living room, where Dom set out the food. He had gotten pad thai, one chicken, one shrimp. "I'll eat whichever you don't want."

I didn't know which I wanted and Dom noticed because he interrupted my thoughts and suggested, "We can also switch halfway through if you'd like."

"You know just what to say to satisfy a woman, don't you?" I blurted before I had the chance to realize what I had insinuated.

Dom just shook his head as he looked down at the ground, the smile tugging at his lips.

I dropped my gaze to the ground, quickly fell to my bottom, and sat on the sofa. Dom lowered himself to the seat right next to me, leaned close, and spoke gently, "One day soon, I'd love to satisfy you without needing to say anything at all."

My head snapped toward him. His face was inches from mine. The heat spreading through my body matched the desire in his dark eyes.

I stared at him in stunned silence. Confident as ever, Dom leaned in and pressed a soft kiss to my cheek. "Breathe, sugar," he prompted me.

It took me a second, but I eventually began to breathe. Obviously, Dom and I had gotten hot and heavy a few times, but hearing him tease me like he just did affected me in a completely different way.

If he hadn't turned away from me and toward the food, I was sure I would have swung a leg over his lap and straddled him. I would have insisted he take the opportunity to do just as he promised.

Dom passed me the shrimp pad thai and a fork before sitting back with the chicken for himself. We ate a bit in silence, our heated stares saying more than we ever could with words. After we switched meals, I broke the silence.

"Thank you for coming over tonight," I expressed.

"All week long, I was waiting for you to invite me. When I realized that it wasn't going to happen, I just took it upon myself. I had a feeling that if I waited for you to invite me, I'd never see you."

My shoulders fell.

"There's no need to be upset, Ekko. I know you're very busy with work and I understand it. When I talked to you on Tuesday night, I already knew how wiped out you were. I was happy, though, that I at least had the forethought to get your schedule for the remainder of the week. This felt like the longest week of my life."

"I thought this week flew by," I countered after swallowing a bite of my food.

"I'm not surprised considering the way you work."

We went back to silence. I had several more bites before I felt full and set the container down on the table. When I sat back on the couch, I turned my body toward Dom's. He finished the remainder of the shrimp and placed the empty container back on the coffee table.

Instead of sitting back on the seat, he leaned toward me, wrapped one hand behind my head, and the other around my waist. My hands instinctively went to his shoulders as Dom fell to his back, taking me with him. Our lips touched and for several long minutes, we did nothing but kiss.

Kiss and touch and moan.

My legs straddled his hips. At the feel of his arousal between us, I rolled my hips. I disconnected my mouth from his and threw my head back. Mere moments later, Dom's lips were touching the skin at my throat, sending another shot of desire through me.

I moaned, craving him more than I had anyone or anything.

His tongue ran along my skin toward my ear, where he pulled away and whispered, "You work too much."

My head fell forward and I rasped, "I know."

He continued to tease me, alternating between nipping at my earlobe with his mouth and trailing kisses along my neck to the base of my throat. "You need to find more balance in your life," he advised on one of his assents up toward my ear. "It's not healthy for you to work like this all the time."

At this point, one of his hands had drifted down over my ass and squeezed me there while the other was planted at my side, just next to my breast. I wanted him to touch me there and if Dom had planned to be noble like he had been the other times we found ourselves in this position, I was going to lose my mind.

"I've got goals," I got out as I moved my hand down his arm to cover his. My fingers moved and wrapped around his wrist and pushed his hand forward while my head fell forward. Dom pulled his mouth from my throat and looked up at me. He gently squeezed my breast before brushing his thumb back and forth across my hardened nipple.

A desperate cry escaped me, and Dom quickly lifted up and flipped us to the opposite end of the couch, where my back was now on the cushions and he was hovering over me.

"You're off for your birthday next week, right?" he questioned me as he tortured me with a hip thrust.

My birthday.

He remembered my birthday.

Nobody had ever remembered my birthday.

Ever.

I shook my head as my feelings overwhelmed me.

Dom stopped moving and stared at me.

"What?" I asked. "What's wrong?"

His hand left my breast and he dropped down to his elbows. "You're working on your birthday?"

I gave him a few quick nods of my head and watched as his face grew sad.

"Why?" he wondered, the tone of his voice almost a desperate plea.

"To be honest, I can't remember a time in my adult life when I haven't worked on my birthday," I answered. "It's not a big deal."

At least, nobody had ever made it a big deal.

"It absolutely fucking is," he insisted. "And I want to

celebrate it with you."

He wanted to celebrate my birthday with me. Even if I didn't have to work, I wasn't sure I knew how to do that.

"Well, my birthday is on Wednesday."

"Your point being?"

"Don't you have to work?"

"I've accumulated a lot of paid time off. This is definitely one of those occasions I'd take time off for. You should take off for your birthday, Ekko."

I laughed and explained, "I don't have paid time off."

"Are you working all day?"

I shook my head. "Just the morning and early afternoon. I'll be leaving work at three."

His body relaxed a bit and he asked, "What do you want to do for your day?"

My eyes widened. "Me?"

He gave me a disbelieving look and noted, "It is your birthday. You get to choose what you want to do. Anything at all."

I was going to lose it. My heart was beating faster, and I could feel the tightness in my throat.

"Really?"

Dom's eyes dropped to my chest, which was rapidly rising and falling. When he looked back up at my face, he wondered, "Why are you so upset?"

I took a deep breath and tried to swallow past the lump in my throat. "Nobody has ever celebrated my birthday with me."

"Not ever?"

I shook my head and looked away.

Dom brought the backs of his knuckles to the side of my face, gently turned it back toward him, and advised, "This is the last time you work on your birthday. From now on, you celebrate with me. Even if this doesn't go where I'm hoping it goes, we will still celebrate your birthday every year from here on out. Got me?"

The fact that Dom thought I was worthy of having a lifetime of birthday celebrations meant the world to me.

He was still looking at me waiting for a response, but I was so consumed with a mix of emotions, the only thing I could do was nod my agreement.

He pressed a quick kiss to my lips and repeated, "So what do you want for your birthday?"

I thought a minute before I confirmed, "Honestly?"

Dom dipped his chin.

"I'd love to just spend it cuddled up with you on your deck by the fire."

"That's all you want?"

He was clearly shocked by my request.

"Yes."

A look I couldn't read washed over his face before he stated, "You've got it, sugar."

I smiled at him, feeling a warmth spread through me. He held my gaze and mirrored it. Then, I remembered what I wanted to share with him.

"Guess what!"

"What?"

"I went to the library yesterday morning and while I was there, I saw they had a new job posted. They're looking for a library assistant. I don't know what it pays, but it's a full-time position and it would be a great way to get my foot in the door for the career I ultimately want to have."

Shifting his body to the side, propping his head up in his hand, he looked down and exclaimed, "That's awesome. Are you going to apply for the position?"

Nodding, I answered, "Yeah. I really hope I get called in for an interview. It would be so nice to have a set schedule and steady, predictable income. Even if it were a little less than I make now, at least I could plan better."

"Plan?"

I'm sure Dom heard the longing in my voice when I replied, "I *really* want to go back to school. The guaranteed income each week combined with a semi-regular schedule would make school much easier to manage."

The look on his face changed. It went from curious and questioning to soft and sweet. "I know there's a lot left to learn about you, but from what I've seen, I have no doubts that you'll make it happen. You're such a determined and hardworking woman."

That was true. Even I had to admit that I worked hard. It's not like I had any other options. I could give up, but then what purpose and meaning did my life have? I would continue to endure what life threw at me because failure wasn't an option.

"Thank you for saying that," I returned quietly.

Dom brought a hand up to the side of my head, captured a lock of hair between his fingers, and continued, "To add to that, you are also a remarkable kisser who I'm convinced is a master of innocent and unknowing seduction."

"I wouldn't say I'm a master at it," I mocked him, laughing.

Lowering his mouth to mine, he stopped inches away from my lips and declared, "I would. Everything you do is a fucking turn-on. It doesn't matter if you're kissing me, sitting there eating Thai food, falling asleep on the phone, or rambling on about a book. All of that and more leaves me struggling to resist the urge to have my way with you."

I wanted Dom. I wanted him so bad that I tempted him, "Well if I were so good at this seduction thing, I would think you would have had your way with me by now. Maybe I'm not giving you the right signals after all."

His fingers left my hair and trailed down over my

collarbone and light across the top of my chest. "You are, sugar," he refuted.

With the way he was touching me, I found it incredibly hard to breathe, let alone respond, so I just gave him a look that I hoped told him I didn't understand. Thankfully, he understood the meaning in my gaze.

"You deserve more, Ekko," he began. "From what you've told me, it doesn't seem like anyone other than Ms. Grace ever tried to give you even an ounce of what you deserved. I'm taking my time with you because I want it to mean something. For the both of us."

I blinked at him in surprise. I never expected to hear him say that. It blew my mind that he thought I deserved something special.

"Are you going to let me romance you just a little bit longer?" he asked.

Romance? He wanted to romance me?

"Yes," I responded, my voice filled with longing.

The grin on his face grew.

And as it did, there was now no doubt in my mind that I was going to end up destroyed soon. It was already bad enough that I craved and missed him the way that I did. If he romanced me, I knew I'd end up falling in love with him. The bad thing about it was that it was likely he'd inevitably realize he settled for me. I wasn't sure I'd survive the fallout from that, but I knew I didn't want to give up the opportunity to be with him, no matter how short the time and no matter what the risk.

CHAPTER 11

Ekko

"I'M LEAVING WORK NOW," I TOLD DOM AS I WALKED FROM the diner to my car.

"I'll meet you at your place. I should be there by the time you get there," he replied.

"Sounds great. See you soon."

We disconnected, and I slid my phone back into my purse as I opened my door and got in my car.

It was Wednesday, and it was my birthday. That also meant that I was currently leaving work and heading home, where Dom was going to meet me so he could commence my birthday celebration.

I was beyond excited for my evening with him. From the moment he told me last Friday that he wanted to spend my birthday with me, I've been counting down the days. Luckily, I've had enough to keep me busy.

I got a call on Saturday afternoon from Alice at the Windsor Public Library. They wanted me to come in for an interview on Monday. Obviously, I was overjoyed that I was going to have an opportunity to convince them that I was the right person for the job, but I spent the entire weekend worrying.

Monday rolled around. For once, luck was on my side

because I didn't have to go into work until the lunch shift and my interview was scheduled for first thing in the morning. Overall, I felt the interview went well, but that didn't necessarily mean I'd get the job. In fact, before I left, Alice thanked me for coming in and stated that they had a few more applicants to interview. I wanted to be hopeful; however, I knew that I had to be realistic.

Dom and I managed to speak with each other on the phone a couple of times over the last few days, but I hadn't seen him since last Friday. He knew about my interview and told me he wanted me to call him as soon as I walked out of the library. It felt good having someone take an interest in what was happening in my life and I enjoyed being able to share it with him. Not only that, he was very good at helping me stay positive. When I told him that there were other people who had applied for the position that still needed to be interviewed, he didn't let me get down on myself. He encouraged me to stay optimistic and I sincerely appreciated him doing that for me.

I pulled up outside my apartment and saw Dom had done just as he said and arrived before me. What was most exciting, though, was that he was standing there leaning against his truck, out in the cold, waiting for me.

He made me feel so special.

I quickly parked and got out of my car. No sooner did I close my door when I felt Dom come up behind me, wrap his arms around my waist, and kiss my cheek. "Happy Birthday, Ekko."

As I leaned back into his embrace, I turned my head to the side to look at him. I smiled and said, "Thank you."

Dom's dimples were prominently displayed, so I took a minute to admire them. He seemed content to give me the time to do it, too.

"I feel bad about you coming here so early. I still need to shower and get ready before we leave."

He pressed a quick kiss to my lips and shared, "I took the day off today and I didn't want to have to wait any longer to hug you, kiss you, and give you birthday wishes. I was half-tempted to come to the diner."

Just as I was about to respond, my phone rang. I stepped out of Dom's arms and pulled the phone out of my purse. When I saw the number on the display, I felt a wave of excitement move through me.

"It's the library," I exclaimed.

"Answer it," Dom encouraged me.

I slide my finger across the phone to answer the call, took in a deep breath as I brought it to my ear, and answered, "Hello?"

"Good afternoon. Is Ekko Rose available?"

"This is," I quickly replied.

"Ekko, this is Alice from the Windsor Public Library. How are you doing today?"

"Hi, Alice. I'm doing well, thank you. And you?"

"I'm great. I just wanted to give you a call and let you know that if you're still interested, we'd like to offer you the library assistant position."

My eyes met Dom's and I gave him a full-fledged smile. He gave me a wink and dimples in return.

"I'm very interested," I assured her.

Alice went on, "Perfect. We'll just need to set up a time to meet and get some paperwork completed. We'd like to have you start just over two weeks from now on the first Monday in December. Your hours would typically be Monday through Friday from nine to five. The position pays fifteen dollars an hour and comes with full benefits after you complete your first thirty days of employment. We can get into all of the details at the meeting, though. Do you have any time to meet next week? I know it'll probably be tough next week with the Thanksgiving holiday."

I wasn't going to tell her that I didn't have anything planned for Thanksgiving. Instead, my eyes dropped from Dom's face to my shoes and I answered, "I am free next Tuesday morning. Would that work?"

"Let me take a look here..." She trailed off. When she spoke again, she confirmed, "That'll be perfect. Can you meet around nine-thirty?"

"I can do that. Thank you so much for calling and for the offer."

"You're welcome. I look forward to seeing you again next week. Take care."

Alice and I disconnected.

I stood there stock-still, my gaze still on the ground. It felt like the opportunity of a lifetime was just dropped in my lap and I needed a minute to process it. I got about thirty seconds to do that before my forehead was planted in Dom's chest. After his hand wrapped around the back of my neck and squeezed gently, he guessed, "I assume that was a job offer?"

I moved my head up and down against him.

"Congratulations," he said softly. "I told you they'd be foolish to choose anyone but you."

Dom took my weight as I tipped my head back and looked up at him. "Thank you for having faith in me. I can't believe I got the job," I rasped, my emotions getting the best of me.

"What did I tell you when we talked after your interview?"

"Keep my head up and my eyes pointed forward."

"Why?"

"Because my future is in front of me and I need to stay focused on that."

He gave me another look of his dimples before he advised,

"Why don't we head inside? It's cold out here and your nose is starting to turn red."

I dipped my chin in agreement.

Once we were inside, Dom suggested, "How about you go get ready and then you can tell me all about the offer?"

"Okay," I replied as I turned to walk down toward my bedroom.

I didn't get more than two steps away when I felt Dom's hand at my elbow. When I turned and gave him a questioning look, he explained, "I told you I couldn't wait to come here to hug you and kiss you. I want to kiss you before you walk away, Ekko."

"You kissed me on my cheek when we were outside."

He chuckled and stepped toward me. His voice was deep and low as he dropped his mouth close to mine. "That was not the kind of kiss I was talking about."

"Oh."

Dom's hands came up on either side of my neck and his thumbs stroked along my jaw. I felt his lips just barely brush against mine briefly before he claimed my mouth. He offered slow, deliberate, closed-mouth kisses and each one made me feel like I was some long-lost treasure that had finally been found. Dom made me feel like I mattered and I couldn't begin to process just how lucky I was to have him in my life.

After taking his time kissing me, never urging me to open my mouth for him to taste more, Dom whispered against my lips, "Go get ready, fun size. I want to get you back to my place so I can give you your present."

I couldn't wait to spend the night cuddled up next to him by the fire, so I didn't delay in moving to do as he suggested.

By the time I walked out of my bedroom, an hour had passed. I took my time, mostly because this was a first for me. Maybe I didn't have fancy clothes or fabulous shoes to wear, but I had an incredible man that believed I was someone worthy. He believed that I deserved to feel special and he was slowly making me feel the same.

I walked down the hall to meet Dom and found him sitting on the couch waiting. It made me feel awful. Just as I was about to apologize for leaving him alone all that time, he stood and walked over to me.

"Ready to go, birthday girl?"

I wasn't surprised he was ready to go. There was *nothing* for him to do here. I had books, which offered me entertainment, but that was about it.

"Yeah," I replied.

Dom and I walked out to his truck and left for his house. After parking the truck in his driveway, Dom came around to open my door for me. He'd done this every time I'd ridden in his truck and it astonished me every time. He was a true gentleman.

When we entered the house, I immediately let out a sigh of relief and removed my jacket. I had missed being here.

"Before I make you dinner, I want to give you some of your gifts," Dom announced.

"What?"

"Your birthday presents," he said, putting his hand on my back urging me toward the kitchen.

When we entered the kitchen, I saw two wrapped gifts sitting on top of the island and one large box underneath it. I froze.

"If those are for me, I'm going to cry."

"Don't cry," he pleaded. "This shouldn't make you upset."

My throat constricted so tight it began to hurt. My hands instinctively pressed together in front of my face and I struggled to breathe. Tears pooled in my eyes and with one gentle caress from Dom's finger down the side of my arm, they spilled down my cheeks.

I took a minute to collect myself and swallow past the tightness in my throat. When I looked up at him, his expression had nothing but concern in it.

"Are you okay?"

I nodded.

"Do you want to open them?"

I repeated the same gesture.

We sat and Dom slid the boxes over to me.

"Does it matter which I open first?"

He shook his head. "Whichever one you want."

I took the smallest box from the top of the pile and began tearing the wrapping paper from it. My belly was a bunch of nerves as I removed it and stared down at the necklace box. When I lifted the top, I saw a gorgeous rose gold bar pendant. It had the word 'Bookworm' engraved on it. I looked up at Dom and gave him a smile, doing my best to not break down into tears.

"This is perfect," I said as I removed it from the box and admired it.

He reached out, took the necklace from my hands, and put it on me.

When he stepped back to look at the necklace resting just below my throat, I couldn't stop myself. I threw my arms over his shoulders and initiated a kiss unlike any of our kisses from earlier in the day. I wanted to pour every ounce of appreciation I had for him into that kiss. I knew it hadn't been a very long time, but the more I was around Dom, the stronger my feelings for him were becoming.

"Thank you," I breathed when I pulled back from him.

He grinned and replied, "You're very welcome."

I moved back to the island and took the next box off the top of the pile. It was bigger than the first box but much thinner. Removing the wrapping paper, I revealed only a simple, white box. Curiosity got the best of me and I quickly lifted the lid to find tissue paper covering the contents. I pushed the paper back, saw what was inside, and burst out laughing.

When I managed to pull myself together, I held up the gift and announced, "These are the greatest socks I've ever seen."

Dom was grinning, his dimples on display, and he was clearly proud of himself for getting me a pair of light and dark blue socks, with a picture of a girl peeking over the top of a book, and the words 'Fuck off, I'm reading' on them.

"As soon as I saw them, I knew I wanted to get them for you," he explained.

"I love them. Thank you so much." I leaned toward him and gave him a quick peck on the lips. It seemed I couldn't control myself; this was the best birthday I'd ever had.

"Open the last one," he urged.

I'm sure I looked like a little kid on Christmas morning when I turned my attention to the last gift. It was a huge box in comparison and when I tried to move it, I noted how heavy it was. I ripped off the paper and uncovered a plain, brown shipping box. The part of the shipping label indicating where the package came from had been removed, so I was stumped. I pulled off the tape and opened the top of the box. After removing the packaging material on top, I saw what was inside and my heart began pounding. I picked up the extra item sitting on top, saw exactly what it was, and felt my knees buckle. Dom wrapped an arm around my waist to steady me and all I could do was stare at the box in total disbelief.

Eventually, I tore my gaze from the box, looked at Dom, and questioned him. "How did you know?"

"I knew what I wanted to get you, but I had Elle help me with the specifics on that special thing on top. For the big part of the gift, when we were there that day Levi helped me with getting your stuff moved in, I heard you telling Elle about how much you liked hers."

Dom had purchased me the same oversized chair that Elle had in her library. The only difference was the color. Sitting on top of the chair, though, was a signed paperback of the first book in one of my favorite romance series.

I stayed silent, still trying to process what he'd done.

Dom spoke again. "I wanted to get you a signed copy of a book that you'd enjoy, but I had no clue which one to get. Elle told me that this set was something you had to have, so I figured I'd get this one to start. If you like it, I'll complete it for you."

"I can't believe you did this," I said, my voice a hair over a whisper.

"Have you read this? Do you like it?" he asked, now clearly worried that perhaps he'd screwed up.

I took in a deep breath and assured him, "I love this series and she's one of my most-read authors." I paused a moment to let it settle in. It barely penetrated when I felt compelled to share, "Dom, this is the nicest thing anyone has ever done for me."

"I'll order the rest of them and when the final one is out, I'll complete it for you."

"What?"

"I don't know. Apparently, there's still one more book that needs to be written, but there aren't any specifics on a release date. I don't care when it is or where things are between us, I want you to promise me you'll tell me when it releases so I can complete the set for you."

My heart was bursting with happiness.

My emotions flooded me. I buried my face in his neck and cried, "You are the most amazing man I've ever met.

Thank you so much."

Dom held me tight, settling me with the closeness and warmth of his body. When I pulled back, I kissed him again and hoped that it expressed even just a fraction of what I was feeling for him.

After we tore ourselves away from the kisses, Dom went about making dinner.

"Can I help?"

He shook his head. "I did a bunch of prep work earlier today. Besides, the birthday girl does not work on her birthday."

"I worked earlier today," I reminded him.

Dom gave me a stern look and noted, "That better be the last time that ever happens, too."

His words made me think back to my phone call from earlier in the day. My new job.

"Well, now that I'll have a new job, I might become fancy like you with paid time off. I guess I have to wait and get the details of that on Tuesday, though."

"Is that when you go back in?"

I nodded. "Yeah. Alice said they want me to start the first Monday in December, but wanted me to come in next week to get some paperwork completed and out of the way."

"At least you'll be able to give the diner enough notice that you'll be leaving," he pointed out.

My mind drifted to Jerry. He was such a kind man and an incredible boss. He and his wife had provided me with steady employment and I was heartbroken that I'd be leaving them.

"Yeah, but I'm going to miss Jerry and his wife, Christie. Not to mention some of my regulars."

Dom looked at me like I was crazy. "You're getting a new job, not moving across the country. It's not like you can't go visit."

"I know."

I watched as Dom began searing the pork chops. While those cooked, he went about combining broth, apple cider, cinnamon and a few other ingredients in a separate bowl. Once the chops had been seared on both sides, he removed them from the pan and put a mix of chopped apples and onion in followed by the liquid mixture.

"When I was in the shower earlier I figured it all out," I started. "This new job is going to pay me nearly ten thousand dollars a year more than I'm currently making. It'll cover my expenses at the apartment and I'll have enough leftover that I can start saving again. I think I can register for school again so that I can start next semester."

"I think this job is going to be the start of a very promising future, Ekko."

I couldn't help but smile. Ever since he'd come into my life, things had started looking up and I was beginning to consider him my good luck charm.

A few minutes later, Dom was plating our dinner. Pork chops with apples and onions. He even made a side of oven-roasted potatoes. It was, by far, the most delicious meal I'd ever had, and it was perfect for fall. I was, once again, left wondering why any of his previous girlfriends ever left him.

After dinner, Dom cleared our plates and brought a small dish over to me with a freshly-baked brownie on it. There was a single candle in the brownie.

"I'd sing, but I'm not a great singer."

I grinned at him and brushed it off. "It's okay. Your cooking skills more than make up for it."

"Make a wish," he urged.

I didn't even have to think of one. I already knew what I wanted. I made my wish and blew out the candle.

Dom stood and got a second plate for himself and a dish

filled with brownies. When he was seated again, we ate birthday brownies. They were phenomenal.

And I sat there trying to ingrain every moment of the night in my mind, fearful that I'd never have something so wonderful ever again.

CHAPTER 12

Dom

"**T**HIS HAS BEEN THE BEST DAY OF MY LIFE," EKKO DECLARED. She was curled up in my lap, the palm of one hand and the side of her cheek pressed against my chest. We'd just finished up dessert and I followed through with giving her the one thing she'd told me she wanted for her birthday.

I couldn't get over it.

When I asked a week ago what I could get her for the special occasion, her response was just this. She wanted to be in my arms, on the deck, sitting by the fire. Ekko had been struggling for so long, just moved into her new apartment, and could have asked for anything she wanted. I don't think the thought ever crossed her mind to ask for anything materialistic. It wasn't who she was.

Of course, that didn't mean she couldn't appreciate nice things.

She was more than appreciative when she walked into the kitchen and saw the gifts sitting there for her. And while I knew she would have been more than satisfied with simply having a quiet night here with me on the deck, I wanted her to have more. Seeing how she reacted to each gift she opened was worth it and with each reaction she had, I fell harder and harder for her.

Having her here in my arms now, cuddled under a blanket by the fire, I was finding that I was in complete agreement with her. This had been one of the best days of my life, too.

"I'm happy to have given this to you today, Ekko."

"I have been meaning to apologize to you, though."

"For what?" I wondered, completely lost as to why she could have possibly thought she needed to apologize to me.

"Earlier at my place...I plan to get a television as soon as I can afford one, but I didn't have any way for you to be entertained while you were there. I feel awful for making you wait all that time with nothing to do."

I hated how she always viewed herself negatively simply because she didn't have the luxuries that most people took for granted. I kissed the top of her head and corrected her, "That's not true."

She pressed her hand into my chest and pulled her head back to look at me. "What?"

Watching the light from the fire brighten her curious face, I felt myself fall a little deeper. I offered her an explanation, "I spent that hour thinking about you. I thought about how proud I am of you for never giving up and how happy I am that you got that job offer. Mostly though, I spent that time fighting every urge to come down to your room so I could have you because I couldn't stop the taste of your lips from completely consuming me."

Despite the chill in the fall air, I didn't feel an ounce of cold. And I was certain the reason for that had nothing to do with the fire burning next to us and everything to do with the sultry woman sitting in my lap.

Her voice was deep and husky when she spoke. "I don't think I told you this earlier, but I have the day off tomorrow."

Christ. Was she saying what I thought she was saying?

"Ekko?" I questioned.

She nodded and added, "Do you think you could help make this day even better for me?"

"Sugar," I got out just before she leaned in and gave me a kiss.

When she pulled back, she pleaded with me, "There's one more thing I'd really love for you to give me for my birthday."

There was no longer any question about it. I couldn't deny the clear intention in her tone.

Fuck, did I want her.

Even still, I made no move to give her what she was asking for and I had no idea why that was the case.

Ekko turned her body a bit, straddled my legs, and pushed the blanket off her shoulders. My eyes followed her hands as they went to the buttons on her shirt. She unbuttoned each button and she did it painstakingly slow. When she had opened the last one, she allowed the shirt to slide down her arms.

I took her in, my eyes roaming over the curves of her little body. She was petite, but she had curves where they mattered. Full, round, perky breasts, a tiny waist, and an amazing ass that I always had the urge to squeeze. Ekko's hands went to the hem of the camisole she had on underneath the button-up shirt, where they lifted it up and over her head.

She was there before me in nothing but a lace-trimmed bra from the waist up and she was the most exquisite thing I'd ever laid my eyes on.

"Ekko—" I repeated her name, only this time my voice was thick with emotion at the sight of her.

Unable to resist the urge to touch her any longer, I ran my fingers up her thighs to her hips. One hand stayed planted at her hip while I lifted the other to the side of her neck. My fingertips began tracing delicately from her collarbone down over the top swells of her cleavage.

As the fire crackled beside us and the light from it illuminated and warmed her soft skin, I continued to move my hands over her body. With each brush of my fingers against her skin, Ekko's breathing quickened.

Her hands fell to my abdomen and gripped my shirt at my sides. Slowly, she began sliding my shirt up, eventually forcing me to take my hands from her body so that she could lift the fabric over my head. Once it was off, I wrapped an arm around her waist as my other hand went to her shoulder blade. Taking my time, I slid my hand underneath the strap of her bra and allowed my fingers to move up over the top of her shoulder, where I pressed a kiss before pulling the strap down her arm.

My mouth trailed kisses over her collarbone toward her neck. Ekko dropped her head back, giving me better access while she rocked her hips over me. I lifted my other hand to the middle of her back and unhooked her bra. Reluctantly, I pulled my mouth back from her throat and watched as the lace-trimmed fabric fell from her body.

She was perfect.

Absolutely spectacular.

I lifted my gaze from her flawless breasts to her seductive eyes.

"You're beautiful," I rasped.

A smile tugged at her lips. As much as I wanted to continue to stare at her, I wanted to pleasure her even more. My hands cupped her breasts and both thumbs swiped over her nipples. The moan she let out shot straight to my dick. Unable to wait any longer, I lowered my mouth to her. Closing my mouth over one nipple, I licked and sucked as my fingers continued to play with the other one.

Ekko's hands were at my shoulders, her fingernails digging into my skin. I didn't know how it was possible, but she managed to grind her pussy down on my cock even harder than she already had been.

Fuck.

I wanted that warmth.

The warmth that would come along with being deep inside her.

I switched sides, teasing her other breast with my mouth. She made it clear that she thoroughly enjoyed it. She moaned and whimpered, her desperation for more becoming more and more evident.

"Dom," she breathed, her voice a desperate plea. "Please."

I couldn't deny her any longer.

Hell, I couldn't deny myself any longer.

"Mouth," I demanded.

Ekko gave me her mouth as my hands dropped to the waistband of her pants. I unbuttoned them and started moving them down her hips. Ekko, keeping her mouth connected to mine, shifted on my lap, allowing me to remove her pants. Then, I had her sexy, little body in nothing but a pair of panties straddling me.

My hands were instantly at her ass, squeezing.

It wasn't enough.

Not for her.

Definitely not for me.

Her hands left my body and moved to her hips. This time, she broke the connection with my mouth as she shimmied out of her panties.

Completely naked, Ekko's desperately hungry eyes came to mine. She was silently pleading with me for something... anything I could give her.

I didn't make her wait.

Gripping one hip in my hand, I brought my other one right to the spot between her legs. The instant my fingers slid through her wetness and I heard her moan, I knew I was gone for her. I applied a bit more pressure and rubbed my hand over her.

Ekko's breathing grew louder.

I wanted more from her and I knew she was eager for it.

I slipped one finger inside her and the moment I did one of her hands gripped my shoulder while the other captured her breast. As my finger moved in and out of her, I watched as Ekko's entire body responded to the pleasure.

She was gorgeous.

Her head was down to the side, her eyes closed, and her lips parted. Her chest was rising and falling rapidly, and her hand was massaging one of her breasts. Her hips angled toward me, seeking further gratification.

She was so tight. I couldn't wait to have her wrapped around me.

A second finger entered her, and my pace picked up. I put my mouth to her free breast, sucking it in and teasing her hardened bud with flicks of my tongue.

Her hand left her breast and wrapped around the back of my head, holding me to her.

"Please, baby," she breathed.

Hearing her call me baby did me in. There wasn't anything I wouldn't give to her. I moved quicker, her moans grew louder. Mere seconds passed before she clamped down on my fingers, her nails dug into the skin at my shoulder, and she moaned through her orgasm. I had to pull back from her to watch. I needed to see her come apart.

Despite the cold, there was a sheen of sweat on her skin. She was gorgeous.

Her satisfied eyes came to mine.

"Kiss me, sugar."

Ekko brought her lips to mine and kissed. With her tongue in my mouth, I began moving my fingers inside her again. She pulled back just a touch and pleaded with me, "I want you, Dom. Please...tell me I can have you. Make my birthday wish come true."

She could have me.

I'd wanted this for months. And after having witnessed her coming, there was no way I wasn't going to see that again. Only this time, I'd make sure it happened with my cock inside her.

I brought both hands to her hips, grinned at her, and replied, "You're getting all of me tonight."

Hopefulness turned to relief in her face before she dropped her hands to my jeans. She worked to get them open, then lifted so I could raise myself and help her slide them down my legs. I pulled my wallet out of the back pocket, tossed the jeans to the side, and set the wallet on the table beside us.

Ekko began moving her body down mine, her hands traveling all over my torso. She'd occasionally dip her head and kiss me, her lips covering multiple spots on my chest and abdomen. The lower she descended, the harder I got. When her fingers gripped the waistband of my boxer briefs, I stopped breathing.

This woman.

This beautiful fucking woman.

There was no doubt she'd be my undoing.

Ekko slid the material down my legs, freeing me. Her eyes widened at the sight of me, her gaze focused on just that one part of my body. After she tossed my underwear to the side, she wrapped her hand around me.

It had been too long. Way too long.

I groaned.

"You're really big," she worried, nervously biting her lip.

Wrapping an arm around her waist, I lifted up and flipped her over to her back. It caught her by surprise, but she quickly recovered when I settled myself over her.

"I think we'll fit together perfectly."

This didn't seem to ease her concern, so I added, "But I'll still go slow. I won't hurt you, Ekko."

She gave me a nod of understanding.

I lifted up, reached out for my wallet, and grabbed a condom. I kept my eyes on Ekko as she watched me sheath myself.

She licked her lips.

Fuck.

Positioning myself at her entrance, I confirmed, "You good?"

"Yes."

Slowly, almost painfully slow for me, I pushed about halfway inside and gave her a minute to adjust to my size. I pulled back and pushed forward again, just as slow as the first time. The difference this time was that I had filled her. I stayed there, resting on my forearms, planted to the root of my cock, and croaked, "Are you okay?"

For the first time since meeting her, I couldn't read her eyes and I started to worry that I had hurt her.

"Ekko," I called. "Talk to me, sugar."

"You're perfect for me, Dom," she exclaimed, a clear surprise in her tone.

I pressed a quick kiss to her lips and said, "I told you we'd fit together."

She smiled up at me and begged, "Please move."

I wasted not another second and moved. I started slowly but quickly found a gradual, steady rhythm so that I could prolong this with her. It had been months since I'd been with anyone and the last thing I wanted was to not deliver for her. With each thrust, Ekko rewarded me. She alternated between closing her eyes and moaning with delight or arching her back and holding on tight. Either way, I didn't care. I loved watching her.

Eventually, I lifted my chest from her and shifted my weight to the palms of my hands. My pace picked up and, within seconds, Ekko was on the verge. I moved quicker, feeling myself getting closer, but knowing I wanted to watch her when she came apart for the first time with me inside her.

"Dom," she breathed.

My name coming from her when she was like this, filled with me, had me close to losing control.

"Baby, I'm going to come," she let out.

"Take it, sugar. Let me see you come apart for me."

Ekko exploded, her body trembling as her orgasm tore through her. Her body was flushed, the light from the fire illuminating her skin. I'd never seen anything more beautiful in my life.

When she came down from her orgasm and I knew I'd satisfied her, I powered harder into her. It didn't take much longer and just a few thrusts later, I gripped the side of the lounge chair with all my strength and buried myself inside her. Ekko's arms wrapped around my neck and she pulled me toward her. I felt her tongue at my throat and that's when I groaned through my orgasm. Ekko's mouth continued to move along my throat until I finished and dropped my head to her.

I lowered her to her back, slanted my head, and dipped my tongue inside her mouth. She took it and gave back just as good. Pulling back a minute later, I rested my forehead against hers and we struggled to catch our breath.

"Wow," she whispered, still out of breath.

I closed my eyes a few seconds, smiled, and agreed, "Yeah. Wow."

A minute later, I pulled myself from her body and announced, "I'll be right back."

I moved to dispose of the condom and when I returned a few minutes later, I nearly fell to my knees. Ekko was on the lounge chair, still completely naked, her arms bent up with her hands beside her head, her eyes looking up at me, and a smile of utter fulfillment on her face. Blinking slowly, she shared, "I can't move. My body no longer works."

I let out a laugh as I lowered myself to the side of the chair next to her and said, "I'll take care of you."

My hands moved to her legs, where I began separating her thighs.

Ekko tensed.

"What are you doing?"

"Seeing to you," I answered as I put a warm cloth between her legs.

I looked up at her and initially saw hesitation in her face. A few seconds passed before she relaxed and dropped her head back to the chair.

After I took care of her, I snagged the blanket from the foot of the lounger and fixed it to cover her before I climbed under, shifted her body, and curled her into me.

We stayed like that for a long while in silence. I knew she hadn't fallen asleep; I could feel it in her body. But I left her to her thoughts for a while. After some time had passed, she finally spoke.

"Thank you, Dom."

The chair shook with my laughter. "Sugar, I can't even begin to guess what you could possibly be thinking you need to thank me for."

"I'm not sure I could ever come close to thanking you for everything I should, but I'll say this for now. Thank you for giving me this today. For giving me my first ever birthday celebration. And I hope you know that even though I'm extremely grateful for the meaningful gifts you gave me earlier tonight, what today means to me has nothing to do with receiving those presents and everything to do with the fact that you believe I'm worthy of them when nobody else has ever done something like this for me. But that's not even the half of it. It's really all about you. Just you and the person you are."

I remained silent, unable to respond to her.

Apparently, Ekko wasn't finished because she completely gutted me when she continued, "I'm really starting to feel something strong for you, Dom. And it scares me. I'll never understand how I could have been so unlucky in my life with just about everything else and still somehow managed to deserve the privilege of knowing someone like you. After all these years, I finally know what it's like to matter to someone. But what scares me most is that with the way my life has been, I know I've just set myself up for serious heartache. When that time comes, I want you to know that I'll hold on to this memory, this day and especially this night, for the rest of my life."

"Ekko, look at me," I demanded.

She tipped her head back and looked up at me.

"I want to make you promises about what lies ahead, but I can't do that because I don't know what will happen. I've felt something for you for months now, and that feeling just got a whole lot stronger. I like what we have between us and I hope it stays good. If it starts not working for either one of us, know that you'll always matter to me. I'm sorry you never had that from anyone before, but I can promise you'll always have that from me moving forward."

She closed her eyes and let out a sigh of relief before she cuddled further into me. I held her tighter. I couldn't imagine how it must have been for her all her life feeling like she never really was important to anyone. I hated that she ever had to experience it, but I also knew I'd make sure she never felt that from me.

A few minutes passed before I spoke again. "So just before things took a turn to a really nice place out here, you mentioned that you're not working tomorrow. Does that mean I can convince you to spend the night with me?"

I felt her smile against my chest.

"I was really hoping you'd invite me to spend the night," she replied. "I miss your bed."

Well, that wasn't exactly what I had hoped to hear.

"Of course," she started again. "As much as I miss the bed, I mostly miss being wrapped up by you while I sleep."

That was much more like it.

Ekko and I stayed outside by the fire for a little while longer. I would have held her there all night, but it was going to get too cold out overnight. So, when I knew that she'd started giving in to sleep, I put out the fire, picked her up, and carried her to my bed, where I wrapped her in my arms and held her close.

Sometime in the middle of the night, Ekko woke me up with her mouth wrapped around me.

Ekko had been worried that she was setting herself up for heartache. I couldn't know for sure, but I didn't think it was possible to find any reason for not wanting to be with her. Being woken up like that in the middle of the night wasn't something I thought I'd ever want to give up.

CHAPTER 13

Ekko

THE SOUND OF MY OWN MOANING WOKE ME.

It took about point two seconds for me to figure out that I wasn't dreaming. I was in Dom's bed, legs spread, with his face between them.

He was feasting on me.

And he was doing one heck of a job of it, too.

"Baby," I whimpered.

Noting I had woken, Dom pulled his mouth back a fraction of an inch and declared, "Just returning the favor."

I smiled inwardly. After being with Dom for the first time last night on his deck and experiencing the single best night of my entire life, Dom carried me up to his bed. We both fell asleep, but sometime in the middle of the night, I woke up craving him. I figured it might be a welcome surprise to wake him with my mouth.

Dom was content to let me play with him for quite some time before he hauled me up his body and had me ride him. Being in control, I went above and beyond to make him feel good. After our middle-of-the-night rendezvous, we fell back asleep.

Until now.

I was being pleasured by the hottest, kindest, strongest,

gentlest man I'd ever met. From the moment I had met him, Dom always amazed me with what seemed like an effortless ability to do anything. From the simplest of things to the most daunting tasks. And through all of that, I'm not sure why I was surprised at just how incredibly talented he was at oral sex.

Dom sucked on my clit as he pumped a finger inside me. Quickly, he'd brought me to the point of no return and, within minutes of waking, I climaxed. Dom worked me through my orgasm before he shifted on the bed, grabbed a condom, and slid inside.

After he delivered a second and third orgasm, he found his release and collapsed on the bed beside me. Dom disposed of the condom and we then both took a few minutes to catch our breath.

I was on my back, my arms resting on the pillow just above my head, when he curled into me, resting his head on my shoulder, and draping his arm over my body just below my breasts.

And that was it.

Everything we did to each other's bodies over the last several hours was magnificent. We'd both managed to experience incredible physical pleasure, but for me, it was so much more than that.

It was in the cuddling afterward. The way he held me close. His fingers running through my hair or tracing delicately down my arm. The constant touch. I hadn't realized how much I'd been craving it until he gave it to me. Those whisper touches made me feel for the first time in my life that I was not only wanted but also like I mattered. Truly mattered.

Knowing now how that felt, I wasn't sure how I'd ever be able to live without that feeling again.

"Good morning," I finally said after a few minutes had passed.

"Morning, sugar."

"That was nice of you," I teased.

Dom let out a laugh and explained, "I figured it was only fair considering you took the liberty to be nice to me in the middle of the night."

"So you're just trying to keep the playing field level, then?"

Dom lifted his head and asked, "Ekko, you just came three times. Add to that the one time in the middle of the night and the two times out on the deck and I'd say this is definitely not a level playing field."

Feeling a bit embarrassed, I looked away and mumbled, "It's been a while."

Dom turned my head toward his and grinned. "There's no need to feel humiliated, Ekko. It's been a while for me, too."

My eyes widened in shock and I confirmed, "It has?"

His chin jerked downward.

"How long?" I blurted before I could stop myself. I quickly followed up with, "I'm sorry. That was rude. You don't have to answer that."

"Since the night I saved you," he answered immediately.

That was more than six months ago. And he was Dom; he was beautiful. He probably could have had any woman he wanted.

"What?"

Dom's arm that was draped across my body gave me a bit of a squeezed before he replied, "I knew from the minute I laid eyes on you that you were the girl for me. I can't explain it; it's just something I felt about you that was different than anything I've ever felt before. As time went by and I watched out for you, I grew more and more attracted to you."

I stared at him, completely shocked.

"Just so you know," Dom continued. "You were absolutely worth the wait, Ekko. I don't regret waiting all that time for you."

"Stop," I ordered. "I can't cry again. You can't keep doing and saying all of this sweet, wonderful stuff. I don't know how to deal with all of it."

"You're going to have to get used to it, fun size. After everything that's happened over the last few weeks and especially after what happened last night, you're mine now. I'm not going to hold back on giving you all the sweetness you deserve."

He was a dream come true.

And that scared the living daylights out of me.

Before I could respond, Dom went on, "Speaking of being mine, I need to ask you something."

"Okay," I replied, nervously.

"Two things, actually. First, as you already know, Levi and Elle's wedding is coming up. I'd love to take you with me. It's the second Saturday in December, so you won't have to worry about needing to work since you will have started your new job. Will you be my plus one?"

I wanted to go with him. I wanted to go so bad, but I'd seen Levi and Elle's home. I had to believe that they had family and friends that were very well off. I wouldn't fit in and I definitely didn't have anything nice enough to wear.

Despite all my negative thoughts, I didn't want to disappoint Dom. "I'd love to be your plus one," I responded.

Dom grinned at me, pressed a kiss to my chest, and rested his head back on my shoulder.

"What's the second question?"

"It's a two-part question. For starters, is the diner open next Thursday?"

"No. Jerry and Christie closed it for the holiday."

His arm tightened around me. "What were your plans for

the day?"

It was Thanksgiving. I didn't have anywhere to be and nothing was open, so my plans had consisted of sitting home and reading a book.

"Reading," I rasped, the feeling of embarrassment creeping back in.

Dom lifted his head again. There was a look on his face that I couldn't read, but he ultimately pushed past it and asked, "Are you willing to give that up for part of the day to spend it with me?"

With the way I felt about him and, perhaps more importantly, the way he made me feel, I would have given up reading for an entire week to spend Thanksgiving with him.

"Are you serious?"

"Yes."

My throat got tight. "I'm going to cry," I warned him.

Dom shifted his body and slid up so his face was closer to mine. His hand came up to cup the side of my face and his thumb stroked along my cheek. Then, his voice was soft when he spoke, "Don't cry."

It was too late. A single tear had fallen. After he swiped it away with the pad of his thumb, he pressed a kiss to my lips. "You break my heart sometimes, Ekko."

"I break yours?"

His eyes searched my face a moment before he responded, "The simplest things mean the world to you. It blows my mind."

Of course, they did. How could he be surprised by that? When you had nothing, when you came from nothing, having anything meant something. And having someone meant everything. I didn't tell him this. Instead, I whispered, "I'm looking forward to Thanksgiving with you."

A satisfied smile broke out on his face, complete with

dimples. He rolled to his back and reached out to the bedside table. Seconds later, his phone was at his ear. Keeping his eyes on me, he waited for someone to answer.

Suddenly, he spoke, "Hey, Mom. I'm just calling to let you know I'll be bringing someone with me next week for Thanksgiving."

He was silent, and I was mortified.

Mom?

He was planning to have me meet his Mom?!

I started panicking. I sat up in the bed, pulling the sheet up to cover my naked body.

"Yes, she does exist. I don't know why you didn't believe me before," he argued, his tone teasing.

He told his Mom about me already. I didn't know what to do with that information.

"Okay. See you next week. Love you."

My heart.

Hearing him tell her he loved her.

"Did you just call your Mom and tell her I was going there with you for Thanksgiving?" I questioned him.

"Yes," he started. "You said you were looking forward to spending it with me."

I raised my brows. "Yes, I know that. I was looking forward to spending it with you. You made no mention of your mom."

"It's Thanksgiving, Ekko. We're going to go to my parents' house and spend the holiday with my family."

"Your family?"

He nodded.

"Who would that be? Mom and Dad?" I worried, unsure if I could handle this kind of pressure.

Dom nodded again and added, "Among others."

"What others?"

"Colton, Memphis, Kendall, and Jojo."

My eyes widened. "Who?"

He smiled at me and said, "My brothers and sisters."

My jaw dropped. "Your parents had five children?!" I asked, disbelievingly.

"Colton and Memphis are my older brothers. Mom and Dad wanted another baby and ended up having my older sister, Kendall. They didn't want her to grow up without a sister, so they tried for another girl and got me. Jolie, or Jojo as we call her, is my baby sister."

Wow. My father never even met me and my mother never wanted anything to do with me. Dom had two parents who wanted their children and cared so much about them that they made sure their daughter didn't grow up without a sister. I couldn't even begin to imagine a love like that.

"You want me to meet your family?"

Dom reached his arm out to me and wrapped it around my waist. After he tugged me toward him and I fell to my side, facing him, he answered, "Yes, I do."

"Will they like me?"

His face dipped close and his voice was low, "They'll love you."

Warmth and longing spread through me. My arms went around his neck and I held on tight. Dom kissed me for a bit before he got up, with me in his arms, and announced, "Breakfast time."

"Yay," I cheered.

Dom chuckled and carried me out of the room.

Then, he made French toast for breakfast while I tried not to get too excited about his family loving me.

"I'm a little nervous," I admitted.

"There's nothing to be nervous about, Ekko. This is supposed to be a night of fun. There will be a lot of people there, but everyone is just looking to have a good time," Dom reassured me.

It was Thanksgiving Eve and we were in his truck on the way to see Elle perform at Big Lou's Restaurant and Saloon. Big Lou's was in Windsor's neighboring town, Rising Sun.

The last several days had been so busy and flew by.

I ended up thoroughly enjoying the day after my birthday because Dom decided to take the day off. He hadn't originally planned it, but when he realized I didn't need to go into work he wanted to take advantage of the opportunity. It was so nice to have an entire, care-free day with him. We even snuck in a trip to the bowling alley.

On top of that, I also got a call from Elle. She told me that she was going to be performing once more before her wedding and was hoping I'd be able to make it out to see her. Luck was on my side once again because Jerry and Christie let all of us know that we'd be closing early today. They wanted to make sure that the staff had plenty of time to spend with family and friends for the holiday. Normally, this wouldn't have made a difference to me one way or the other, but now that I had someone to spend it with, my perspective had changed.

Dom and I were both back at work on Friday. I had to work the weekend, but he came over to my place on Sunday since I only ended up working through the lunch shift. I gave Jerry and Christie my two weeks' notice. They were sad to see me go but completely supported me. To top it off, they told me that I'd always have a job there if I found myself in need of one. While I hoped I never had to take them up on it, I appreciated their kindness tremendously.

Monday was another full day at work. Dom and I didn't

get to see each other; though, we managed to connect that evening over the phone. On Tuesday, I went in to meet Alice at the library to sign all of the necessary paperwork to start my new job. Completing that paperwork felt so good. I felt like I was one step closer to living my dream, a dream that only a few short weeks prior I had just about given up on. That afternoon, after a quick stop at the mall for something, I was back at the diner and worked until close.

And finally today, I worked nearly the entire day. It was so busy at the diner. I hadn't expected it to be as busy as it was, but the consensus was that nobody wanted to cook the day before they had to prepare Thanksgiving Day feasts. I didn't mind because by the time we closed tonight I had had one of my best days ever for tips at the diner. I wasn't sure if it was the holiday spirit or something else, but whatever it was I was grateful.

In fact, ever since that first night I stayed at Dom's, my financial situation had improved. I had managed to get two months' worth of rent payments put in the bank plus a little extra. My kitchen was stocked, and I was no longer worried about where my next meal was coming from.

"It's just...well, I've never really done this before. I don't know what to expect."

Dom reached across the center console, wrapped his fingers around my thigh, squeezed, and said, "To enjoy yourself. That's all you need to do tonight. It's going to be fine."

I covered his hand with mine, stared straight ahead, and tried taking a few settling breaths to calm myself.

A few minutes later, Dom had pulled into the parking lot. Big Lou's was a two-story building with a massive deck on the first level that wrapped around three sides of it. There was an outdoor staircase that led up to the second-floor balcony. We got out of the truck and Dom began guiding me toward the staircase.

"The first floor is the restaurant," he explained, putting his hand to the small of my back as we climbed the stairs. "The saloon is upstairs. That's where Elle will be performing."

Dom and I came to a halt at the entrance, where he stopped to chat a minute with the bouncer. Dom was a big man and the bouncer rivaled Dom's size.

"Can it be?" the bouncer asked.

Dom laughed as he shook the bouncer's hand and replied, "Hey, Cliff. How's it going?"

"What's it been? Six, seven months?" Cliff asked.

Dom shrugged as he wrapped his arm around my shoulders and pulled me in toward him. "Cliff, this is my woman, Ekko."

Cliff looked down at me and offered a friendly smile. "Nice to meet you, Ekko."

"You too."

His eyes went back to Dom. "Now it makes sense."

Dom didn't try to fight the grin from spreading on his face. "We'll catch you later, Cliff."

At that, Dom ushered me inside as Cliff called out, "Have a good night!"

"What makes sense?" I asked, looking up at Dom.

He gave me a gentle squeeze and answered, "I used to come here regularly. That stopped after I met you. There was no point in me coming here to find a lousy hook up when I already met the woman I wanted to be with."

His words melted my heart.

Dom held my eyes a moment before looking across the saloon. "Come on," he urged, nudging me. "Levi, Elle, Cruz, and Lexi are all here already. I'll introduce you to Lexi."

We made our way over to Dom's friends, but before he could say anything, Elle walked right up to me, pulled me in for a hug, and exclaimed, "Hey, Ekko! I'm so happy you could make it!"

"Me too," I responded, hugging her back. "I'm so excited to watch you perform."

I had to be honest. It was such a new experience for me to have someone approach and greet me the way Elle had. She was such a bright and fun-loving woman with a carefree attitude. Even though I was a little out of my element, I had to admit it felt good to be welcomed like that.

When Elle pulled back from me, she turned and greeted Dom. After acknowledging Elle, Dom turned back to the group and went about making introductions.

"Ekko, I think you might remember Cruz," he started.

I had.

And it was nothing short of embarrassing. Twice now I'd been around Cruz and both times I'd been in rather awful predicaments.

"Yeah," I responded, directing my attention to Cruz. "It's nice to see you now when I'm not needing someone to rescue me."

Given what happened at Ryan's a few weeks ago and adding that to me being nearly abducted a few months ago, he very easily could have made judgments about the kind of person I was. Instead, he chuckled and never made me feel bad about the fact that I was who I was.

"It's good to see you again, darlin'. Happy to see you've healed nicely, too."

There was that as well. Cruz had also seen me with blood pouring down my face. I didn't have an opportunity to let myself get too caught up in that because the other woman that was there cut in, "It sounds like all the ladies in this group have been in trouble at some point."

My brows pulled together as I looked at her, waiting for further explanation.

"I'm Lexi," she introduced herself as she held her hand out to me. "I'm Cruz's girlfriend."

I extended my hand to her and shook. "Hi, Lexi. I'm Ekko."

"Don't feel bad about needing their help. Elle and I have both already been there," she pointed out.

"You have?"

She nodded. "I was kidnapped and nearly thrown into a sex-trafficking ring. Thankfully, some quick thinking on my end mixed with this group of very determined men made it so before anything bad could happen, I was found along with many other women."

I gasped. My eyes darted back and forth several times between Lexi and Dom before ultimately settling on Lexi. "The same one he was working?" I asked, pointing to Dom. "The same one that he and Cruz made sure that I didn't become a victim to?"

Confusion washed over her face as she looked to Cruz. His face softened, and he leaned in. "Ekko was the girl in the attempted abduction I told you about," he explained.

Realization dawned in her features and her head snapped back toward me. Apparently, she knew about what had almost happened to me.

"Are you okay?" she wondered.

"Me?" I shot back, disbelievingly. "I should be asking you the same question. I was fortunate enough that these guys showed up before it was too late."

Her expression changed as she leaned back into Cruz. "I am the best I've ever been...in more ways than you can imagine."

That was good to hear, and I was in awe of Lexi's resilience. I couldn't even begin to think what I would have done if Dom and Cruz hadn't been there that night.

Before I could respond, Elle spoke. "I've got to head back and get ready to go on stage in a few minutes. I'll catch up with all of you afterward."

We waved her off as she turned to walk away. Levi was right by her side the entire time.

"Isn't he going to watch her show?" I asked Dom while he pulled out a chair for me at the reserved table in the front of the room.

"He will," Dom began. "Just offstage, though. Ever since things went down for her with her stalker, he doesn't like to be more than a few feet away when she's performing. The threat is no longer there, but I think it's still in the back of his mind."

"Wow," I marveled, completely blown away. I thought that it was just Dom who was protective, but it was evident he kept good company.

Dom sat down to my left and Lexi sat off to my right. While we waited for Elle's performance to begin, Lexi and I made conversation. To start, she asked about what I do for a living. It felt great to be able to share the news about my new job with another person. What made it even more special was the fact that she seemed truly interested in learning about me.

Of course, I wanted to know more about her and what made her the strong woman she was. I wasn't sure if she wanted to talk about it, but I asked her about the details of what happened when she was kidnapped. If it bothered her to talk about it, she didn't let on. She gave me the story, and when she finished, I was in complete shock and amazement. Truthfully, I didn't think I would have had the courage to do what she did. Recalling my own experience, I remembered feeling helpless as I kicked and screamed and wanted to know how she found the courage to save herself.

That's when she shocked me even further.

Lexi told me that years ago she had been raped. It

happened when she was in college and she never fought back then. Healing from that took her years, so when the opportunity to fight for herself arose again, she took advantage.

"I'm so sorry," I said, unsure if that was even enough.

"Thank you. I'm doing great now, so please don't worry."

My discussion with Lexi ended at that moment because Dom tapped me on the shoulder and pointed in the direction of the stage. "That's Lou. Elle's about to start."

For the next hour and a half, we listened to Elle. She was phenomenal. I'd heard about her, but there was nothing quite like witnessing it with your own eyes. Her voice was exquisite. After her set, Elle and Levi joined the group again. The six of us hung out together for a while and I learned a bit more about everyone.

"Wes and his crew didn't show up tonight," Dom stated. There was a bit of a questioning tone in his voice, though.

"My brother is overly concerned with Charley right now," Elle replied. "She's so pregnant, due any day, and is utterly exhausted. I met up with her earlier this week and insisted she stay home tonight. I know they all wanted to be here, but my soon-to-be nephew is more important to me. Besides, I know we'll see them all tomorrow and they'll be at the wedding in two weeks."

"It's the same with Zane and Emme," Levi added. "Zane is being extra cautious since Emme's still a month away from delivering their twins, but my sister-in-law is determined. Zane called me earlier today and explained that he had to bribe Emme. He promised her several dances at the wedding if she stayed in tonight."

Wow.

Brothers and sisters-in-law and babies.

Family.

Something I wanted more than anything else, more than I

wanted to become a librarian.

"If you guys don't have plans and are looking for something to do tomorrow night, we'll all be meeting up at Zane and Emme's place. You're welcome to stop by," Cruz offered.

Trying to tamp down the excitement I felt at the prospect of being included with such a wonderful group of people, I directed my hopeful gaze to Dom. He looked down at me and his face warmed before he turned to the table and announced, "Ekko's meeting my family tomorrow. Depending on what time the festivities end at the Moore residence, we can swing by Zane and Emme's for a bit before heading home."

When I looked back at the group, I found smiles of excitement from the girls and approving nods from the guys. The conversation continued to flow after this, but I was too caught up in my thoughts and feelings to really get involved in it. I was only a few hours away from what I had a feeling was going to be the best Thanksgiving of my life.

CHAPTER 14

Ekko

I T WAS THANKSGIVING MORNING AND I WAS HARD AT WORK IN MY kitchen.

Last night, after Elle's show at Big Lou's, Dom brought me home. I really wanted to wake up with him this morning, so I asked him to spend the night. He did, but he left early to run home, shower, and change before we needed to leave to go to his parents' house.

After Dom left, I got to work on making some pies. Earlier in the week, I had asked him about what I could bring today, and he insisted that it wasn't necessary. Maybe that was true, but I refused to go there empty-handed.

My apple pies had just finished in the oven and were sitting on the countertop cooling while I put together the ingredients for my no-bake pumpkin pie. Once I had combined all things pumpkin and pumpkin spice with a few extras, I filled the crusts and covered the pies.

An hour later, after I had showered, gotten dressed, and put on some makeup, there was a knock at my door.

Dom was right on time.

I opened the door to let him in.

The minute he came in and shut the door behind him, he gave me a once-over and said, "You look amazing."

Feeling proud of myself, I returned, "Thank you. I wanted to make a good first impression with your family, so I kind of took myself shopping on Tuesday after I left the library. It wasn't the outfit I really wanted, but it was on sale. Even still, it's much nicer than anything else I have."

Dom put his hand to the back of my head and brought his lips to mine. After kissing me, he pulled back and stated, "You want to buy new clothes to make yourself feel good, or because you work hard and deserve to treat yourself to something nice, you do it. But don't buy them because you think you need to impress my family."

I dropped my gaze from his and took a step back. "Dom," I started. "You know how awful my situation was. I'm certainly not living in the lap of luxury now, but I'm doing better. I don't want your family to think I'm total trash."

His eyes flared, and he took a step toward me. "What did you just say?"

Evidently, that was the wrong thing for me to say. I tried to backpedal and explain myself. "You have two parents and four siblings. I have nobody. You have a nice home, a beautiful truck, two motorcycles, and a great job. Up until a few weeks ago when you walked into my life, I was living out of my car, rationing any food I had, and working at a diner."

"You were living out of your car for two days," he pointed out.

"My living situation prior to that wasn't much better. I was with a drug dealer," I countered.

"You didn't know he was and the minute you found out, you left," he shot back.

I looked away again and my voice got soft. "I know. I just…I just don't want them to know how awful things were for me. I hate that you even know. It's so embarrassing."

Dom brought his hand up to my jaw and nudged my head

back toward his. "Nobody needs to know anything you don't want them to, but I'm going to tell you now that I do not *ever* want to hear you call yourself trash again, Ekko," he warned.

"Poor choice of words," I tried to brush it off.

He knew it and he didn't let me get away with it. "You've thought that from the first night I brought you to my place. You told me you didn't want to go with me because you had no business being near someone like me. I had an inkling then that this is what you were thinking, but decided not to call you out on it given the situation. I'm not holding back on that anymore."

I gasped.

He held my gaze.

I couldn't argue with him. It was the truth. That's precisely how I felt. And try as he might to get me to see it different-ly, I'd lived for twenty-nine years knowing where I stood on the social status scale. Being lucky enough to get back into an apartment, land a new job, and date the most incredible man I'd ever know wasn't going to change my perspective.

"Just please promise me you aren't going to tell them," I pleaded.

"I promise, but you need to not be ashamed of who you are."

It was a holiday, we had to go, and I didn't want to spend the day arguing with him, so I gave him a nod and a smile. I'm not sure if that convinced him, but he let it go.

"Are you ready to go?" he asked.

"Yeah, I just need to get the pies. Will you help me carry them? I've got four made."

"I told you that you didn't need to bring anything."

I turned and started walking toward the kitchen as I re-plied, "I know, but I didn't want to go without anything, so I made two apple pies and two pumpkin."

As I walked into the kitchen I heard Dom chuckling as he followed behind me. Our disagreement forgotten, we loaded up the pies and made our way over to his parents' house.

Twenty minutes later, Dom was pulling into the driveway lined with cars and my nerves had skyrocketed. I hadn't noticed until he parked and reached across the center console, but my leg was nervously bouncing.

"Relax," he said softly. "They'll love you."

My head bobbed up and down with understanding, but I was only mildly reassured. I hoped I'd make a good first impression with the people I presumed Dom held closest in his heart. I had a feeling Dom could still see the worry in my features.

"Stay put while I come around to help you out," he instructed.

I did as he asked, mostly because I was too consumed with worry to do anything else.

Once Dom made it to the passenger side of the truck, he opened my door and held his hand out to me. As I moved to step out, Dom pulled me toward him and caught me around the waist. My feet never touched the ground and I instinctively wrapped my legs around his waist. Before I had a chance to think, Dom captured my mouth with his.

While our tongues tasted and hands roamed, the last bits of anxiety melted away. All that existed was the two of us and I realized that no matter what else happened, if I only had him, I could be happy with that.

The sound of a car door closing caused me to pull back from Dom. I tensed as we both looked to the side. A man, just as tall, but not nearly as bulky as Dom, was striding toward us with a smirk on his face.

Despite the cold outside, I was certain my cheeks were flushed with embarrassment. I began wiggling in Dom's arms.

He got the hint and lowered me to the ground.

"Looks like it's a Happy Thanksgiving for you," the man said to Dom before turning his attention to me. "I'm Dom's older and much wiser brother, Colton. Are you Ekko?"

My eyes rounded, shocked that he already knew my name.

"Hey, asshole. If she weren't Ekko, this would be one hell of a way to ruin the holiday, don't you think?" Dom finally addressed his brother.

Colton didn't take his gaze from me. He simply grinned and declared, "With the way you talked about Ekko for months, I knew she couldn't have been anyone else."

Dom had been talking about me for months.

I stood there in silence, too stunned to move. Either Colton thought I was crazy and decided to get away or he realized I was too dazed to form a coherent sentence because he ended, "I'll catch you two inside."

Once Dom and I were alone again, I found my voice. "Why am I not surprised?" I practically exploded. "Leave it to me and my horrible luck to have that happen. Why did you do that? Why did you kiss me?"

Dom's hands framed my face as he bent and lowered himself to be eye-level with me. "Sugar, relax. I kissed you to take your mind off everything. And it worked perfectly until Colton showed up. He was just joking with us; you need to stop worrying."

My eyes filled with tears. "I really want them to like me, Dom. I want it more than you can imagine and I don't want to do anything to screw that up," I whispered.

His thumbs stroked back and forth over my cheekbones. "You are an amazing woman, Ekko. That, in and of itself, is enough to make them like you. You also make me a very happy man. And that will make them love you."

"Are you sure?" I worried.

"I promise."

I closed my eyes and took a deep breath. I needed to trust him. More than that, I needed to find a way to start believing in myself. Dom was showing me that I was someone worth knowing.

"Okay," I agreed.

Dom pressed a kiss to my forehead before we opened the back door to the truck and pulled out the pies.

A minute later, Dom ushered me through the door from the garage leading into his parents' house. We walked right into a room just off the kitchen. Dom managed to carry his two pies while keeping one hand at the small of my back. I appreciated the comforting touch from him.

As soon as we entered the kitchen, he set his pies down and took mine from me. There was an older woman that I knew immediately had to be Dom's mother standing there. Her back had been turned when we walked in, but the second Dom had set the remaining pies down, she turned around.

I could see her mind working as she assessed me and waited for an introduction. Dom walked right over to her, gave her a hug and a kiss on the cheek, and wished, "Happy Thanksgiving."

She gave him an adoring look, returned the sentiment, and brought her curious gaze to me.

"Mom, this is my girlfriend, Ekko. Ekko, this is my mom, Angela."

Dom's mother waited about three seconds before she walked over, pulled me into her arms, and announced, "Happy Thanksgiving, Ekko. I'm so happy to finally meet you; I was beginning to think he made you up."

"I'm real," I assured her. "And Happy Thanksgiving to you as well, Mrs. Moore."

"Angie, please. Everyone calls me Angie."

Before I could respond to her, I was distracted by the voices entering the kitchen. When I looked to my left, I saw an older man I believed was Dom's father, two younger women that had to be his sisters, his brother, Colton, and another guy I suspected was Dom's other brother, Memphis.

Dom wasted no time in introducing me to the remaining members of his family. All of them were warm and welcoming. Dom's father, Bill, gave him an approving nod after he greeted me. Colton and Memphis had a way about them that was similar to Dom. They struck me as the protective type. Kendall and Jolie, or Jojo as they called her, were a breath of fresh air, instantly folding me in their arms. They had a kind and caring nature about themselves. The siblings all bared a physical resemblance to each other in one way or another, but their mannerisms and personality are what told me they belonged to the same family.

I felt an immediate connection with Jojo. I didn't know if it was because we were closest in age or if it was because she was, by far, the most outspoken of the group. That was saying something since they were all outgoing and friendly.

After we got introductions out of the way and Angie ordered us into the dining room, I realized my nerves had melted away. I was silently kicking myself for having gotten so worked up for no reason. Even though your relatives didn't necessarily always reflect the kind of person you are, I should have known that Dom wouldn't have subjected me to a group of people that wouldn't have been accepting of me.

We sat down to eat, and the conversation immediately started flowing. I expected to be under some scrutiny, but it wasn't ever unwelcome or nasty.

"So, what do you do, Ekko?" Kendall asked.

"I'm actually in the process of changing jobs right now. I've been working as a waitress for quite some time now, but I just got a new job as a library assistant at the Windsor Public Library. I start just over a week from today on the first Monday in December."

"That's cool. What does a library assistant do?"

"Mostly, I'll be responsible for a lot of the clerical duties: checking books and materials in and out, shelving materials, assisting patrons with questions, and helping out with library programs to name a few. But my goal is to become a librarian. I'm hoping to start school again next semester."

"Will you have to go away to school?" Bill asked, an edge of nervousness in his tone.

I shook my head. "No. I have a semester left to finish my undergraduate degree. Then, I'll be taking courses online for my master's in library science."

"How did you and Ekko end up together?" Memphis asked Dom.

He thought for a moment before he responded, "I went to the diner one night when she was working."

Memphis and Colton both narrowed their eyes at him. They didn't believe him.

"Don't push it," Dom warned, knowing their thoughts.

"What?" Jojo cried. "What did I miss?"

Dom ignored his sister and looked at me. "Ekko, let me tell you about my family and what they do. "Mom is a school teacher and Dad's an attorney. Kendall's a nurse, Jojo is a massage therapist, and Colton and Memphis are detectives for the Rising Sun Police Department."

That explained a lot. Kendall and Jojo both had nurturing personalities that it was only fitting they worked in professions where they took care of others. Dom's brothers knew he wasn't being entirely truthful because they'd been trained to spot it. I didn't like that they had reason to mistrust him, or more specifically, me. And it was all because I made him promise that he wouldn't tell them the truth about my situation.

I figured if there was any time to make a good impression on them, it was now. And because I was trying to accept that I was someone who was worthy of companionship and a little bit of good luck, I didn't think there was any time like the present to start showing that I was worthy.

"Dom and I got together after he came into the diner a couple weeks ago, but we met before that," I announced to the table. Suddenly, I felt his hand wrap around mine under the table. He was offering me encouragement. "I'm not comfortable getting into all the details of what happened right now, but I'll tell you this. I found myself in a bit of a rough spot a few months ago that led me into a pretty bad situation, which could have been catastrophic, but Dom happened to be there that night to help me."

When I finished speaking, I braced myself for their reaction. I had expected to see looks of disapproval. I mean, Dom's family was so put together. They were all wildly successful and it wouldn't have been out of the realm of possibilities that they'd see me as someone who was unworthy of their son and brother. Instead, I received glances of approval for me and smiles filled with pride for Dom.

From that point forward, any lingering tension I felt was gone and I could thoroughly enjoy spending time getting to know Dom's family. The conversation shifted to other topics and I never once felt left out.

We spent most of our day with Dom's family, but as the evening rolled around and everyone started leaving he asked, "Did you want to stop by Zane and Emme's place?"

I leaned in and answered, "I'd love to, but I have to work tomorrow morning. I think it's going to be busy with holiday shoppers out and about."

"It's up to you. If you want to stop over, I have no problem going. If you'd rather call it a night, that's okay, too. There will be other opportunities to meet everyone."

"I don't think it'll be a good idea for me to be out late tonight. You should probably take me home. But if you want to go visit with your friends, you should."

Dom lowered his mouth to my ear and whispered, "I'd rather visit with you."

Heat spread through me. "That works for me," I said softly.

Dom and I said goodbye to his family before we took off back to my apartment. Even though he'd already insinuated it, I still wanted to confirm that he was going to spend the night with me. All of the festivities for the day had worn me out and I wasn't sure I'd ever been around so many people at once, but I knew I didn't want to be alone tonight.

We got ready for bed and a few minutes after we'd been curled up in each other's arms, I spoke. "Thank you for giving me my first Thanksgiving worth remembering."

Dom kissed my hair and whispered, "My pleasure, Ekko."

"You're so lucky."

"Lucky?"

I sighed, trying to figure out how to tell him how I felt without making it seem like I was having a pity party. It wasn't that I believed he didn't appreciate what he had in his life, but I wanted to make sure he knew just how fortunate he was.

"You know that I've always been a reader, but it dawned on me tonight how reading has impacted my life. When I was younger, and I read, I thought it was an escape from my life and my situation. Now that I'm older, I see it for what it really was. Reading only took me farther into my life. It showed me the reality of my own and what I didn't have."

"Money and things aren't everything," he declared.

I took in a deep breath and blew it out. "I know that, but love and a sense of belonging are. And I didn't have that. I've never had that from anyone other than Ms. Grace. You have the most amazing family. Seeing you and all of them today just showed me how much I missed out on. I'm not feeling sorry for myself; I'm just really happy you've had that in your life."

Dom's arms tightened around me. "I am, too."

"I do wish, though, that I had someone in mine. I had it briefly with Ms. Grace, but then it was just loneliness. I would have given anything to not have to feel that."

"You've got me now, sugar."

The moment I heard him say those words, I felt myself melt farther into him. I pressed a kiss to his chest and whispered, "I know, baby. I'm trying to get used to this feeling."

"Take all the time you need; I'm not going anywhere."

I gave Dom another kiss. My hands began roaming over him and I made it very clear what I needed from him. Seconds later, he took over and made it so I didn't regret missing the chance to visit with his friends.

CHAPTER 15

Ekko

"I JUST GOT IN MY CAR," I SAID TO DOM AS I HELD MY PHONE between my ear and shoulder. I was sliding my hands back and forth trying to warm them while I waited for my car to heat up.

"Okay. I'm finishing up a few things here at the office and then I'll be leaving," he replied. "I'll meet you at my place. I should be there not too long after you get there."

"Alright. I'm going to take a shower when I get there and then I'll start something for dinner."

"Sounds good. See you soon."

Dom and I disconnected. The temperature gauge on my dash had barely moved and I was freezing. I couldn't wait to get in Dom's shower and warm up. I put the car in drive and pulled out of the lot.

It was just after four o'clock on Monday and I was getting my first day off since Thanksgiving. This was one of those oddball years that had five Thursdays in November instead of the usual four, which was precisely why I worked at the diner today instead of having my first day at the library. The days that followed the holiday were incredibly busy at the diner. I worked all day Friday, Saturday, and Sunday. I was in early today for another shift but thankfully was done for the next day and a half. I didn't have to go back to work until Wednesday afternoon, and then I'd just need to work every day until Saturday. My last shift at the diner was scheduled to start on Saturday morning and end just before the lunch shift. Then, I'd start my new job next Monday. I couldn't wait.

Not long after I got off the phone with Dom, I was pulling into his driveway. When I got out of the car, I was surprised to see George, one of my regulars from the diner, walking by.

"George?" I called. "What are you doing here?"

"Hey, Ekko. I'm just out for a little exercise. I live in the neighborhood, a couple doors down," he answered as he pointed in the opposite direction. He took a minute to think and his expression changed. "Do you live here?"

I shook my head. "No. My boyfriend lives here. It's date night, I guess you could say. I missed seeing you this week since we were closed on Thursday."

He held his hands up and waved them in front of his chest. "I do not go out in this holiday shopping madness. More often than not, I'm a grumpy old man. Dealing with droves of holiday shoppers and the hustle and bustle of the season is more than this cranky man can handle."

I offered a friendly smile and urged, "Well I hope you'll stop in this week because it's my last week at the diner."

"No kidding?"

"I got a new job at the Windsor Public Library. I start next Monday," I explained.

George let out a chuckle and said, "I stop in to the library every now and then. I'll still see you around occasionally."

A shiver ran through me the longer I stood in the cold. "That's perfect. I've been a bit bummed that I won't see my co-workers and regulars at the diner anymore, so I'm happy to hear I'll still be able to see you."

He offered a friendly smile in return.

"I better go in and you better get home. It's so cold out here."

"And it's only going to get colder," George added as he gave me a nod and took off down the sidewalk.

I grabbed my bags out of my car and ran inside to get out of the cold.

Once inside, I wasted no time in moving up the stairs to take a shower. I hopped in and did my business quickly, but stood there enjoying the warmth from the water. After giving myself ample time, and finally having the feeling back in my limbs, I turned off the water and got out.

Just as I wrapped the towel around me, I heard a knock on the bathroom door followed by Dom's voice, "Ekko?"

It startled me, but I recovered and answered, "Yeah?"

Dom didn't respond. Instead, he opened the door and came inside.

"Hey, baby," I greeted him, sliding my hands up his chest and around his neck.

Dom wrapped his arms around my waist, pulled me close, and kissed me. "Missed you, sugar," he shared when he pulled his mouth from mine.

While we had spoken to each other every day since then, we hadn't seen one another since we woke up on Friday morning and I took off to work.

"I thought you were going to be downstairs when I got back," he remarked. "Did something happen on the way home?"

"No, sorry. I saw one of my regulars from the diner walking by when I got here, so I chatted with him. That delayed me a bit. But then I got in the shower and was still too cold to get out when I finished so I stayed in a little longer."

The next thing I knew, I heard the thud of shoes and the clanging of his belt on the tile floor. After he pulled his shirt over his head, he asked, "Are you still cold?"

I wasn't, but I could certainly play the part. "Maybe a little," I teased, tipping my head back and pressing up on my toes.

Dom lowered his head and brought his mouth to mine. His hands went to the top of the towel, pulled it apart, and let it fall to the floor. Seconds later, with his mouth still connected to mine, he was carrying me to the bed.

His body hovered over mine as his hands caressed the skin up and down the sides of my body. When his lips left mine, I nearly cried at the loss. But Dom had plans. Plans that involved trailing kisses down my throat and chest, where he cupped my breasts in his hands before sucking one nipple in his mouth.

A shot of desire ran through me and landed right between my legs. My back arched as I let out a moan. My response to his touch and teasing only served to motivate him. He worked that much harder to please me. Dom kissed his way down my body, his mouth eventually finding its way between my thighs. One lick through my wetness and I was gone.

"Baby," I rasped as my hands fisted the sheets.

One of Dom's hands was splayed across my belly, the other at my hip, as he continued to lick and suck—as he continued to devour me. It didn't take long for Dom to work me up, but just before he sent me soaring, I lost his mouth.

When I groaned and whimpered, clearly indicating my displeasure with his decision not to see me through, he gave me his most reassuring tone. "Patience, Ekko. I'd never leave you like this."

I watched as he removed his boxer briefs and hastily slid on a condom. Then, it was nothing but urgent need between us. Dom's body came over mine as he slid inside and filled me. My hips lifted and lowered to match and meet his thrusts. Since I'd been so close to the edge moments before it didn't take long for the splintering sparks of pleasure to travel through every inch of my body. My eyes closed as I moaned, "Baby."

I barely had a second to come down from my orgasm when Dom lifted my legs at my knees and drove himself in deeper and faster.

A feeling of awe swept through me.

His strength.

And power.

And control.

I could feel the urgent and desperate need he had for me with the way he moved and the sounds he made. Seeing it sent another thrill of desire flooding through me. Instantly, I felt the sensations building again and I needed more.

"Harder, Dom. Please," I begged.

His pace picked up, his thrusts grew stronger, and his voice was a low growl when he got out, "Beautiful...so damn gorgeous."

He continued to work me until my orgasm slammed into me, causing a scream to escape. I'd never been a loud lover, but there was something about him that forced the sound to leak from deep in my lungs.

A deep roar filled the room as Dom found his release and buried himself to the root of his cock inside me. I watched as it tore through him, saw the beauty of it, and knew I'd never want to live without him in my life.

It wasn't until an hour later when Dom and I were downstairs preparing dinner together. We had cuddled a bit after our rendezvous before Dom got up to shower while I got dressed and started some prep work on dinner. He had joined me in the kitchen a few minutes ago and we were preparing some chicken noodle soup.

When I mentioned something to him yesterday about

how cold it was outside, he suggested that we have chicken noodle soup tonight. It had been a long time since I'd had it, but I couldn't hold on to those memories forever. I decided to put my negative thoughts aside for him and agreed.

We sat down to eat and, after getting several warm bites of the delicious soup in my belly, I blurted it out.

"The last time I had chicken noodle soup, it was cold, and I was eating it out of a can."

Dom's spoon clattered on the bowl as it fell from his hand. "What?" he asked.

I told him the story about being a hungry fifteen-year-old girl sitting on the tattered mattress on the floor of her dirty apartment trying to ration the food in that can so it would last another day. I also explained how that same girl had a plan to do something more for herself, but that plan was blown to bits when she ended up in foster care three days later.

"Christ, Ekko. I knew you had it rough when you told me about Ms. Grace, but I never realized just how bad it was for you."

I shook my head, hating that I'd made him upset. "I didn't intend to ruin your night tonight, Dom. I haphazardly made that declaration because I was comparing those two situations in my head. I'm grateful I've got a much better experience with chicken noodle soup now. That's all."

His hand wrapped around his spoon again before he shared, "You didn't ruin my night. You're here with me and we're both happy. There's not much that can ruin that."

I leaned toward him, gave him a kiss on the cheek, and whispered, "Thank you, baby."

Dom and I finished our dinner in a comfortable silence, content to just be in each other's presence. There was no need for us to fill the time with conversation. We seemed to be able to easily sit there with each other and just enjoy having the company of one another.

After dinner, Dom and I moved to his living room, where he turned on the television. We were on the chaise portion of his massive sectional. Dom's legs were outstretched, and my body was pressed against the length of him with my head resting on his abdomen. Dom asked if I would mind watching a hockey game. Lorenzo, who was one of Dom's co-workers, had a brother who played for the NHL and his team was playing. I didn't much care what we watched and told him that. I was happy just being warm, curled up next to him.

When the game ended around nine-thirty, Dom switched off the television. He didn't say anything, but I didn't mind. I was enjoying the feel of his fingers alternating between scratching my head and running through the strands of my hair.

"That feels nice," I hummed with my eyes closed. My voice was a mix of complete bliss and sleepiness.

Dom didn't respond. He just kept doing what he had been doing until he shifted one of his legs underneath my body. My head was still resting on his abdomen with my arms wrapped around his waist, but my body was now between his legs.

Dom moved his hands to my shoulders and began massaging. I couldn't stop the sound that escaped my lips, my moan indicating just how much I enjoyed what he was doing. When he'd sufficiently loosened up my shoulders, he announced, "I can't wait for you to start working at the library. I hate how demanding the work at the diner is on your body. Lift up a second so I can get out from under you. I'll give you a full-body massage."

I lifted my head and asked, "Really? It would be awfully unkind of you to tease me with that."

He grinned at me and assured, "I wouldn't tease you about that. That would be cruel."

I lifted my body a bit so Dom could slide out from underneath me. I fell back to my belly on the sofa while Dom went in search of some lotion. When he came back, he lifted my shirt over my head and pulled my pants down my legs, leaving me there in just a pair of panties. Then, he settled his body on top of my booty and was careful to not crush me with his weight.

As he worked the muscles in my back and my arms I was reminded of the sheer power he had. I could feel the strength in his hands and loved how great he was making me feel. I hadn't really realized just how much a toll constantly working like I had been was taking on my body until he reached my lower back. He alternated between using the heels of his palms and his thumbs to work my lower back and the top part of my ass.

"This is the most amazing thing I've ever felt," I groaned.

Dom chuckled as he got up off my body. "I think you're telling me a story now."

"I'm serious," I insisted. "I've never felt this good in all my life." Dom's hands began moving down my legs and I let out another groan. "Yep," I went on. "There's definitely nothing better than this."

"We'll have to see about that," Dom challenged. "I'm not sure how it's possible that you forgot so soon, but maybe I'll have to remind you just how good I can make your body feel."

"No, no, no," I protested. "This is perfect. I'm not complaining."

His hands moved in long, delightful strokes up and down each of my legs. With each caress, I found myself drifting closer and closer to sleep. Just before I completely drifted, he stopped rubbing my legs and held my feet in his hands.

Oh. My. Goodness.

My feet.

My poor battered feet hadn't ever been massaged.

"I lied," I spoke up.

"Oh yeah?"

"This. Just this. You could rub my feet from now until forever and I'd never want another thing. Holy cow, that feels amazing."

The strength of his hands on my clearly tired and worn out feet was like nothing I could have imagined. I couldn't begin to comprehend how his hands weren't feeling sore after he'd been so generous with his massage, but he'd given my feet just as much attention as he did my shoulders and back. In fact, my feet may have been given a dose of extra special treatment.

When he finished with my feet, Dom trailed his fingers up the backs of my calves and over my thighs with a feather-light touch. Two fingers landed in the spot right between my legs. Thoughts of sleep had vanished and my eyes shot open. Dom must have seen this because there was an edge of humor in his voice when he gently rubbed his fingers over me and teased, "Are you sure I can't make your body feel better than I just did?"

"Hmm?"

That was the only response I could formulate.

"I feel like you've given me a challenge, fun size," he joked, finding and circling my clit.

I bit my lip, trying to fight the urge to moan.

Suddenly, he flipped me to my back. The heat and desire in both of our eyes was undeniable. His fingers slipped underneath the waistband of my panties. Once they'd reached their destination, his mouth descended on my breasts. I couldn't take it.

"Okay," I breathed. "You win. This is better. Way better."

He smiled against my nipple before sucking it in once

more. Then, he lifted his head and looked at me.

"I was sure I'd get you to see this my way," he taunted me, his dimples on display, clearly proud of himself.

Seconds later, my panties ceased to exist, and Dom proved to me just how wrong I'd been. Afterward, he carried me upstairs and tucked me close to him. Despite my lack of clothes and the cold temperatures outside, I'd never felt warmer.

Dom

I heard her whimpers and my eyes shot open. It was still dark, so I knew it was sometime in the middle of the night. I glanced over at the nightstand and saw it was just after two in the morning.

She groaned again.

"Ekko?" I called, nudging her shoulder.

"I'm sorry, baby. I didn't mean to wake you," she replied.

"What's wrong, sugar?"

Her body tensed and she remained quiet. I lifted up on my side, my right arm holding me up. My eyes adjusted enough to the dark that I could make out her features. Those alone told me enough. Ekko was in pain.

Instinctively, my hand reached over and cupped the side of her face, where my thumb stroked back and forth across her cheek. "Talk to me," I urged her.

She hesitated a beat and finally answered, "It's just stomach cramps."

Cramps?

Had it been a month since I first brought her back here?

"Your period?" I wondered.

She shook her head. "Not yet, but once I start feeling like this, I know it's coming in the next few days."

"Have you taken anything?" I asked.

"No."

"I'll get you something," I stated as I rolled out of the bed and went downstairs to grab her some water and painkillers. Before I went back to the bedroom, I grabbed the heating pad.

When I walked back into the room, I flipped on the light on my nightstand. Her eyes squeezed shut briefly and she slowly opened them again.

"I feel horrible," she said as she sat up in the bed.

"I'm sorry," I responded, hating that she was in pain.

"No, that's not what I meant. I feel awful for waking you. You have to work tomorrow," she clarified.

I handed the water and painkillers to her as I sat down on the bed. "So, if I was sick, injured, or just not feeling well, are you saying you wouldn't wake up to take care of me?"

"Of course I would," she answered without hesitation.

"Precisely."

She tossed back the pills, chased them with the water, and fell to her back again. "Ugh. It's my stomach and my lower back. This is the absolute worst."

"Your back?"

"Yeah. It never used to be like this, but for the last year or so it's gotten worse. Now I have this awful cramping in my stomach, pain in my back, and even down into my thighs sometimes."

That didn't sound normal to me. "Have you seen a doctor?"

"It's PMS, Dom. What's a doctor going to do for me other than tell me it's part of life?"

I shrugged. I wasn't sure, but I didn't like seeing her in pain. I stood and walked over to her side of the bed. I plugged in the heating pad and put it on her belly.

"This should help take the edge off a little until the meds kick in. Just try to relax and go back to sleep," I started as I began rubbing her back.

"I can't fall asleep with a heating pad plugged in," she worried.

"Yes, you can. I'll take care of it after you're asleep."

She closed her eyes and murmured, "I'm so lucky to have you."

I pressed a kiss to her cheek and continued to rub her back until she fell asleep. It hadn't been quite twenty minutes when I turned the heating pad off, unplugged it, and climbed back into bed beside her.

It was difficult to find sleep again as my mind drifted to the thoughts I'd pushed to the back of my mind when I arrived home about ten hours ago. Something had started at work. I didn't know what the outcome was going to be, but there was a case I was working on that was giving me bad vibes.

Really bad vibes.

Rarely, if ever, were my instincts wrong with something like this. My goal, though, was to try to figure out what was going on and get it sorted as quickly as possible. I didn't want the stress I'd certainly feel from it leaking into the newfound peace that Ekko was working toward.

CHAPTER 16

Ekko

Good luck today.

That was the text I received this morning from Dom. It was my first day at my new job and while I was slightly nervous, I was mostly excited.

I finished getting ready, walked out to my car, and tapped out a reply while I gave my car a minute to warm up.

Thanks. I hope it goes well!

Not even a minute had passed when my cell chimed with his response.

It will be. They chose you because you were perfect for the job.

I sent him a reply in the form of an emoji. The one blowing a kiss. Sadly, he never sent one back. Not that I expected it. I mean, as sweet and charming as Dom was, he did have his limits. I never took him as the kind of guy to send an emoji, but I didn't hold that against him either. He'd been an absolute blessing over the last month.

As the days had passed since that night at the diner, he'd proven on more than one occasion just how incredible he was. In fact, when I had inadvertently woken him up in the middle of the night a week ago, he wasn't angry. When the unbearable pain in my stomach had pulled me from the comfort of my own sleep, he went out of his way to care for me. I knew he'd never given me any reason to doubt how caring he was, but sometimes it was still difficult to wrap my head around.

Ryan hadn't ever gotten up with me in the middle of the night. And my mother certainly never took care of me. Even as a kid. It was a wonder I even survived my childhood—how I managed to clean up my own vomit at the tender age of eight is beyond me.

I shook my head, attempting to rid myself of the negative memories and focus on the good I was experiencing now. I had succeeded in getting myself back into an apartment, I was on my way to a new job, and I had the most amazing boyfriend. While I couldn't be certain of just how long my good fortune would last, I knew enough to appreciate it while I had it.

I arrived at the library with ten minutes to spare. I gave myself one last pep talk before I got out of my car and went inside. When I had come in to complete the paperwork just before Thanksgiving, Alice told me to seek her out when I arrived on my first day here. So, I walked in and went straight to the circulation desk. There were two women there, one who looked to be about my age and another who looked to be in her late-fifties or early-sixties.

"How can I help you?" the younger woman asked.

Offering a friendly smile, I replied, "Hi, I'm looking for Alice."

"Are you Ekko?"

I gave her nod.

She stuck her hand out for me to shake and introduced herself. "I'm Kate. It's nice to meet you. Alice mentioned that you'd be starting today. I only remembered because you have such a unique name. I love it."

I liked her instantly. "Thank you."

"I'm the archivist here," she shared before she pointed

to the woman standing next to her. "This is Judith; she's the librarian."

"It's so nice to meet you both," I replied.

For the first time since I arrived, Judith spoke. "Please, call me Judy. I'll let Alice know you're here. She'll give you the grand tour and start your training."

"Thanks," I said before she turned and walked away.

"You look familiar," Kate stated. "I feel like I've seen you before."

I shrugged and guessed, "This place is like a second home to me. For a long time, if I wasn't working, I was here."

Her brows knitted together. "So...you don't come here anymore?"

"I do," I corrected her. "It's just that I was working a lot at my previous job and had very little free time. I have a boyfriend now and so I was spending some of my free time with him."

"Oh, yummy," she joked. "That's at least a good reason not to come in here as frequently. How long have you guys been together?"

"It's new. Only about a month."

She laughed. "I'm not much further ahead. My man and I have only been together about three months. I love this stage, though. He's so sweet and attentive."

I rounded my eyes. "You're so right. That's how my last relationship was. It started fine, but then I just felt like I didn't matter one way or the other. This one, though, has been amazing from day one. I don't want to think about that changing."

She held both hands up and announced, "Fingers crossed for the both of us."

At that moment, Alice and Judy had returned. "Good morning, Ekko. It's great to see you again. Are you ready to get started?"

I perked up. "Yes!" I exclaimed.

Alice and Judy both grinned at my enthusiasm. While Judy got back to work, Alice took me on the grand tour to start my day.

I had spent my entire day learning most of my job responsibilities. Alice didn't want to throw too much at me for the first day, so she said she'd teach me about half of it today and the remainder tomorrow.

There were things Alice covered today that I already knew since I spent so much time in the library and there were other things I had to learn. While circulation desk procedures weren't something I'd had any experience with, shelving returned and used materials was a breeze. The Dewey Decimal System was like a second language to me.

In addition to learning how to check materials in and out of the library, I also had to learn about processing fines, issuing library cards, and repairing and reconditioning library materials. I couldn't remember the last time I felt excited about my job.

I liked the people I worked with at the diner and always made the effort to give my patrons a good experience, but being a waitress was just a job. It wasn't something that made me feel alive.

And while I adored Jerry and Christie, they weren't people I was going to call up and chat with when I was having a bad day. The library had Kate and I really liked her. We ended up taking our lunch break together and she shared a lot with me. I learned more about her in one thirty-minute lunch than I had about any of my co-workers at the diner for the years I'd been there.

I was surprised at how quickly I felt comfortable with Kate. She was just one of those people that, with her outgoing and quirky personality, you couldn't help but like.

After lunch, I was back at it with Alice. I spent the rest of my afternoon learning the ins and outs of the mechanical functions of library equipment and sorting and processing the mail.

A few hours later, I was back in my car and completely in my glory. My first day had ended and it was, without a doubt, something special. Roughly thirteen years from the day I told myself I was going to get a job at the library and make something of myself and I was finally seeing that happen.

On that thought, I pulled out of the lot and went home to my apartment.

About nine and a half minutes after I walked through the door of my apartment, there was a knock at it.

I opened it to find Dom standing on the other side. "What are you doing here?" I asked as I stepped back to allow him to come inside.

Once I closed the door, he gave me a kiss on the cheek and answered, "I wanted to hear how your first day was."

"You came here just for that?" I asked, disbelievingly.

"Yes." His response was short and sweet, but a moment later he grew concerned. "Does that bother you?"

Bother me? How could it?

"Not at all. It's just…unexpected."

The second the words were out of my mouth I realized they weren't true. Perhaps with anyone else, they would have been accurate, but Dom had proven he wasn't like everyone else. I should have expected he would care enough to know how I liked my new job and I felt awful for grouping him with the others who let me down.

"I'm sorry, that's not what I mean," I quickly corrected myself. "Thank you for coming by to talk with me about it. It means a lot to me that you care."

Dom and I moved out from in front of the door and sat

on the couch. My place still didn't have all the bells and whistles, but I was slowly adding personal touches when I could afford them. Those were few and far between because after I'd set aside the money for rent, I was putting the rest into saving for school. While I knew that I could apply for federal student loans, I wanted to wait to take those out until I was going to school for my master's. I was a little too worried about my bad luck leaking in and creating an even more desperate situation for me.

Once we made ourselves comfortable, I bubbled, "It was the *best* day ever. I love my new job."

"I'm so happy for you, Ekko."

I offered him a genuine smile and went on, "Since Alice is the manager, she showed me the ropes and I met a couple of my co-workers, who were all very nice to me. Judy is the librarian and she's one of the sweetest women I've ever met. I didn't get a chance to really talk with her much because she was always busy doing something. There were several other people working different positions that Alice introduced me to throughout the day, but I feel like I made a connection with the archivist, Kate. We're right around the same age and I think we're well on our way to becoming good friends."

Dom wrapped his arm around my shoulders and curled me into his body. After kissing the top of my head, he surmised, "Sounds like you had a really great first day. And I'm sure you'll become great friends with your co-workers."

With my cheek pressed to his chest, I let the events from the day run through my mind. It really had been the best day.

"I love it there," I sighed after a few minutes had passed. "It feels like I'm where I meant to be."

"You deserve this, sugar. I'm so proud of you for working so hard to get what you want. With everything you've been through, there's not a lot of people who could endure all that and keep going. You'll get back to school and get your degree before you know it."

I gave him a squeeze before I responded, "Thank you for believing in me. It feels so good to have someone there to support and encourage me."

Dom held me just a little tighter. After we sat together in silence for a few moments, he asked, "How's the belly pain today?"

I tipped my head back to look up at him. "Much better. And my period should be gone within the next day or two."

Dom leaned down and kissed me on the forehead.

"How was your day?" I wondered.

He sighed. "Not over yet, unfortunately."

"What?" I asked, putting a palm to his chest and sitting up.

I watched as a look I couldn't read washed over his face. "I've got a case I'm working on right now and I wasn't quite finished when I left work to come here."

"Why did you leave then?"

His face softened. "It was your first day. I knew how important and special it was to you, and I wanted to be here when you got home so you could tell me how it went."

"Is it a bad case?" I worried.

"I don't know yet," he huffed, clearly frustrated. "It's a bit of a mystery at this point, but I'm working on it."

I didn't like hearing this. Dom never really spoke much about his work to me. Other than the one case that I had been involved in months ago, he kept his work life private. I guess it made sense, considering he was likely always working on confidential cases, but now that I was hearing this it worried me.

"Is there anything I can do?"

He shook his head. "Just focus on accomplishing your

goals. I'll get it worked out. One way or another, my team and I always figure it out."

"Well I hope it's nothing too serious," I said. "What time do you have to go back to work? Do you have time to eat dinner first?"

He grinned. "I won't be able to focus much if I don't eat something. Are you inviting me for dinner?"

My shoulders fell. "I would love for you to stay for dinner, but I can't make you a fabulous meal like you always do for me. I had originally been planning to make a batch of turkey chili. It's so warm and comforting when the weather is like this."

"Sounds good to me. I'm sure I'll love it," he agreed. "Can I help?"

"No!" I exclaimed. "You rarely let me help at your place and you have to go back to work tonight. I'm doing this tonight, but you can certainly talk to me while I cook."

"Can I kiss you for a minute before you do that?"

"You could, but that would delay me starting the chili, which once all the ingredients are combined, will need to simmer for at least twenty minutes. I thought we could use that time for making out."

His eyes got dark and he advised, "You better get to work then."

Before I hopped off the couch, I gave him a quick peck on the lips. Not quite fifteen minutes later, I had tossed all the ingredients in the pot and set the stove to the low setting to simmer. Then, Dom and I spent the next twenty minutes acting like high school kids with out-of-control hormones.

Dom finished his dinner in perfect time. His phone rang the second he put his spoon in the empty bowl. After fishing his phone out of his pocket, he looked at the display and held it to his ear. "Michaels? What's going on?"

I watched as he listened to whoever Michaels was speak. I also watched as his body grew visibly tight.

"Leave it for me. I'm on my way."

Dom disconnected the call and brought his eyes to mine.

"I've got to go and get back to work." It was clear from his tone that he was not happy about having to leave. I couldn't say that I didn't understand his frustration.

I took a sip of my water before I stood to walk him out.

When we got to my front door, I stepped in close to him and wrapped my arms around his waist, pressing my cheek to his chest. Dom engulfed me in his arms.

"Thank you for coming by to see how my day went. It means a lot to me that you cared enough to do it."

I felt Dom's lips on the top of my head. After he kissed me, he spoke. "I wanted to make sure you had a good day."

I tipped my head back to look up at him and teased, "You could have called, you know?"

"Then I wouldn't have been able to see your beautiful face," he remarked while simultaneously dazzling me with his dimples.

He was the sweetest man.

"How'd I get so lucky?" I wondered.

Dom didn't answer me with words. Instead, he lowered his head and touched his mouth to mine.

"Thanks for dinner, Ekko."

"You're welcome."

"I'll talk to you later."

I gave him a nod and wished, "Good luck with your case, baby."

At that, he gave me one final kiss before he turned and walked out.

After he left, I finished up my dinner and cleaned up the kitchen. Then, I spent the rest of my night figuring out my plan for returning to school. Tomorrow, I'd stay a little later after work and use the computers at the library to get all of the necessary applications completed so that I'd finally be able to finish my last semester and get my undergraduate degree.

With any luck, I'd have something to celebrate soon.

CHAPTER 17

Dom

"I GET THE FEELING THIS IS THE SECOND PIECE," TRENT Michaels said to me as I walked into his office.

Trent worked at Cunningham Security with me. He was a genius when it came to anything tech related. This didn't mean that he couldn't handle his own out in the field; he was just utilized better behind a computer. As a result, he spent a good amount of his time in the office, especially when the guys were out on cases that required someone to be watching their backs from a controlled environment. Because of this, he happened to be at the office when a new piece of the case had arrived.

I had an indication a few days prior to Thanksgiving that something wasn't right. I got proof of it the Monday after the holiday. Then, later that week I had received a delivery at the office. It was a plain white envelope with my initials, D.M., on the front of it. When I opened the envelope, I found a puzzle piece inside. A single corner piece. It was about the size of my palm and looked like a close-up picture of the ground, a street perhaps.

When I was at Ekko's place not more than fifteen minutes ago and Trent called telling me another envelope had arrived, I knew I was going to find another piece to the puzzle inside.

Apparently, he felt the same since he'd just said those words as he held the envelope out to me.

Taking it from him, I bit out, "I really hope there's a bit more than some fucking pavement to look at."

Sure enough, there was a puzzle piece inside. It was also a corner piece about the same size as my palm. The good thing was that it wasn't of the pavement, but it was still useless.

The sky.

I was beginning to get irritated with this.

Looking up at Trent, I announced, "It's the sky. The fucking sky."

"There's something on the back."

I looked back down and flipped over the piece. The word 'You' was printed on the back. Just underneath that was the letter 'f' and a sliver of another letter. Unfortunately, the way the puzzle was cut ended the letter there.

"What is it?" Trent asked.

I held the piece out to him. After he took it from me, I stated, "I'll be right back. I've got to get the other one out of my office. I need to see if there's anything on the back of that one."

I made my way back to my office and yanked open the top drawer of my desk. Pulling out the envelope I dug out the piece and flipped it over. There was nothing on the back.

"Damn it!" I shouted.

"What's going on?" Pierce asked as he passed by my office.

"I don't know yet," I clipped, my irritation evident. "That's the problem."

Pierce was concerned and followed as I walked out of my office back toward Trent's. "Does this have to do with the puzzle piece Michaels told me about?"

"Yep. I just got another one."

"Anything on that one," Trent asked as Pierce and I walked

back into his office.

"Nothing," I returned as I tossed it down in front of him.

Pierce walked over and looked at the two pieces. After inspecting them, he asked, "Didn't you get a note delivered, too?"

"A week ago, today."

"When did the first piece arrive?"

"Thursday."

Pierce contemplated the pieces a minute and guessed, "With any luck this guy is methodical, and you'll have another piece on Thursday."

"And if he's not?" I challenged.

Trent and Pierce both shrugged their shoulders.

"How was this piece delivered?" I questioned Trent.

"Taped to the front door. I already checked the camera. He walked right up, taped it to the door, and pushed the buzzer on the intercom."

I shook my head in disbelief and took a step toward him. "That's the kind of information you lead with, Michaels. Can you pull it up so we can check it out? Do we know the guy?"

"He's covered," Trent explained as he hit a couple buttons on the keyboard in front of him. "He was dressed in all black, wearing gloves, a ski mask, and a hooded sweatshirt. There's nothing on the video that'll help."

He turned his computer screen and showed us the footage. It was just as he described. There was nothing that would help.

"So, a note that says 'worthless' along with two puzzle pieces, neither of which shows anything of substance," Pierce recalled the evidence of the case. "Who did you piss off?"

"That's a loaded question," I shot back. "That could be any number of people given this line of work, but nothing in particular that stands out."

"There's nothing you've worked on over the last couple of months that someone might be feeling the sting from still?"

"Nothing obvious. Unless…" I trailed off.

"Unless what?"

"Ekko's ex. It wasn't really a case that I worked on, but that whole situation happened not long before this started. Maybe he's feeling the need to seek out revenge after we barged into his place the way we did."

As I looked back and forth between them, Trent sat back in his chair and Pierce crossed his arms over his chest.

"Isn't he a drug addict?" Trent asked. "Do you think he's with it enough to pull this off?"

"He told Ekko he only sells," I started. "I don't know how true it is, but if that were the case it's certainly a possibility."

"I don't know; I'm not so sure about that," Pierce chimed in. "I was there that day and, while you certainly intimidated and embarrassed him, I don't think that guy has it in him."

In an instant, the wind was out of my sails. I wasn't going to leave anything up to chance because I really didn't know the guy, but I had a feeling Pierce was right. Ekko's ex-boyfriend didn't strike me as the kind of guy who'd do something this methodical. And considering he didn't really seem to be torn up over the loss of Ekko, I didn't see any motive other than a bruised ego. It didn't make much sense that he'd be behind this. Nevertheless, I'd still do some research and look into him.

"Maybe you could ask her? See what she thinks about the possibility of him doing this?" Pierce suggested.

"No," I immediately shut him down.

"That was definitive," he noted.

"She's just gotten out from under him and started a new job today. She doesn't need to be worried about this. She knows I'm working on a case, but she doesn't know anything about it. I don't want to bring this stress on her."

"Even if you could put an end to this faster?"

A downward jerk of my chin indicated that going to Ekko and revealing details of the case to her was not an option, even if her ex was involved. In fact, the possibility of him being involved was even more of a reason I didn't want her knowing. With any luck, I could solve this case on my own, and get it done quickly, without her ever knowing just how stressed I was over it.

Pierce let out a laugh and quipped, "I never thought I'd see the day."

"What?"

"When you are no longer the life of the party because you're so far gone for a girl."

Without a shred of doubt in my tone, I assured him, "I'm still very much the life of the party, Reynolds…it's just a different kind of party."

Pierce and Trent both laughed. It was nice to have a bit of lightheartedness in the room when moments ago I was feeling very agitated about this puzzle. Even still, I couldn't relax too much if I was going to make sure that I solved the case quickly.

"I'm going to take a few hours and go through some of my last couple of cases," I explained. "Maybe something will pop out."

"Want some help?" Trent offered.

I shook my head. "I'm good for now, but I might need your help if I figure anything out. At this point, I think it's going to be a needle in a haystack until I get more puzzle pieces."

My friends both gave me nods of acknowledgment before I picked up the puzzle pieces from Trent's desk and walked out. I knew I was grasping at straws at this point by going back through my caseload from the last few months, but sitting around waiting for someone to make their move wasn't my thing. Even if the time I spent wasn't going to lead me to an explanation, I couldn't simply sit back and do nothing.

Three hours later, I'd been through several months' worth of cases and I was no closer to having even the slightest clue as to what the puzzle pieces were about. It was late, and I was frustrated, so I decided to call it a night.

I didn't know what it was, but something about this case was really bothering me. Much more than nearly any other case I'd ever remembered working. I was almost certain the reason for it was the planning and systematic way in which the person behind it was handling it. I also had absolutely no idea where to start looking for clues and that aggravated me.

After shutting down my computer and putting the puzzle pieces back in my desk, I snatched up my keys and left. It was relatively late. As much as I wanted to go back to Ekko's place to see her, I decided against it. She had just started her new job this week and I didn't want to be the reason she showed up to work sluggish.

By the end of the week, I had moved from being frustrated to downright pissed. I received another puzzle piece. The third corner. And it was the opposite pavement piece. The back had nothing on it, so it only served to just irritate and infuriate me. Someone was playing a game with me and I didn't like it one bit.

I had managed to do a bit of investigative research on Ekko's ex-boyfriend. While I couldn't be a hundred percent certain he wasn't involved, my gut was telling me that he wasn't the guy behind this. He spent too much of his time wrapped up in himself and his clients.

This was really the only silver lining. I hadn't wanted to think that the case was headed in this direction. There was nothing to indicate that this had anything to do with Ekko, so I tried to use that to calm myself when I started feeling frustrated about the situation. I kept telling myself that it could be worse and that she could be involved.

At this point, it was Friday evening and I was taking the rest of the weekend off to be with my girl. We had Levi and Elle's wedding to attend tomorrow and I wanted to be there to celebrate with them completely.

When Ekko and I spoke earlier in the week, I had asked her how she wanted to handle the wedding weekend. I explained that I was more than happy to have her stay at my place tonight or, if she preferred, we could stay at hers. She claimed she didn't care, but then also suggested that I'd probably be more comfortable in my own bed since it was bigger than hers. To be quite honest, I would have slept on the floor if it meant I was with her, but I took her hint to mean that she wanted to be at my place.

I had just arrived at her place to pick her up. Other than Monday after she'd had her first day at her new job and I stopped by to visit her, I hadn't seen Ekko all week. We'd talked on the phone at least once every day, though, and we texted frequently.

But I had missed her.

More than I'd ever missed a woman.

Once she opened the door to her apartment, I took a second to let out a breath, feeling relieved finally seeing her beautiful, smiling face after so many days. But it was only a second because I needed more than just that. I stepped inside, pushing the door closed behind me, as I wrapped an arm around her waist and put one hand at her ass. After I lifted her up, she wrapped her legs around me and dropped her lips to my mouth.

Apparently, Ekko had missed me at least just as much as I had missed her. She immediately parted her lips and allowed my tongue to invade her mouth while her hands remained planted on the beanie covering my head. We kissed each other for several long moments. Any lingering tension I felt over my case melted away with each stroke of Ekko's tongue over mine.

When Ekko pulled her mouth back, she wrapped her arms around my neck, rested her head on my shoulder, and shared, "I missed you so much this week, baby."

I gave her a gentle squeeze and returned, "Missed you too, sugar."

We held on to each other for a bit, truly enjoying our reunion.

"Guess what?!" she suddenly jolted in my arms.

"What?"

She grinned from ear to ear and said, "I'm starting school again in January. I contacted my school and they're letting me come back for the spring semester. I'll be able to finish my undergraduate degree in just a few months!"

"That's awesome! I'm so proud of you."

She dropped her head to my shoulder again and hugged me.

"Are you all packed up?" I eventually asked.

Ekko lifted her head from my shoulder and looked at me before she responded, "I think I've got it all packed. Well, other than a dress for tomorrow. Are you sure you don't mind going with me to the store tonight so I can find something?"

"Not at all. In fact, I called in reinforcements."

Her brows pulled together. "Reinforcements?" she asked.

"Jojo is good at this kind of stuff," I explained. "When I talked to her a couple days ago and told her we were going to be going shopping today so you could get a dress for the wedding, she insisted on meeting us there. I wanted to make sure you were okay with it first before I told her it would be alright."

"She wants to go shopping with us?"

I nodded and added, "She said she saw a dress there that was perfect for you and she's dying to see it on you."

Ekko just stared at me in disbelief. I waited for her to respond, but she never did.

"Ekko, what's wrong?"

Her eyes welled up with tears. "Your sister wants to go shopping with us and help me choose a dress."

"If you don't want her to go, that's okay. I can tell her—" I got out before Ekko held her hand up and cut me off.

"No!" she exclaimed. "I want her to go. It's just that…I've never had a girls' shopping trip before."

I smiled at her. "Well, it's just Jojo this time and I'm going to be there, so it's not officially a girls' shopping trip. But I think you should plan a real one soon. My sisters will definitely be up for it."

"Really?"

"Of course," I assured her.

Ekko bit her lip, a failed attempt to tamp down her excitement over the prospect of having real friends with whom she could spend her time.

"Are you ready to go?" I asked.

She nodded her head furiously, no longer trying to hide how she truly felt.

I lowered Ekko to her feet and followed her to her bedroom, where I grabbed her overnight bag for her. Once she confirmed she had everything she needed for the weekend, I made a quick call to Jojo. She told me she'd meet us in twenty minutes, so Ekko and I got in my truck and took off.

Two hours later, Jojo was walking out of the dressing room with a huge smile on her face.

"It is absolutely perfect on her," she announced. "I knew it would be."

"Is she going to come out here so I can see it?" I wondered.

Jojo shrugged her shoulders. "I don't know. She has it on and keeps looking at it in the mirror, but she seems unsure about it. I'm not sure why because it's absolutely perfect for her."

"Is it too short or too revealing? We are going to a wedding. Maybe she's just being hesitant because she thinks the style isn't appropriate for the occasion."

My little sister gave me a look that told me she was seriously beginning to question me. "Do you think I'm an idiot? I know where you two are going and the dress is perfect for it. Maybe it's the shoes…" She trailed off.

"Shoes?"

Jojo looked back toward the dressing room before directing her attention to me again. "Ekko seemed to love the dress the minute she put it on. She asked my opinion on shoes and when I told her what I thought, she started questioning the dress."

I had a feeling I knew what was going on. "Tell her to come out here so I can see the dress," I requested.

I waited while my sister went back into the dressing room to get Ekko. A minute later, she walked out and I had to admit Jojo was right. The dress was perfect for Ekko.

"It looks beautiful on you," I said softly.

Ekko smiled at me, but I could see the trepidation quickly wash over her face. She looked down at the ground. I didn't want to make her more uncomfortable so I glanced over at Jojo and confirmed, "You said there were shoes you thought would look great with the dress?"

She gave me a nod.

"Ekko, what's your shoe size?"

Her eyes shot to mine. "What?"

"What's your shoe size?"

"Six and a half. Why?"

I pulled out my wallet, handed Jojo one of my credit cards, and ordered, "Go get the shoes she needs for this dress. Meet us back here."

Given I never handed my credit card over to my sister in a mall ever in my life, she wasted no time and took off toward the shoe department.

I took a few steps toward Ekko and asked, "What's wrong?"

"Nothing."

"Jojo said you loved the dress and then started acting funny about getting it. Why?"

She shrugged her shoulders. "I don't know. I just thought maybe I'd look around and see if I could find something else that might look nicer."

"This dress is perfect, Ekko. I want you to get this one."

Her worried eyes came to mine. "I can't," she rasped.

My hand reached out to the tag on the dress under Ekko's arm. Three hundred and seventy-five dollars.

"I've got it," I told her.

"Dom, no. This is too much."

"It's a dress. One that was made for your sweet little body. And it's one that I want you to have. The whole reason you need a dress is because I invited you to go with me to Levi and Elle's wedding. I'm getting you the dress."

Her shoulders slumped. "I feel like such a failure sometimes," she whispered.

"You're not a failure. You've been working your ass off for a long time, just switched jobs, got into a new apartment, took over your cell phone bill, and just got things squared away to start school again for the spring semester. Cut yourself some slack."

"I hate that I can't do this for myself."

I pressed a kiss to her forehead. "I want to do this for you."

She shook her head. "I'm not sure I'll ever be able to come close to doing for you what you've done for me."

"I can't even begin to tell you all that you do for me, sugar. It's not about money."

Ekko gave me a small smile.

"Go get changed. When Jojo gets back with your shoes, I'm going to take two of my favorite girls out for dinner. Then, you and I are heading back to my place."

Ekko's eyes heated. She knew what was in store for her, so she scurried off and got changed.

A couple hours later, after we'd gotten Ekko's new dress and shoes and I had taken her and my sister out for dinner, I took my girl home.

CHAPTER 18

Ekko

"**T**HAT'S A LOT OF CARS."

My voice had an edge of anxiety, but mostly I was dumbfounded at just how many people were in attendance.

Dom and I were in his truck and had just pulled into the parking lot at the venue for Elle and Levi's wedding.

Dom reached across the center console, wrapped his hand around mine, and said, "They've got a lot of people who love them."

Love.

Something I thought I experienced in my relationship with Ryan.

Now, being with Dom, I knew that what I had with Ryan wasn't love. In the beginning of our relationship, things were okay...good even. He was nice enough, showed an interest in me, and we got along well. Somewhere along the line, about halfway into our relationship, that feeling fizzled for me and it never really came back. It saddened me to know I stuck around simply because at the beginning of the end, I was desperate for a connection to anyone. And at the end of it, I stayed because I was desperate to survive.

It was different with Dom. The spark, the intensity of

emotion, was always there. I knew it was still very early in our relationship, but this feeling was different from what I felt with Ryan. I didn't want to compare the two relationships; however, it was hard to miss how consuming the connection I had to Dom was.

"They're very lucky," I replied, my voice giving me away. It was filled with hope. Hope that I'd one day get to a place where I'd have people in my life who loved me.

Dom simply smiled at me before he leaned over and gave me a quick kiss on the lips. When he pulled back, he instructed, "Stay there. I'm coming around to help you out."

I watched as Dom got out of the truck and opened the back door on his side. He pulled out his jacket for his suit and put it on. That alone was enough to make a girl fall in love. From the moment I met him, I felt an undeniable attraction to Dom. His protective and nurturing disposition drew me in. The size and power in his body captivated me. And the dimples hooked me.

But now he was all that he was, and he was all of that in a suit. He was divine. He exuded confidence and strength with each step he took, something that would leave most people quaking in their boots. When he opened my door and helped me out, though, all of that tough, hard exterior that strangers saw melted away.

I looked up at him after he closed the door. He wrapped an arm around my waist and his face softened as he looked at me.

Just like it always did.

I loved that.

I loved him.

The realization hit me full force and I nearly stumbled. Dom was quick to catch me. "Are you alright?"

I couldn't tell him.

Could I?

What would I do if I told him how I felt, and the feeling wasn't mutual? Dom made it clear he cared about me; I didn't doubt that. But love was something else entirely. Knowing how I felt about him, I wasn't sure I would be able to handle knowing he didn't feel the same.

"I'm good," I started. "I think I've got to get used to these shoes."

Dom held my hand as we walked across the parking lot to the venue. Elle and Levi had decided to have their wedding at the Parks Ridge Ski Resort in Rising Sun. I hadn't ever been to the resort before, but I already knew it was going to be beautiful inside.

Once we entered the building that was off to the right of the main lodge, we were directed to the second floor, where I immediately understood why they chose this location. The views were breathtaking and provided the perfect backdrop to a markedly romantic occasion.

Dom guided me down the aisle toward a row of empty seats. We sat down and were joined a few minutes later by some of the guys from Cunningham Security. It surprised me that Levi didn't have any of his co-workers in his wedding party.

I leaned into Dom and stated softly, "I thought you guys were all close."

"We are."

"Didn't he want to have any of you in the wedding?"

Dom wrapped his arm around my shoulder and shook with a laugh. "Including Levi, there are nine guys who work closely together. Levi also recently hired a tenth guy to handle some things in the office, plus we have Deb who works as the receptionist. Considering he's got two brothers plus Elle's brother, Wes, they would have had a really large wedding party."

"I can't imagine being in a position where I'd have to choose who to not have in my wedding. It seems like such a wonderful problem to have."

Dom's fingers squeezed my shoulder in response.

I didn't want to be a downer, but being here made me realize just how much I didn't have. And it had nothing to do with money.

It wasn't much later when the ceremony started. As I watched Levi and Elle join their lives together, I felt a pang of jealousy wash over me. They both had been nothing but kind to me and I was truly happy for them, but I wanted what they had. More than I wanted to become a librarian, I wanted to feel like I belonged somewhere. That I belonged with someone. Dom felt like that person for me, but I wasn't sure I was it for him. I'd never be able to give him what he deserved. I'm sure to anyone who saw me, I looked like a typical woman at a wedding…overcome with such emotion and on the verge of tears. It was true, but my emotions went deeper. I was longing for something I wasn't sure I'd ever have.

The ceremony concluded, and I took a deep breath. I didn't want to ruin Dom's evening, so I did my best to push the self-loathing thoughts to the back of my mind. I was going to try to turn the rest of the night around.

Roughly an hour later, Dom and I were seated at a table for the reception in the ballroom. Between the end of the ceremony and now, Dom had introduced me to more than a handful of people and I was worried I'd have to remember everyone's name. I was typically good at remembering names, but this was overwhelming.

"I'll be right by your side all night," Dom whispered into my ear. "You won't have to worry about forgetting who someone is."

A rush of air left me. That was a relief.

"Would you like another drink?" he asked.

"I'm good for right now," I replied. "I'm a lightweight, so I should probably wait until I have some food in me before I consume any more alcohol, though. It could be disastrous otherwise."

Dom laughed. "I'd take care of you."

"I have no doubts about that," I joked back.

Over the course of the next few minutes, the parents of the bride and groom, the bridal party, and Levi and Elle were all introduced. Shortly afterward, dinner was being served, drinks were flowing, and the music was playing. Once dinner was finished, Levi and Elle shared their first dance together before the bridal party joined them for the next song. Following that, Elle and her father danced together before Levi and his mom did.

After all the formal dances had finished, the wedding guests were invited to join in the festivities on the dance floor.

"Let's go," Dom declared as he stood from his chair.

"Are we leaving?"

He gave me a disbelieving look. "We're going to dance."

"I don't...I don't dance," I stammered, fear having taken over, rendering my body completely stiff. It's not that I had any issues with the act of dancing. I simply hadn't ever done it and didn't know how.

Dom wasn't going to accept that because he slid my chair away from the table and held his hand out to me. "It's a slow song, Ekko. It's easy, especially since you'll be in my arms."

Dom's arms were always a haven for me, a place I always felt safe, so I figured I could trust he'd see to it that I didn't make a fool of myself. On that thought, I placed my hand in his and allowed him to guide me to the dance floor. Keeping my hand in his, he pulled it up to his chest between us as he wrapped an arm around my waist and pulled me into his body.

My wide eyes stared up at him. All I got in return was the softest, sweetest smile, complete with dimples. With that, Dom showed me how to dance. It really was easy, especially considering I just had to follow his lead. When the song ended, he lowered his mouth to mine and kissed me. It was filled with such tenderness and I found myself melting farther into him as the music flowed into another song.

"What are the chances I'm going to be able to talk you into staying out here with me when the music is no longer slow?" he suddenly asked.

My body stiffened. "I'm not sure that's a good idea. I have no idea what I'm doing."

"I'll teach you," he offered.

I thought on it, knowing I needed to let loose and have fun. "Okay, but I think I might need another drink or two in me before I can do it."

"I can make that happen."

At that moment, a hand tapped Dom on the shoulder. We both looked to the side to see Levi's father, David, standing there. He was looking at Dom when he asked, "Would you mind if I cut in for a song?"

Dom looked to me, silently confirming I was comfortable with it. After I dipped my chin in agreement, Dom stepped to the side and held on to me until I was in David's embrace.

"How are you doing, Ekko?" David wondered.

"Very well. Thank you."

We spent the remainder of the song chatting. Once I congratulated him on his son's marriage, we moved the conversation to other topics. I brought him up to speed on all the new things happening in my life with school and work. He was genuinely interested in hearing about it and I had to admit to myself just how good it felt to have that. It made me a bit nostalgic, wondering why my own father never even stuck around to see me come into the world. I had no idea who he was.

When the song ended, David and I parted ways. He walked in the opposite direction to his wife while I turned toward the table Dom and I had been seated at for dinner. Dom was standing with his back to me as he talked with a man and a woman. I recognized them as part of the bridal party but didn't know who they were.

As I made my way through the crowd, Dom turned to the side and I stopped in my tracks. I couldn't move. He was holding a baby. A baby that looked brand new. It was, by far, the most beautiful thing I'd ever seen in my life.

I'm not sure how much time passed, but I was eventually pulled from my catatonic state when Dom looked in my direction. His eyes found mine and he grinned. I walked the rest of the way toward him. Once I was by his side, he said, "Ekko, this is Elle's brother, Wes Blackman, his wife, Charley, and their newborn baby boy, Taj."

I held my hand out to them. "It's so nice to meet you."

"You too, Ekko," they replied in unison.

I looked to the baby in Dom's arms and gushed, "He's beautiful. Congratulations!"

"Hey Wes," Dom interrupted. "Why don't you take your wife out for a dance? Ekko and I will hang with Taj."

Charley looked a bit nervous, but Wes immediately thanked Dom and ushered his wife to the dance floor.

"She didn't seem too comfortable leaving her baby with us," I noted.

Dom pulled out my chair so I could sit before he lowered his body in the chair next to me. "It's not us. She's overly protective. He's the only blood family she's got."

Maybe there was hope for me after all.

I dropped my eyes to Taj and felt a sense of longing wash over me. I couldn't wait to be a mother. No matter what else

I could accomplish in my life, I knew that I'd put more effort and energy into being the best mom I could be.

"Do you want to hold him?"

Looking up in Dom's eyes, I nodded. Seconds later, I was holding a sleeping Taj in my arms and I was so content. I sat there staring down at the beautiful baby boy, wondering how my mother was able to see me as a baby and not feel an overwhelming sense of obligation to protect and nurture me. Taj wasn't mine and I had just met his parents, but I knew looking at him that I'd sacrifice myself to protect him.

His whole hand held on to my one finger as I brushed my thumb across his knuckles. I felt myself getting emotional, but thankfully, an interruption broke me out of my thoughts.

"How's my nephew doing?" a very pregnant woman asked as she came up and pressed a kiss to Taj's head.

"He's your nephew?" I wondered.

"I'm Emme, and Charley's my best friend," she stated. It was then Dom jumped in and explained that Emme was Levi's sister-in-law. She was married to Levi's brother, Zane, a professional snowboarder who was standing right beside her. That is, he stood there only long enough to be introduced to me because he pulled up a chair for his wife.

"Sit, sweetheart," he encouraged her gently. "I don't want the girls making their debut tonight."

My eyes rounded. "Girls?"

Emme huffed as she sat down. "Twin girls. I'm in the home stretch now. I think they'll be here early and I'll have them in time for Christmas."

"That's so exciting!"

She smiled as she dropped her head to rest against Zane's hip. He was still standing beside her. "It is," she agreed. "But I'm utterly exhausted at this point."

Emme was adorable, but it was no surprise she was so

tired. I couldn't imagine having to prepare for two babies.

Dom and I spent the next little while talking with Emme and Zane until Wes and Charley joined us again. Sadly, I had to give up Taj, but I was beyond grateful for the time I could hold him.

As the evening wore on, I had another drink and Dom managed to get me out on the dance floor. With the liquid courage in my body, I had loosened up enough to not care how stupid I may have looked on the dance floor. I certainly wasn't as reserved as usual, but I wouldn't have considered myself to be drunk. I was happy about that because I learned the one thing I had been hearing about so much to be true.

Dom was the life of the party.

This wasn't the first time I'd seen him show just how much fun he could have. It was, however, the first I'd seen it in a setting with such a large crowd. I also noticed that most of the guys he worked with weren't as willing to step out on the dance floor. Dom was certainly my opposite when it came to his outgoing personality, but I truly believed that was one of the things that made him perfect for me.

Several hours later, we had arrived back at Dom's house. After we'd showered together, we climbed into his bed, where Dom was on his back and had curled me into his body.

"I had such a good time tonight," I shared, with my cheek pressed to his chest.

"Me too. I'm glad you enjoyed yourself."

We both went silent for a few minutes before I finally spoke again. "You looked pretty incredible holding Taj."

I felt his body vibrate with laughter beneath me. "I thought the same thing when I saw you holding him."

"Do you want to have kids one day?"

"Yes."

"How many?"

"Four."

I lifted my head and rested my chin on his chest. "Four? Really?"

"At least. I mean, I'd be fine with five, too."

I stared at him in disbelief.

"Don't you want kids?" he asked. I sensed a bit of worry in his tone.

"I've always wanted a big family. I want lots of babies. And I want to give them everything I never had."

Dom didn't reply.

I decided to continue, "I want to be the best mom in the world."

"I have no doubts you'll be exactly that," he remarked.

"You think so?"

"I know it."

I put my head back down on his chest. A few moments of silence passed before I said, "I love that you want the same thing as me."

Dom squeezed me before he replied, "Me too, sugar."

CHAPTER 19

Ekko

TAKE THE GOOD WITH THE BAD.

I had been repeating that in my head for longer than I could remember.

My life, until recently, had been filled with very little good and a whole lot of bad. I tried not to let it get me down, but it wasn't easy. That's not to say that I didn't have any good; it's just that there wasn't much of it. At least, not until recently.

Until Dom.

From the moment he walked into my life, the scales began to tip favorably in my direction. It wasn't always great, and I expected to still experience hiccups along the way, but I was no longer feeling completely weighed down by my bad fortune.

Over the last few weeks, I had been experiencing an abundance of positivity. First and foremost, I adored my job. Each day, I looked forward to what that job brought me in terms of personal fulfillment. Beyond that, it gave me something I couldn't remember ever having.

Friendship.

Kate and I had forged a solid friendship. What I loved about it was that it wasn't built on pity or obligation. While she didn't know the deep, dark truth of my past, I found that she was someone I could trust to be a true friend. She shared details of her life openly and she did it without shame or fear of judgment. I loved that about her and wished I could be as confident as her.

The week after Levi and Elle's wedding, Kate and I were having lunch together when she blurted, "I think I'm in love with him."

"What? Who?"

"Brett."

Brett was Kate's boyfriend and I'd learned a lot about him in the short time I'd been working with her at the library. He worked construction and, from everything Kate told me, put in a lot of hours to make a good living. Most importantly, she never complained about the way he treated her.

"You think you're in love?" I asked.

After taking a bite of her sandwich, she nodded and added, "It just hit me this morning while I was getting ready. I love my sleep and Brett knows it. I stayed at his place last night and struggled to wake up this morning. Even though he's got the more physically demanding job, he doesn't let exhaustion stop him from giving a hundred percent of himself to me when we're together. He woke up this morning, made breakfast, and brought it to me in bed so that I could get those few extra minutes."

"He sounds like a keeper, Kate."

She stared off in the distance for a brief moment before she agreed, "Yeah, I think he is. I know it's early still, but it feels so different with him, Ekko."

"I know what you mean," I chimed in. "I had the same feeling this weekend with Dom."

Kate grinned at me. "Spill the beans!"

A feeling of excitement swept through me at the fact that I was about to share something so personal with someone I considered to be a friend.

"Obviously, there's that mutual physical attraction, something I'm sure you've got with Brett," I started. She nodded in agreement. "Well, for me, with Dom it's been so much more than that. It's the little things that he does, the selfless acts, that do it for me. He goes out of his way to make my life easier. Better. And he protects me in a way that nobody else ever has."

"He sounds so dreamy," she sighed.

"He really is. He's perfect. When we were at his boss's wedding this weekend, I saw him holding a baby. I stopped walking and could barely breathe seeing that."

Kate's smile grew even larger. "Ah, seeing a man holding a baby. Is there anything better?"

I nodded and explained, "Yes…seeing the man you love holding one."

"Have you told him?" she wondered.

I shook my head. I wanted to, but I was too scared. "What about you? Are you going to tell Brett how you feel?"

She scrunched up her nose. "I'm not sure I can do it. I feel like he should know, but I want to be sure he feels the same."

I completely understood her mindset because I couldn't imagine telling Dom what he meant to me only to find out that while he cared for me, the feeling wasn't exactly mutual. I knew what I felt for him was so strong that if the feelings weren't reciprocated, it would lead to a heartbreak from which I wasn't sure I would ever be able to recover.

"I hear you on that," I concurred.

Kate and I spent the rest of our lunch swooning over our men, trying to come up with ways to get them to admit their feelings to us first. Neither of us was going to commit to following through on those plans, but it was still fun to think about.

I ended up getting a surprise that same afternoon when

George walked through the front door of the library. He didn't smile when he saw me, but it was rare that I ever saw him really smile. When he used to come in to the diner every week, he was always so grumpy. He was harmless and he was never downright rude to me, so I looked beyond it and found it endearing.

"Hi, George," I greeted him as he walked up to the circulation desk. "How are you doing?"

"The diner's not the same without you there," he returned. "Figured if I was going to be able to see your pretty face again, I'd have to make a trip here."

My heart melted. "Oh, George. I'm sorry. I really need to try to make some time to stop in over there. I miss Jerry and Christie, too."

"Make it a Thursday or a Friday," he instructed. "Those are my days."

"Friday?" I questioned.

He shrugged his shoulders. "I had to add another one to the mix."

Grinning at him, I promised, "I can do that."

At that, George took off and browsed the shelves. I helped him check out a few books and watched as he left the library. It warmed my heart to know that he missed seeing me at the diner and that prompted him to make the effort to come and visit me at my new job. I didn't have many people in my life who cared about me, so I knew I needed to make a real effort to visit him at the diner soon.

The weekend after the wedding, I experienced even more good fortune. I finally had my first girls' shopping trip. Kendall and Jojo must have spoken with their brother because they reached out to me earlier in the week and insisted the three of us plan a shopping trip. Since the Christmas holiday was coming up, they wanted to get their shopping done. I couldn't spend boatloads of money, but I had been putting a little bit aside for the last few weeks. My only hope was that I'd have enough to get something that Dom would truly enjoy.

"Please tell me you have suggestions," I begged his sisters. "I feel like I've been going crazy trying to come up with something to get him, but I'm certain he already has everything I think of."

"He's going to love anything you get him, Ekko," Kendall began. "He's easy to please and so laidback. Trust me, as long as you're with him, he's going to be happy."

I sighed. "That's not very helpful."

She shrugged her shoulders and went on, "Maybe not, but it's the truth."

While Jojo didn't give me any specific ideas, she at least attempted to help me out. "He's all about having a good time. For Dom, life has always been about doing what he had to do to make it fun. Kendall is right. He's going to love whatever you get him; that's going to be because it's coming from you. But if you want to get something that you know is really going to make his day, try to figure out something that'll incorporate the things he likes most. You and having fun."

She was right.

They both were.

Dom loved having a good time. And he always seemed to have a good time when he was with me. I just needed to figure out how I was going to put those two together to give him something he'd remember.

After a full day of thought and running ideas past his sisters, I finally came up with the perfect gift. I shared part of my idea with Kendall and Jojo and they both agreed it was brilliant.

Sure enough, just over a week later I started wondering if my bad luck was going to start rearing its ugly head. It was

Monday morning and it was Christmas Eve. Dom and I had originally planned to spend the day together yesterday, but something sudden came up at work for him and he needed to go in. Even though I told him to come by when he finished, he never showed. I wasn't too worried about him because he reached out to me late last night and explained that he might be a while and not to wait up.

I knew he had an incredibly important job and I would never give him grief about having to work late or unexpectedly. Even still, I couldn't help but worry that our first Christmas together would fall victim to my usual misfortune.

Deciding that sulking in bed would do me no good, I got up and made my way out to the kitchen.

Breakfast first.

If after breakfast I still hadn't heard from Dom, I'd send him a quick text message just to make sure he was okay. I had a feeling he probably worked so late that he was just catching up on sleep.

As I stood in front of the open refrigerator contemplating what to make for breakfast, I decided that breaking out the bacon to eat alone wouldn't be nearly as enjoyable as it would be if Dom were with me. I barely had an opportunity to peruse the shelves when I heard a knock at the door.

Considering the only people who knew where I lived were Dom, Levi, and Elle, it was safe to assume Dom had arrived. I raced over to the door, unlocked it, and yanked it open. I was stunned at the sight before me.

Dom was standing there with a Christmas tree.

Stepping back from the door to allow him to come inside, I shared my surprise. "You got me a tree?"

Dom carried the tree into the apartment and set it down in front of him just inside the door. He pressed a kiss to my cheek and said, "I wanted you to have one for our first

Christmas together."

My heart.

This man.

I put my hands to his shoulder, pressed up on my toes as he lowered his head, and I kissed him.

"You are the best thing that's ever happened to me," I rasped when I pulled back.

Dom gave me a wink and suggested, "How about I get this set up and then we can go out to get decorations for it?"

"Can I make us breakfast first? I splurged and bought bacon."

He chuckled. "Well, we can't have that going to waste. I'll get this in the stand while you start breakfast."

That afternoon, following a bacon and egg breakfast, Dom took me shopping for decorations for the tree. After deciding on the decorations I wanted, we went back to my place. As I stood there in my living room, hanging ornaments on my tree, I couldn't help but steal glances at Dom. I managed to do it for the longest time without being caught, but he finally noticed.

"You've been giving me that weird look ever since we got back here," he started. "Care to tell me what it's all about?"

And here I thought I was doing a great job of being sly.

I shrugged my shoulders, feigning nonchalance as I looked away with a smile tugging at my lips, and answered, "I just like you."

Not looking up, I heard movement before I felt Dom's arms around me. One was at my waist, the other in my hair on the side of my head opposite of him. He gave me a gentle nudge, encouraging me to look at him. When I did, Dom pulled me close to him and whispered, "The feeling's mutual."

I smiled at him, letting the feeling of pure happiness wash over me. While I couldn't be certain, I had a feeling Dom was doing the same because his dimples were on full display.

He lowered his head to mine, his lips just barely brushing mine. My eyes closed and my mouth swept across his. When he was through with allowing me to take my time teasing, Dom's grip in my hair stiffened a bit and he completely captured my mouth. His tongue slipped past my lips into my mouth and I gave mine in return.

The arm he had around my waist tightened as he lifted me up off the ground. My legs immediately wrapped around him. Keeping his mouth connected to mine, Dom started walking.

I quickly pulled back and cried, "Wait!!"

He stopped and waited for an explanation.

"We need to put the star on the tree," I pleaded.

"We'll do it later."

My eyes went to the nearly-completed tree and my smile faded. Dom set me down and urged, "Get your star, Ekko."

I darted over to the couch, where I had set all of the bags from our trip to the store. I fished the tree topper out of its bag and held it out to him.

"I can't reach," I mumbled.

He closed the distance between us, but instead of taking the star from me, he bent down and wrapped his arms around my thighs and lifted me up. Dom walked back toward to the tree and declared, "Now you can."

Once I had successfully affixed the star to the top, Dom set me back down on my feet. He gave me about five seconds to marvel at it before wondering, "Is the tree good now?"

I gave him slow, gentle nods in response as I whispered, "I love it."

The next thing I knew, Dom bent and pressed his shoulder into my belly as one of his arms wrapped around my thighs again. I was off the floor the next instant with the perfect view of his stunning backside as he walked us down the hall toward my bedroom.

Dom and I had planned to spend Christmas Eve at his place, so after a couple rounds of fun in my bedroom and a home-cooked dinner that we ate in front of the tree, we packed up my things, locked up my place, and left.

The next morning, enfolded in Dom's arms, I looked up at his face to find him already awake looking down at me with such adoration. He gave me his dimples before he said, "Merry Christmas, sugar."

His words and the look in his eyes warmed me to my core. I'd been awake for mere moments, yet I already knew this was going to be the best Christmas ever.

"Merry Christmas, baby," I returned the sentiment. After giving me a kiss, I asked, "What's the protocol for presents? Do we need to have breakfast first or can I give you your present now?"

Dom let out a chuckle. "We can do whatever you want."

"Presents!" I exclaimed, jumping out of the bed in my camisole and panties. Dom was in his birthday suit and I planned to use that to my advantage.

I had set my bag with Dom's wrapped gift and my counterpart to it on the bed just as he sat up. As I pulled the present out of the bag, Dom eyed me curiously. He took the wrapped box from me and I felt it necessary to give him a heads up about what to expect.

"It's nothing fancy," I warned him. "Just something fun."

When Dom's eyes went to the gift and were no longer focused on me, I slid my hand back inside my bag preparing for what was ahead. Quickly, Dom tore the wrapping paper away from the box.

"Ahhh," he sighed. "This is going to be fun!"

I moved quick. Lifting my arm from the bag, I aimed the high-capacity dart gun at Dom and blasted a few shots at him while I shouted, "It's only fun if you can get your opponent!"

Dom jumped out of the bed, snatched up a pair of boxer briefs, and started tearing the box apart for his weapon. He would still have to get his darts loaded into the magazines, so I eased up on shooting him. Once he had it open, I watched him work like a professional. It was then I realized he probably worked with real guns on a regular basis and I might need to rethink my approach.

I slowly crept toward the door of the bedroom, blasted off a few more shots, and ran out of the room as I yelled, "Good luck finding me!"

Descending the stairs as quickly as possible, I took off toward the dining room. I was small enough that I was pretty sure he wouldn't see me when I draped my body, belly down, across the seats of three chairs on one side of the table. As I waited for Dom to come searching for me, I did my best to calm and control my breathing from my sprint down the stairs.

Apparently, Dom was in the right profession because I saw him before I heard him. He slowly paced around the room, easily using his height and size to scan the area for my whereabouts. Unfortunately for him, his height was a disadvantage in this particular match.

I held my breath as he entered the dining room and walked around the table. When he began to retreat, I took my shot at his backside, aiming high and hitting the middle of his back. Dom spun around, clearly caught off guard by the blast. Pulling my bottom lip in between my teeth, I bit down hard in an effort to stifle the burst of laughter threatening to give away my location. Unfortunately, I didn't succeed and accidentally let out a snort.

Suddenly, my vision was filled with the sight of Dom's body lowering to the ground. When his eyes met mine, he grinned and teased, "Killer hiding spot, fun size, but I'd say you've got yourself in quite the predicament now. Wouldn't you agree?"

I narrowed my eyes. "You wouldn't shoot me in the face," I dared him.

"You shot me when I was unarmed and naked!" he countered.

"I stayed away from the important bits!" I defended my actions.

Dom shook his head before he stood and pulled the chairs out slowly. Cautiously, I rolled to my back and sat up.

"I'm grateful you are willing to see there was an obvious disadvantage there," I offered as I stood up.

He nodded and admitted, "There was a pretty significant disadvantage, but I think you've failed to realize that there is always going to be one between us in this game."

"How so?"

The look on his face turned devilish. "I might be big, but I'm still pretty nimble. I'm betting, considering you probably don't have much shooting experience, that your aim is going to be off. I'll be able to avoid a majority of your shots. I shoot regularly and rarely miss a target."

Crap.

Dom held his gun up and added, "Let's not forget that you've already blasted through twenty-six darts. I still have all of my ammo."

Twenty-six? How did he know?

Pointing my gun at him, I started to shrink backward out of the dining room, never taking my eyes off him. Dom kept his feet planted and laughed at me. When I had cleared the room and knew I could take off, I pulled the trigger and ran. Magically, Dom avoided all of my shots and somehow managed to fire three shots, all of which hit me.

We raced throughout the house, firing our weapons at one another. I fired randomly whenever I saw Dom. He was precise and accurate, only shooting when he knew he'd hit his target. Before I knew it, I was crouched down behind a wall around the corner from him and I was out of ammo. I wouldn't have been surprised if Dom knew it, too.

"Care to give up?" I goaded him.

He let out a grunt and called back, "I'm just getting warmed up, Ekko."

"Shit," I hissed under my breath.

"What's wrong? Are you out of ammo?" he taunted me.

I needed a plan.

Taking in a deep breath, I stood and turned the corner into the living room, where Dom had his body shielded behind the couch. The floor and furniture were covered with lime green darts. I couldn't even fully assess that situation, though, because Dom's eyes were narrowed on me. I held my empty hands up and admitted, "I'm out. You can take your shots now."

He cocked his head to the side, seemingly unsure of why I was giving up.

My fingertips slipped under the straps of my camisole at my shoulders. My hands went through, followed by my arms. I pushed the shirt down over my breasts and exposed them to him.

His eyes focused on my breasts.

I moved the shirt over my hips and allowed it to fall to the floor. Dom followed the camisole's journey down my legs before his gaze went to my hands gripping the material of my panties. I shimmied my legs back and forth until they joined my top at my feet. Dom still had the gun in his hand, but his knuckles had turned white.

My plan was working; I had to keep going.

I brought my hands to my breasts, cupping their weight in my palms and brushing my thumbs over my nipples.

Dom swallowed hard.

Keeping one hand at my breasts, the other traveled down my body right between my legs. I touched myself for not more than ten seconds before Dom moved. He was on his knees and he set the gun down at my feet. His hands instantly wrapped around the backs of my thighs, holding me in place as his mouth closed over me.

My hands left my body and gripped the back of his head, pulling him closer, urging his tongue inside. Dom didn't disappoint. He worked me harder, relentlessly pleasuring me and bringing me to the brink of an orgasm in a matter of minutes.

"Baby," I moaned.

I was nearly there when Dom pulled away. He stood and opened the bottom drawer on the end table where he'd put a stash of condoms a couple weeks ago. While he worked to open the packet, I sat on the edge of the couch and pushed his boxer briefs down his legs. His erection jutted out from his body and I couldn't help but to wrap my mouth around him. Dom cupped the back of my head gently as I moved my mouth along his length, sucking him in, wanting to make him feel just as good as he made me feel.

After giving me a few minutes to enjoy him, Dom pulled himself from my mouth and sheathed himself. I fell to my back on the couch as he hovered over me.

"Guide me in, sugar," he instructed.

I did as he asked and before I had a chance to think about it, Dom had filled me. My legs wrapped around him instantly, my need to keep him close taking over. As Dom began to thrust his hips, I lifted mine to meet his. No sooner did we get into a steady rhythm and I was so close to orgasm when Dom pulled out and shifted on the couch. Dom was seated and pulled me over him. My thighs were straddling his and I began quickly lifting and lowering my hips over his, desperately trying to find my release.

When Dom could no longer stand to have me in control, he held my hips in his hands and relentlessly powered himself into me.

"Yes, Dom."

The look in his eyes, the force of his thrusts, and the feel of his hands on my body sent me over the edge. My body tensed over his, pleasure coursing through every nerve inside me. I hadn't gotten through my orgasm when Dom found his release, holding my body firmly in place, as he called out, "Fuck, Ekko."

A few minutes after we came together, I framed Dom's face with my hands and pressed a kiss to his lips. When I pulled back, I said, "I don't care that I lost. This has been the best day of my life."

Dom's hand caressed my bottom. "I didn't win."

I jerked my head back from his. "What?"

"The number one rule in a situation like that is to never allow yourself to become distracted. You cleverly took advantage of my weakness for your sweet, little body and I succumbed. You won this battle, sugar."

"I guess I did, but I get the feeling you still believe you were handsomely rewarded."

He laughed and kissed the tip of my nose.

"Lift up. I want to get this condom off so I can give you your gift."

"Wait!" I cried. "I want you to know that I didn't have a lot of money to spend, but that I wanted to do something special for you for Christmas. So, while what I did this morning was so much fun, I didn't feel like it was enough to show you what you mean to me. I don't have another gift for you to open, but I want us to take a trip one day to soon to Grand Teton National Park. You've taught me over the last few months that material things really don't matter. It's how we choose to live our life that counts. I want to spend a day exploring a place that's been in my backyard my whole life that I've never been able to visit. And I want to do that with someone who's made my life so much better from the moment he's been in it."

"I'll go anywhere with you, Ekko. Anywhere you want, anytime you want."

I smiled at him, kissed him, and lifted my body from his. Then, I prepared myself to continue having the best day ever. Dom and I cleaned up the darts that were all over his house, had breakfast together, and he gave me my gift. He'd gotten me a laptop. Knowing that I was preparing to start school again, he didn't want me having to go back to the library just so I could do my schoolwork. I was so grateful for him and the effort he put into getting something so thoughtful.

We spent the rest of our afternoon and evening with his family before we went back to his place for the remainder of the night.

And when I went to bed that night, I never expected that my good luck streak was about to end.

CHAPTER 20

Ekko

THREE WORDS.

I'd just heard the three words that had the power to change my entire life.

It was Wednesday, just over two weeks after Christmas. I had been working every day at the library and had started school again on Monday. I was attending classes in the evening and, even though I had long days, I was so happy to finally be working toward my goal.

Dom and I had gotten back into our work routines. Now that school had started for me, I had a feeling our time together would be even less. I tried not to let it get me down, though, because I knew this would be a short-lived hiccup and that there was an end in sight.

And everything had been going great until tonight.

Tonight, when I heard those three words.

"I'm sorry, Ekko."

Words that could have only meant bad news was to follow.

I left work at five o'clock and because it was my night off from school, I took advantage. I had scheduled a doctor's appointment. I'd gone through another excruciatingly painful period and decided to get checked out since I finally had health benefits.

My doctor noticed the trepidation in my features in response to her apology and explained, "I think you might have endometriosis."

I had heard the term before but didn't really know much about it.

"What does that mean?"

She gave me a sympathetic look. "Essentially, the lining that typically grows inside a woman's uterus every month doesn't just happen inside your uterus. The tissue can attach to the outside of the uterus, your ovaries, fallopian tubes, and other internal parts."

Even though I was a bit relieved to know that there was an explanation for my extreme pain, none of this sounded good.

"Okay, so you said you think I might have it. How do we confirm and what does this ultimately mean for me moving forward? Am I just going to have painful periods from now on?"

"There's a concrete answer for one of those questions, but the other two aren't so simple. Based on the things you've told me today about your symptoms and the pelvic exam I did, I'm confident there's some level of endo, but I don't know yet how severe. To see the extent of it, we'd need to do a bit more testing. Now, you've said you're experiencing the sometimes-debilitating pain a few days prior to your period and then in those first few days after getting it along with excessive bleeding. Luckily, you aren't having the pain during or after sex or with bowel movements and urination. There are some things you can do to help, but it's going to be a matter of trial and error. What works for one woman may not work for another."

My schedule was tight right now, but the pain I experienced sometimes was enough to take me down for the count for a couple of days. If there were things I could do that would help, I was up to trying them.

"I'm willing to do what I can to make it better," I assured her.

She offered a genuine smile and praised, "That's great. There are lots of options that I'm happy to discuss with you. In addition, we can discuss your plans for a family."

A family?

"What?" My voice was barely a whisper. "Does this mean I won't be able to have any children?"

"A large majority of the women diagnosed with endometriosis only end up finding out that they have it because they're experiencing issues with infertility. It is then that they get diagnosed with endo. It's not impossible to get pregnant, but it can be very difficult."

My gaze went to my hands in my lap. I felt like I had been punched in the gut. For as long as I could remember I always wanted a large family. In the last few months, my desire for one had grown.

And Dom. As one of five children, he wanted lots of babies. What if we stayed together and I couldn't give them to him? I wouldn't do that to Dom. I loved him too much to take that away from him. No matter how desperately I loved him and wanted to be with him, I would never allow myself to take away his dream. My bad fortune didn't have to become his.

"Ekko?" the doctor called, pulling me out of my thoughts. When I brought my eyes back to hers, she explained, "Let's not get ahead of ourselves just yet. We can set up the appointments before you leave to get the additional tests done and confirm the severity of your diagnosis. Then, we'll work together to come up with the best options to pursue so that you can still have everything you want in life."

I was too stunned, too hurt, to speak so I simply nodded.

"I'll step out so you can get dressed. Come out when you're ready. I know it's easier said than done, but try not to worry too much just yet. If you have any questions for me between now and your next appointment, don't hesitate to reach out to me, okay?"

"Okay."

At that, the doctor left the room and I sat there in stunned silence for a few minutes. I knew she told me not to get ahead of myself, but a lifetime of disappointments and struggles led me to believe that the outlook was grim.

I hopped down off the examination table, removed the gown, and got dressed.

When I scheduled this appointment, I had done so because I was overdue and because I was hoping for an explanation as to why I was having such severe pain every month. I never expected to hear what I did today and now I wasn't so sure if I'd have rather lived in oblivion.

After seeing my doctor just outside the examination room, I explained that I needed some time to process everything, but that I'd call next week to schedule the follow-up appointments. She urged me to get on the schedule since it would be several weeks before I'd be able to get in for the additional testing anyway. I went ahead and scheduled, but truthfully was relieved I had time. I wanted to take a few days to myself to figure out what I was going to do with what I'd just learned.

It seemed as though I would have the time, too. Since I needed to keep my school and work schedule in mind, I could only make an appointment for a Wednesday when I got out of work. This meant I couldn't get an appointment for nearly five weeks, but I didn't really mind. Delaying the onslaught of more bad news was completely fine with me.

Wednesday evenings had become my grocery shopping days since I typically spent my weekends with Dom. Tonight, once I left the doctor's office, I skipped the store and went straight home.

My phone dinged with a text from Dom just as I climbed into my bed.

Hope you had a great day. I'm working late tonight on this case.

Just seeing his name pop up on the screen was enough to send me over the edge. My belly twisted at the thought of losing him. Simply thinking about how this was going to affect him was more than I could handle. It wasn't something I could do via a text message, though, so I gave him a typical response.

So sorry you have to work late. It's been a long, busy day, but I just got into bed.

He responded almost instantly.

Wish I was there with you. Good night, sugar.

Me: Good night, Dom.

My text had indicated I was ready for sleep, but my mind wouldn't let me settle down and drown my sorrows in my dreams. Instead, I was replaying the words the doctor had said, a real-life nightmare.

It's not impossible to get pregnant, but it can be very difficult.

A thousand questions and possible scenarios filtered through my mind. All I could do was wonder how I was going to tell Dom the truth.

I woke up Saturday morning to a not-so-gentle knock at my door. Having done my best to remain elusive for the last few days, I had a pretty solid idea of who was at the door. Dom had texted and called me a couple times since Wednesday night. I didn't want to completely ignore him, but I was still so torn up over the awful news the doctor had given me.

As a result, my mood had shifted, and I was not ashamed

to admit that I was sulking. When Dom called, I answered, but kept the conversations brief. My responses through text message were short and sweet.

Unfortunately, though not surprisingly, I had a feeling my time was up and that Dom was going to want some answers.

Opening the door, I saw I was not wrong.

Dom stood there, his head covered by a beanie with his nose and cheeks slightly red from the cold, and he wore a serious expression on his face. I swallowed hard and took a step back as I greeted him.

"Hey."

He stepped inside, slammed the door shut behind him, and cut to the chase.

"What's wrong?"

Okay, so this was angry Dom. For a brief second, I understood Ryan's fearful expression a few months ago. He'd said two words, but his anger was still so palpable. If I didn't truly believe that deep down he was such a good guy, I might have started feeling worried about what he could do to me with that anger.

Apparently, I took too long assessing him because he spoke again.

"Ekko? What's wrong?"

"Why do you think there's something wrong?" I asked, stalling for more time.

After giving me an incredulous look, he clipped, "You've gone silent the past couple of days. If I wasn't so busy at work dealing with this nightmare of a case, I'd have been here sooner. To be honest, I should be at work right now and not here."

"So why are you here then?"

He became a bit more agitated. "I hope that's not a serious fucking question."

My shoulders slumped. He knew something was wrong

and I was playing stupid. I was doing everything I could to delay the inevitable.

Shaking my head, I delivered the three words to him.

"I'm sorry, Dom."

"I don't like the sound of that."

Me either.

I turned away from him and walked into the living room. Dom followed behind me. I turned around to face him and allowed my gaze to travel from the sneakers on his feet, up his jean-clad thighs, over his torso, to his concern-filled face.

This was going to be the worst thing I ever did in my life.

"This isn't going to work," I murmured.

He raised his brows in question but said nothing in response.

"I'm really sorry," I repeated. My throat was so tight, I barely recognized the sound of my own trembling voice.

"You're sorry?" he eventually replied.

I nodded as tears blurred my vision.

"Why?"

"I'm sorry because I don't want to upset you," I confessed the truth.

He took in a deep breath and clarified, "I don't want to know why you're sorry. I want to know why you think this isn't going to work?"

Now it was my turn to remain silent.

"What happened?" he pressed for more.

"Nothing."

Dom closed the distance between us, so much that our bodies were touching. "Something happened...something changed. I'm going to figure it out, Ekko. You'd make my life a hell of a lot easier right now if you'd just tell me what it is."

"My feelings have changed," I mumbled.

"You're lying to me," he shot back.

"I'm not."

His fingers came to rest on the skin at my wrists and began slowly traveling up my forearms. "You don't feel anything for me anymore?" he asked.

I struggled to remain unaffected by him. His hands reached my shoulders and started moving over my collarbones.

"Feeling my hands touching your skin does nothing for you?"

My lips parted.

My heart pounded.

His voice went even deeper. "Are you saying that if I kiss you, it'll mean nothing?"

In a flash his mouth was on mine, one of his hands cupping me behind my head, the other going to the side of my throat. It was a desperate, claiming, possessive kiss and I could do nothing but give in to what it made me feel.

My legs were going to give out on me.

Dom must have suspected it because he kept his mouth planted to mine, but dropped an arm to my waist.

As we kissed, the reality of the situation flooded me. My emotions took over and I was torn. I loved him so much I wanted to hold on and keep him forever, but I also didn't want to cost him his dreams. It was going to be hard enough for me to accept that I might not ever be able to have children and I knew I couldn't possibly expect him to endure years of struggling to have something he wanted.

Dom's mouth left mine and began trailing down my throat.

"You want to give up on us?" he asked, with his lips inches from my skin.

"You deserve so much more than I can give you," I rasped back. "You deserve someone who can give you everything you want."

He pulled his head back to look at me. "Why not you?"

I couldn't bring myself to say it.

He didn't wait for an answer either. "All I want is you, sugar," he whispered before he pressed a soft kiss to my lips. "Just you."

I love you, I thought.

"Dom...this isn't going to work," I maintained.

With both of his arms around my waist and his face buried in my neck, he insisted, "It will. Whatever you're feeling, we'll work through it."

His mouth moved down my body, following the top hem of my tank. He loosened his embrace and brought his hands to my hips, where he squeezed gently before sliding his hands up my sides to my breasts.

I was finding it harder and harder to stand my ground.

He swiped his thumbs over my nipples.

"Baby," I breathed.

"You like the way I make you feel?"

"So much."

"I love the way you make me feel, Ekko," he began as he lifted my shirt over my head and exposed my naked breasts. As he worked to remove his jacket and shirt, he continued, "There isn't anything I want right now that I don't have with you already."

Not yet.

His hands were on my hips, pushing my shorts and panties down my legs, as he captured a nipple in his mouth. He continued to tease me while he unbuttoned and dropped his pants.

"This isn't helping, Dom. You're confusing me and complicating this."

Dom finished removing his clothing, stood tall, and lifted

me up in his arms. With my legs wrapped around his waist and our faces only inches apart, he said, "I'll take it. If you're confused, that means there's still a chance I can convince you to change your mind."

"But," I got out before I felt him filling me.

"Just feel, Ekko," he urged as he took the final few steps toward the wall, rested my back against it, and began moving inside me.

And so I did.

I felt everything.

Something about being with Dom like this at this moment was different. I couldn't be certain, but I had a feeling it had a lot to do with the fact that I knew what I was giving up. For so many years I'd had nothing but horrible circumstances to endure. And while I always managed to just barely get through them, my life had always felt like one long uphill battle. He came into my life and it was instantly better. It filled me with dread thinking about having to give him up.

But I couldn't be selfish.

Not with this.

Not with something so incredibly important.

And I knew that if he was aware of the real reason why I couldn't stay with him, he'd never allow me to walk away from him...from us.

If I didn't, I'd always have it lingering in the back of my mind. I'd always regret not giving him the chance to get everything he wanted in life.

"Tell me, sugar," he whispered against my lips as he slowly pumped his hips.

"Dom," I replied, my voice filled with sorrow. His name came out as a plea and I felt myself fighting against the tears still threatening to fall.

His chest pressed against mine, his mouth moved along

my jaw toward my ear. "Just tell me what happened. I'll fix it."

You can't.

I didn't answer.

He didn't say anything else either.

There was no need for words. Dom's body collided with mine, my thighs tight to his sides, and with each thrust, I couldn't do anything but let what I felt for him consume me. I wouldn't be selfish with Dom's future, but I'd be greedy now.

Just one last time.

One last time before I let him go.

Even though he didn't need to because I already knew how wonderful he was, Dom was clearly on a mission to prove something to me. He gave it to me hard, fast, and slightly rough. Not rough to the point he hurt me, but enough that I'd still feel him long after he was no longer between my legs.

My body, as it always did with him, responded quickly to Dom. So, while my mind wasn't ready for it to end, I couldn't stop myself from giving in to the physical pleasure and coming apart around him while he kissed me through his own orgasm.

A few moments later, pinned against the wall with Dom still inside me, he asked, "Are you over your crazy idea to end what we have between us?"

I didn't want to be, but I had to do it.

I shook my head and answered, "I'm sorry, Dom. We can't continue this."

His head jerked back. "You're serious?"

I swallowed hard and closed my eyes. "Please don't hate me," I begged.

"I don't understand," he started, the tone of his voice bordering on angry. "After everything you've gone through, everything you've fought for in your life, you're just going to throw us away? And without an explanation?"

"I really did not ever want to hurt you," I rasped, struggling to get the words out.

He pulled out of me and made sure I was steady on my feet before he looked away and began picking up his clothes. For the next minute, he stayed quiet and kept his focus on getting himself dressed.

Dom started walking away from me, but suddenly stopped and turned back so he could completely shatter my heart. "I fell in love with you, Ekko. Hard and fast. And, honest to God, I believed you were the girl for me. Someone I wanted to have a family and grow old with. There's not a doubt in my mind I would have spent the rest of my life doing what I had to do to prove to you just how special you are and what you mean to me. You keep telling me you're sorry. I guess I should apologize, too. I'm sorry I'll never be able to show you just how much I love you."

I couldn't speak.

I held his gaze, my lips parted in shock, but I remained silent.

He waited a few seconds, I'm certain hoping I'd change my mind. When I didn't give him what he wanted, he just shook his head at me, completely disappointed.

Dom turned and walked to the door. With his hand on the knob, he looked back at me. "Just took you without protection," he clipped. "I was caught up in what I was feeling, not thinking straight. From a pregnancy standpoint, it was one time. It's not likely, but that's all it takes. If you're concerned about your health, you've got nothing to worry about. I've always worn a condom and I am tested regularly."

I gave him a nod. It was all I could muster up as I continued to tell myself that I was doing this for him.

"Take care of yourself, Ekko."

At that, he opened the door and walked out. My knees buckled, and my back slid down the wall as I slowly crumpled to the floor. I fell to my side and cried.

Dom loved me.

And because I loved him, I did what I had to do to make sure my bad luck didn't take away his dreams.

CHAPTER 21

Dom

"**S**HE'S IN AGONY."

Over the last few days, it felt like a rain cloud that refused to just unleash its impending storm had been hanging over my head. It was Thursday nearly two weeks after I'd walked out of her place that Saturday morning and I'd been going through the motions under that cloud ever since.

There were two things weighing me down, one much more than the other.

Ekko.

My beautiful girl.

Sometime during the last two and a half months, I'd fallen in love with her. And just when I thought the time was right to share that sentiment with her, she broke things off with me. It was completely out of the blue and unexpected. I only noticed a few days prior that she started getting quiet, but I never suspected that this was where things were headed. In fact, I worried that I would have been the one to hurt her somehow. Of course, not intentionally, but the fact remained that I had the power to devastate her.

Or so I thought.

I always knew that Ekko was tough. She was nothing if

not a fighter. Unfortunately, one of the things that I loved most about her was the one thing that pulled her away from me. Once she had her mind made up, there was little anyone could do to change it.

What Ekko failed to realize was that I am just as stubborn. While my attempt to convince her that we belonged together was unsuccessful, I wasn't going to just walk away without a fight. I knew if I had any chance to win her back, though, I'd have to figure out why she suddenly wanted nothing to do with me. The way that she responded to me Saturday morning told me that this wasn't simply a matter of a relationship no longer working for one individual. Ekko was still very much connected to me. And I was determined to make sure she stayed that way.

Sadly, I had been struggling with accomplishing what I wanted to with her because my case was taking too much of my focus. Ekko meant too much to me to allow what we deserved to have to take a back seat. So, as much as I hated having to do it, I enlisted the help of some reinforcements.

Elle.

Jojo.

Kendall.

I couldn't be sure they'd get me any information that I needed, but it was worth a shot. To be honest, it was more an attempt for me to feel better about the situation with Ekko. I couldn't devote the time I knew was necessary to fix things with us, but I had to know she was doing alright.

I started with Elle because I believed she could make an appearance in Ekko's life and it wouldn't seem suspect. Apparently, I was right because Elle was now in my office at Cunningham Security updating me on Ekko.

"Agony?" I questioned.

Elle's face was filled with sorrow. "Yeah, she's not doing

well at all. But she's definitely trying to cover it up and be strong."

"That sounds like her," I sighed as I sat back in my chair.

"Yeah, until she can't be strong anymore."

I sat up straight again and asked, "What do you mean? Did she say anything about us?"

"I feel like I'm in a tight spot," Elle started. "I know you asked me to do this for you and I agreed, but I also don't want to betray her. It's not lost on me that she doesn't have a lot of friends; I want to be a good friend to her. That said, I wouldn't consider myself a good friend if I saw what I did last night and didn't do something to help her, so I'll tell you this. She did tell me that you two were no longer together. When I asked her how she was handling it, she broke down. I was glad we decided to get together at her place last night instead of over her lunch break. She wouldn't have been able to go back to work with how broken up she was. I felt horrible for her."

"So why did she do this?"

Elle shrugged. "I honestly don't know, Dom. She just kept saying that you deserved better than she could ever give you. While I don't know all the details of her past, it's not hard to see that Ekko's had a rough life. Maybe she thinks that she won't ever measure up to some standard."

I shook my head. "I sure hope that's not what it is. She knows I don't look down on her and I never would."

"I know that. And I think she does too. But there's something else going on with her. You just need to figure out what it is, because that girl is so madly in love with you."

My stomach twisted. "You think she's in love with me?" I asked, my voice rough.

Elle reached across my desk and wrapped her hand around mine. "I know she is, Dom. Don't give up on her because love like you two have is hard to find. Letting it go would just be tragic."

Unable to speak, I gave Elle a nod.

"I'm going to head out and let you get back to work. Good luck."

"Thanks, rock star."

She offered a friendly smile and a wink before she said, "You saved my life. This was the least I could do in return."

Elle left, and I sat there dumbfounded for a moment. If what Elle said was true and Ekko really did love me, it made no sense to me why she'd not want to be with me. Ekko was so determined. There was no way this was simply a matter of feeling like she didn't measure up to some impossible standard. If that's what she thought, Ekko was the kind of woman who'd find a way to lift herself up to that level. This was something else. Something I, unfortunately, couldn't put much more time in today.

I pulled out my phone, found the name I needed, and tapped on the screen. Three rings later, Jojo's voice came through the line.

"Hey, bro!" she greeted me.

"Hey, Jojo. I need you to do me a favor," I informed her.

"Anything. What do you need?"

I took in a deep breath and let it out before I replied, "I know you are planning to meet up with Ekko this weekend on my behalf. When you do, just do it as her friend. I'll figure out another way to find out why she decided to break things off."

There was silence on the line for a moment. "I don't understand."

"Elle met with her last night and just stopped by to tell me about it. Ekko's really torn up about the two of us. I just don't want you prying further and upsetting her. She's had enough in her life to make her cry; I don't want to be the reason she sheds any more tears."

"Dom, I'm not cruel!" Jojo cried. "Yes, you asked me to do this on your behalf, but I like Ekko. She's my friend and I'd never purposely hurt her. And you're my brother. I love you and I know how much you're hurting. If I can find a way to take that pain away from you and Ekko, I'm going to do it."

I don't know why I even questioned her. My sister didn't have an evil bone in her body. She loved her family and friends hard and would go to great lengths to protect those she cared about. "Love you, Jojo."

"I know," she shot back. "Love you too!"

I disconnected the call and decided to get back to work. Before I did, though, I wanted to reach out to Ekko. She would be in the middle of her morning at work, but if she really was torn up over this, I didn't want her thinking I held a grudge. And the way I left things when I walked out of her place would easily have her believing I thought the worst of her.

Miss you, sugar.

Satisfied that I had at least tried to do something positive about the situation, I had to switch my mindset to the nightmare I needed to solve. Over the last few weeks, I'd been receiving puzzle pieces. There was no rhyme or reason to the arrival of them. They weren't arriving on the same day each week. I had been receiving one a week through the week before Christmas. Then, the following two weeks I didn't get anything. Last week, I received the sixth piece.

Based on the way it was coming together, I could tell this puzzle was going to have a total of nine pieces. The six that I'd already received were the three along the bottom, which were all the pavement. There was nothing on the back of those. I had the one from the top corner showing the sky with the word 'You' and a sliver of the letter 'f' on the back of it. The last two pieces I'd received were the outer edges of the middle row. While those pieces had nothing on the back of them, they were the first two pieces that finally gave me something.

I now knew where the picture had been taken and it was unsettling, to say the least. Not only were they delivered in the mail at my house, but those two puzzle pieces showed me that someone had taken a photo outside my home as well. The photo had been taken from a distance because my actual house wasn't visible in the photo yet. Even though I knew from the surrounding area that it was my home, there was nothing indicating what the focus of the photo was going to be other than the actual house. I had a feeling the last three pieces were going to tell me that and I was hoping that I'd be getting another photo this week. Considering it was Thursday, there wasn't much time left. Of course, whoever was behind this didn't much care about my lack of patience.

Those two weeks over the Christmas and New Year holiday drove me crazy. On one hand, I was able to keep my focus on enjoying the time with my family and with Ekko, but on the other, I thought I was going to lose my mind not knowing what was happening. Perhaps I should have been grateful for the reprieve, but I wasn't.

I pulled all the pieces of the puzzle out of my desk and put them together. Then, I did what I had been doing for weeks now. I stared at it. Sadly, my research of old cases didn't really give me any clue as to what could be happening since there were so many that could have easily had someone angry at me. I was going through those, but it was a long process that was taking some time to go through to eliminate any with confidence.

"Nothing new yet?" Pierce's voice filtered into the room.

I looked up from the puzzle and shook my head. "This is, by far, the most frustrating case I've ever worked on. I've got nothing to go on. Someone knows my name and where I live.

I don't even know what they want."

Pierce came into my office and sat down. "What did that note say again?"

"Worthless."

His eyes narrowed as a contemplative look washed over his face. I had worn the same expression many times over the last several weeks as I tried to figure out what it all meant.

Frustrated, I pulled the pieces of the puzzle apart and stood. Dropping them into the big manila envelope I had been keeping them in, I looked at Pierce and explained, "I'm going to see if I can figure out where this shot was taken from. It's from a distance, but maybe I can narrow it down to a specific spot."

"You want a second set of eyes?"

"If you've got a set to spare, it'd be appreciated."

He gave me a nod as he stood and walked out of my office ahead of me.

When we arrived back at my place, we looked in the direction where the photo had been taken from.

"Judging by the angle of the photo, I'd have to say it narrows it down to anywhere between the gray stone house on the left and the timber house off to the right," Pierce pointed out after we'd studied the area for a while. "Do you know any of the homeowners in those houses and in between?"

I shook my head and announced, "No, but I'm going to figure out who owns them."

Just then, I noticed the mailman approaching in his mail delivery truck. He was still a few houses away and was moving slow given the amount of snow that had accumulated over the last week.

"What are the chances I'm going to get another puzzle piece in my mail today?" I asked Pierce.

"It would be awfully convenient," he noted.

When the driver approached, he held out the mail and lamented, "I'm sorry. I just noticed this morning that one of those slid down between the seat and the center console. If it's anything time-sensitive, I'm willing to vouch for our error and the delay."

"Don't worry about it," I said as I took the pile of mail from him.

He took off and I thumbed through the mail.

Two.

There were two envelopes addressed to me with no return address, just as the other puzzle piece deliveries had been. One had been postmarked a few days prior to the other.

"Let's go," I ordered.

Pierce quickly followed behind me into my house. I dumped the envelope out. While he began assembling the pieces, I opened the new ones. The two completed the outside frame of the puzzle.

"Take off the top one and flip it over."

I took the new pieces and attached them to the second piece I'd received what felt like ages ago. Pierce and I stared at the haunting message that had been printed on the back of the puzzle.

You took everything from me.

"What the fuck does this mean?" I barked. "And what does my house have to do with it?"

"Maybe it's this guy's way of letting you know that he knows where you live," Pierce suggested.

"Okay," I agreed. "But why?"

Pierce threw his arms up and out to the side. "Apparently, you took everything from him."

"This makes absolutely no sense whatsoever. I mean, yeah, there are plenty of people that we've all had the privilege of bringing down, but I'm not responsible for their choices."

"Maybe a case of adultery?" Pierce guessed. "Perhaps a significant other left their partner after you shed light on the infidelity in the relationship."

It made sense.

And I'd solved my fair share of cases that involved a cheating spouse. Some of those cases involved cheating spouses who had children. So, it wasn't completely unreasonable to think that if one spouse left the other and took the children that there'd be ill will directed at me.

"It's a possibility," I confirmed. "I guess it's time to see what I can find out about who owns those homes. Maybe that'll give me a bit more to work with until I get the final piece here. Although, I can't imagine that it's going to give me anything other than a picture of my house."

My phone buzzed in my pocket. I pulled it out and my breath seized.

I know. I feel the same.

Ekko missed me, too. I instantly typed out a response.

Let's get together. I know you have school, so we can meet this weekend if that works for you.

I realized she must have been on her lunch break because three dots inside a conversation bubble showed up immediately.

I don't think that's a good idea. We aren't together anymore and it'll just complicate things.

Me: We can do it somewhere out in public. How about bowling? This way there's no pressure.

I watched my screen intently hoping she'd agree. It took a little longer for her to even start typing, but her reply finally came through.

I'm sorry, Dom. I can't.

"Fuck," I muttered under my breath.

"Everything okay?" Pierce asked.

I had forgotten he was there.

I slid my phone back into my pocket as I shook my head. "Ekko broke things off nearly two weeks ago."

"Really? I thought you two were solid. What happened?"

Shooting him a look of frustration, I answered, "Consider it another unsolved case."

"I'm sorry, man. I know she was special to you."

"She is," I corrected. "I'm doing my best now to balance these two situations, but I really wish I could get this damn case solved so I could focus on her. She's got something else going on and I need to figure out what it is."

"Let's get back to the office. We can get Trent the addresses for those homes so he can locate the owners' names. Then, I'll help you dig through some of your older cases and see if we can make a connection."

"Appreciate it, Pierce."

With that, we picked up the puzzle and put the pieces away. I tucked the envelope under my arm and we left.

As we drove back to the Cunningham Security offices, I couldn't help but let my mind wander to Ekko. I loved knowing that she was missing me, but I hated that she refused to see me. While I never expected our relationship to end this abruptly, or at all for that matter, it was truly a shock to me that she was willing to completely cut me out of her life. After everything I'd learned about her, I never suspected she'd be able to just walk away without ever seeing me again.

That realization felt like a knife to the gut and I wasn't too proud to admit that my heart was broken. My only hope was that I'd be able to soon figure out what pulled her away from me and how I was going to fix it.

There was no way I could let go of her.

I just needed some time and a clear head to get her back.

CHAPTER 22

Ekko

"**Y**OU'RE DEAD ON YOUR FEET," KATE ANNOUNCED AS SHE walked into the break room at work. "Did your man keep you up all night?"

I lifted my head from the table and looked at her. With one look at my red-rimmed, puffy eyes, her smile died.

"Are you okay?" she asked as she sat down next to me at the table.

Kate didn't know what had happened. The first week following my break up with Dom, I managed to hold myself together while I was at work. During the few days that we had lunch together, I kept the conversation away from the subject of my non-existent relationship by engaging her in the details of her own or by talking about things going on at school.

It was now Thursday afternoon on week two following the most devastating experience of my life and I'd finally succumbed to the pain. It started last night. Elle and I got together at my place because Wednesdays were my night off from school. It was the first we were seeing each other since her wedding at the beginning of December. I had missed her and wanted to hear how things were going for her and Levi adjusting to married life.

After telling me all about her honeymoon, Elle pulled out

her wedding album. I flipped through, feeling happy for her and the love that she found. About three-quarters of the way through the album, though, I lost my composure. Elle's album had been arranged in chronological order of her wedding day. Things took a turn for me when I reached the reception portion of the album. I had completely forgotten until that moment that Elle's photographer had gotten a photo of Dom and me at the wedding.

In fact, it wasn't just one photo; there were three of them. Dom's arm was wrapped around me in all three as he pulled me close to him. I remained focused on the camera in the first two, Dom was like that in only one of them. In the second one, his attention was on me and the look on his face was nothing but pure adoration. In the third photo, I had tilted my head back to look up at him. We were both smiling and happy, blissfully unaware of anything going on around us.

I stared at those pictures for what felt like an eternity before realizing Elle was talking to me.

"I had those printed for you," she said as she dug through her bag and brought out a folder. The moment she slid it into my hands and I flipped it open to see us inside, the tears started. I quickly closed the folder and her album so I wouldn't ruin them, and Elle immediately pulled me into her arms.

I told her that Dom and I were no longer together, letting her know that I was the one to break things off, but I never gave her the full truth. I didn't tell her that I loved him enough to let him go so he wouldn't have to give up his dream of being a father to lots of children.

Elle stayed with me for a long time, waiting until I'd calmed down before she left. Unfortunately, once she was gone and I was alone in my bed, the tears flowed again. They had done so most of the night, too. With very little sleep, I somehow managed to pull myself together enough to get to work on time and get through the first part of my day.

Now that I was on my lunch break, I found I was struggling to keep it together. So, I rested my head on the table and tried to do some deep breathing to settle myself down. I hadn't gotten very far before Kate walked in. And now she would know the truth.

"I ended things with Dom about two weeks ago," I blurted.

"What?! What happened?"

Kate didn't know Dom. She wasn't friends with his friends. She was my friend. And I wanted to do something I hadn't ever had the opportunity to do before now. I wanted to tell her about my troubles and cry on her shoulder.

This didn't mean that I didn't value my friendship with Elle. It's just that I knew she had a loyalty to Dom as well and she was so sweet that she'd want to do what she could to help. That would involve her telling him the truth.

So, I told Kate because I could and because I wanted her support. I explained how I'd been having painful periods for months and how I finally went to see a doctor a few weeks prior. I told her about the diagnosis.

"I don't understand," she started. "What does your diagnosis have to do with you not wanting to be with Dom?"

My shoulders fell. "I do want to be with him. I love him. It's just that we had a conversation back at the beginning of December after we went to that wedding. We talked about children. The both of us want to have a large family with a lot of kids."

"Isn't that a good thing?" she wondered.

"Yeah, it was a great thing. Until I got this diagnosis and learned that it can make it difficult to have children."

Kate reached over and gave my hand a squeeze. "Oh, Ekko. I'm so sorry. Did they say you won't be able to get pregnant at all or that you might have a hard time with it?"

"My doctor said it's not impossible, but that it can be very difficult."

I watched as my friend grew angry on my behalf. "He didn't feel strongly enough about you to stick by your side through this?"

My eyes rounded. "He doesn't know. I didn't tell him."

"How did he respond when you ended it?"

"He tried to convince me not to and he practically begged me to tell him why."

Kate kept her head pointed straight at me, but her brows furrowed and she did a lip curl while her eyes stared off to the side. "So, let me get this straight," she began after a moment of silence. "You love Dom. He makes you happy. You're miserable without him right now. And you broke things off with him without telling him the reason even after he asked you why and tried to get you to change your mind. Do I have that right?"

I gave her a nod.

"What are you thinking?" she nearly shrieked. "Ekko, please know that what I'm about to say is because you're my friend and I care about you."

"Okay," I responded hesitantly.

"You're an idiot!"

"What?"

I couldn't believe she just said that to me.

Kate was so fired up she stood and started pacing. "Finding someone who makes you over-the-moon happy is not easy. Dom did that for you. And you broke it off without even telling him the real reason for it. Don't you think he deserves to know so he can be the one to make the decision about what he wants?"

"I don't want to guilt him into staying with me. I couldn't

bear to have him stick by my side out of obligation now, and then years down the road, regret that we're struggling to have even one child. He wants at least four kids and it would be unfair of me to take that away from him."

"So you took yourself away from him instead?" she asked, incredulously. "Did you ever think he was able to discuss having that many children with you because he finally found someone with whom he would be happy having those kids? Is it even a remote possibility that without you he might not even want kids?"

I made a feeble attempt to defend myself. "I'm sure he still wants kids. You don't just give up on a dream because someone does something to throw a wrench in your plans."

She stared at me in disbelief.

"You did."

I jerked back at her statement. The weight of the situation settled around me and I realized she was right. I gave up on my dream of having a family with a man who would love me.

Kate must have realized she struck a nerve because she didn't wait for me to respond. "Have you spoken to him since you ended it?" she asked.

Swallowing past the lump forming in my throat, I struggled to get out, "He sent me a text earlier today and I just sent him a reply before you came in here."

"What did he say?"

I couldn't bring myself to repeat it.

He missed me.

I pulled up the text on my phone and handed it to her. She read it and looked at me. A tear leaked from my eye and Kate scanned my face a moment before she pulled the chair next to me and engulfed me in a hug.

"I've said my piece," she started. "As your friend, it's my job to tell you when I think you're making a mistake. I've done that. It's also my job to be there to comfort you and support you in whatever decision you make that you feel is right for yourself in a situation like this. That's what I'm going to do now."

Kate fulfilled her duties as my friend and comforted me. Nearly two weeks of not having him around me had taken its toll and I took advantage of having someone there who cared enough about me to see me through it. Kate no longer scolded me for my choice. Instead, she held me in her arms and made me feel better just by being there.

"Thanks, Kate," I finally said when our lunch break was nearly over.

"You're welcome. I'm here anytime you need me."

Saturday rolled around, and it was the official two-week mark since I'd last seen Dom. It was also the day I was getting together with Kendall and Jojo. I had questioned whether it was a good idea to meet up with Dom's sisters and had initially hesitated, but Jojo was persistent. In the end, she managed to convince me.

We had originally planned to meet at Jojo's apartment, but she called me this morning and said she'd pick me up. I had no idea what was going on, but I wasn't going to fight her. I knew she wouldn't accept it if I declined anyway.

When ten-thirty rolled around, there was a knock at my door. Opening it, I found two bright, smiling faces on the other side.

"I hope you're ready for a day of fun," Jojo bubbled.

My brows pulled together as I stepped back to allow them to come inside. "Where are we going?" I asked, walking toward the kitchen to grab my purse.

"First up would be my place of employment," she announced.

"What?"

"We're having a spa day," Kendall explained. "Massages, facials, manicures, and pedicures."

"A spa day?" I worried, though I couldn't stop myself from imagining just how wonderful it would be to have one. I was certainly doing better financially than I had been in months, but I was not in any position to treat myself to an expensive day at the spa.

"Yep," Jojo confirmed. "Perks of the job mean that I get to bring one friend once every three months for the works at a highly discounted rate. But you don't need to worry about the costs because Kendall and I want to treat you."

I had made it to the kitchen, turned to face them, and insisted, "Oh...no, you can't do that. It's too much."

Kendall walked toward me, took my hand in hers, and said, "When a friend is fresh off a breakup, her girls have to be there for her to see her through that."

"But," I stammered, wondering if they knew that I was the one who broke things off with Dom. "Do you know what happened?" I finally asked.

They shook their heads, but it was Jojo that spoke. "We know you two aren't together anymore and that it was your choice. If you want to share any of that with us, you can. If you don't, that's okay, too. Dom's our brother and we love him, but you're our friend. So, while you take the time to figure out whatever it is that you need to figure out, we'll be here for you doing what women do for each other when one of their own is going through a breakup. For you, today, that means you're getting a day at the spa to relax."

"There's no pressure from us, Ekko, for anything other than a day of rejuvenation. We just want you to know that you're important to us and that we're here if you need us," Kendall added.

I shook my head slowly back and forth as I took a few deep

breaths, hoping to stave off the emotions that were threatening to send me into a tailspin.

"You're all so good to me," I murmured. "And there isn't anything I can do for you in return."

"One day I'm sure we'll both suffer through some heartache," Jojo started. "All you've got to do is be there to lend a shoulder to cry on."

I tilted my head and gave her a small nod. "I can do that."

Dom's sisters engulfed me in their arms and held on to me for a moment before pulling back. Jojo ordered, "Now, let's get out of here so we don't miss our appointments."

At that, the three of us left and made our way to the spa. Not much later, I never imagined I could have felt as great as I did. The facial was refreshing and the massage, even though it wasn't nearly as wonderful as the one Dom gave me, was incredibly relaxing. While the girls and I were getting our manicures and pedicures together, I worried that we'd struggle to find things to talk about or that they'd try to get me to talk about why I ended things with Dom.

I was genuinely surprised to find that they respected my right to privacy and never once asked about it. In fact, they set me at ease by jumping right in with their own non-existent boy troubles.

"Maybe I'm just being too picky," Kendall put in when the conversation came up. "I mean, I've been on a couple dates over the last few weeks. And while all of the guys were nice enough, there wasn't even one with whom I was interested in going on a second date."

"At least you're getting official dates, Kendall," Jojo scoffed. "I can't land a date no matter what I do."

I jerked my head in surprise. "Are you serious?"

"Totally," she sighed. "I've been told that I'm too outgoing and some guys are intimidated by that."

"That's such a bunch of crap," Kendall said.

"Maybe I need to start toning it down," she suggested.

"No!" I cried. "Don't change who you are. The right guy is going to love you just as you are and he'll love everything about you."

As soon as the words were out of my mouth, I regretted saying them. Obviously, I didn't want Jojo smothering a part of herself just so a guy wouldn't be intimidated by her larger-than-life personality, but I regretted that I couldn't take my own advice.

Both Kendall and Jojo looked at me and I had a feeling they knew exactly where my head was. Thankfully, they didn't call me out for being a hypocrite. Of course, not knowing my reasoning for leaving their brother was probably one of the biggest reasons.

Kendall quickly chimed in, "I guess it'll all happen for us when the timing is right. Until then, we can have spa days followed by lunch and a girls' night in with a bottle of wine and some sappy movies."

"Totally!" Jojo exclaimed before turning her head in my direction. "Are you up for it, Ekko?"

I grinned at them and nodded.

With freshly painted fingers and toes, the three of us took off for lunch. Afterward, we went to Kendall's condo and I had my first girls' night ever. I had to be honest with myself and admit that for those few hours I was with his sisters, there was a brief respite from the pain in my heart over losing Dom.

CHAPTER 23

Ekko

"**T**HIS CANNOT BE HAPPENING RIGHT NOW," I MUMBLED under my breath.

It was Friday morning, the week after my spa day with Kendall and Jojo and nearly three weeks since I'd last seen Dom.

Empty was the best word I could come up with to describe how I was feeling. Sadly, I wasn't sure that Dom was still feeling the same. Other than the one text message I'd received from him when he told me he missed me and asked me to get together with him, he never reached out again. I couldn't say I blamed him. He was thrown away and when he made an attempt at friendship, I shut that down, too. The more time that passed, the more I didn't like who I had become.

Apparently, I was seeing the error of my ways because my bad luck was making an appearance once again.

I woke up a little earlier this morning so that I could make a quick stop at the diner for breakfast on the go. I hadn't had an opportunity to go grocery shopping. I hadn't felt up to going during my day off from school during the week, so planned to do it on Sunday. And I would have gone on Sunday, but I had to spend Sunday doing schoolwork. Schoolwork that I would have usually completed on Saturday. That didn't happen when

Kendall and Jojo ended up changing plans on me last minute and my time with them ended up being much longer than I had originally anticipated.

When I made my plan to stop at the diner this morning, I accounted for a little extra time so that I'd be able to chat for a few extra minutes with my old co-workers, which is precisely what I did. I also managed to fulfill my promise to George because he was also at the diner this morning. Unfortunately, he couldn't stay long and ended up leaving before I'd even gotten my breakfast. Even still, I was happy that I had the chance to see him, even though it was brief, and I'd had such a great morning catching up with everyone else. Of course, I was now regretting that because when I went back out to the parking lot, my car wouldn't start.

I couldn't be late for work.

I also couldn't go back into the diner and ask for a ride.

They were right in the middle of the breakfast rush and one of the waiters had called out this morning. There was no way they'd survive the rush with another staff member down, even if only for thirty minutes.

The bus stop was right down the road. I wasn't the best with distances, but I didn't think it was more than a mile away. I could walk to the bus. It was bitterly cold, but I didn't have any other choice. I grabbed my things out of the car, locked it, and took off.

About ten minutes into my walk, I was frozen and ready to cry. I wasn't going to make it to work on time. I needed to call and let them know, so I dug my phone out of my pocket.

Just as I was about to dial the number, I heard a man's voice call, "Ekko?"

I looked up to see a familiar face looking at me from the truck pulled up alongside the curb. Unfortunately, I couldn't remember the name of the man and my face must have made that fact known.

"It's Pierce," he reminded me.

"Right, I'm so sorry. Hi Pierce." He was one of Dom's co-workers. One who had been there the day I had my stand-off with Ryan.

"What are you doing walking out here in this weather?"

I looked down the road to where I needed to go. "I was just at the diner and my car won't start. I'm walking to the bus stop because I need to get to work on time, but I'm going to be late anyway."

"The bus stop is at least another mile down the road, so I'd say that's an accurate assumption. Hop in," he urged.

"I'm sorry?"

"Get in the truck. I'll take you back to your car so we can see what's wrong with it. If it's not fixable, I'll give you a ride to work."

"Oh, you don't have to do that."

"I do," he corrected me. "Because if Dom finds out that I knew you were walking out here in the cold and didn't make sure you were taken care of, he'd kick my ass. Please help me out and get in the truck so I don't have to end up in a fist fight today."

Evidently, Dom hadn't shared the news of our breakup with his co-workers. I didn't want to break the news to Pierce that it wasn't likely Dom would fight him, so I simply rounded the front of his truck and climbed in.

"Thank you," I offered.

Pierce noticed I was shivering, turned the heat to full blast, and began driving back toward the diner. When he pulled into the lot and pulled up next to my car, he ordered, "Give me your keys so I can check it out. Stay here and warm up."

I felt bad that he'd be out in the cold for me, but had a feel-ing he wouldn't be swayed. In addition, I didn't want to be the reason he ended up getting to work late as well, so I handed the keys over.

While I tried to regain the feeling in my feet, hands, and face, Pierce inspected my car. A few moments later, he was opening the door to his truck and popping his own hood.

"Your battery is dead," he declared. "I'll jump you and you should be good."

"That's about the best news I've heard in quite some time," I practically cried as I put my hand to the door handle to get out.

"Don't even think about it. Stay where you are until I get it fired up and we get some heat in that car."

I stayed put and waited while Pierce ran jumper cables from his truck's working battery to my car's dead one. He got in on the driver's side of my car and the next thing I knew it fired up. Relief swept through me. I didn't really have the time or the money to deal with car troubles.

After unhooking the cables and closing the hoods, Pierce climbed back in his truck.

"You should be good to go now. Your lights weren't left on, so there's a draw on the battery somewhere. As soon as you can, especially if it's been a while since it's been replaced, you should get a new one in there."

"You're a lifesaver, Pierce. Thank you so much for helping me."

"It's not a problem."

"Is there anything I can do to thank you?"

He shook his head. "Actually, yes. If you have any more car trouble, don't go out walking in this weather. We've got a nasty storm coming tonight. If you need help, call someone."

I gave him a nod and replied, "I will."

At that, I moved to get out of the truck. When I opened the door, Pierce called out, "Ekko?"

I turned back to look at him and answered, "Yeah?"

"He misses you," he stated and paused a moment. "I know it's not my business and it's probably not my place to get involved, but he's my friend. I hate seeing him so upset because it's just not who he is. I've never seen him like he is now. Dom's always been one to roll with the punches and not let things get to him. You've gotten to him, sweetheart."

I was wrong. Clearly, Dom had shared what happened between us.

"It's not that easy, Pierce."

He threw his hands up and said, "I know. I'm not going to pretend to understand what's going on. I just thought you should know that if you're having any doubts or regrets about your decision, you should call him. He loves you, misses you like crazy, and will do anything to make it right for the both of you."

I was going to cry if I didn't get out of his truck. "I'll keep that in mind," I promised even though I knew that there were some things that couldn't be fixed. I was broken and, no matter how much he might have wanted to, Dom couldn't make this better.

Pierce gave me a friendly smile and a nod.

"Thanks again."

With that, I got out of the truck and hopped into my car. Then, I took off to work and arrived only two minutes late. I explained what happened and found that nobody was even remotely upset with me.

Throughout the day, particularly during the downtime, I found my thoughts drifting to the words Pierce said to me that morning. In my haste to free Dom from a life of struggle if we ended up together for the long-term, I never really took the time to consider how it would affect him now.

And it seemed that everyone around us believed I was

making a huge mistake. When I took the time to think about it, I had to seriously consider that they couldn't all be wrong. I couldn't deny that there was a lot of love between the two of us, even if I hadn't had the chance to tell him how much I loved him.

My mind took me back to my conversation with Kate and how she had said that I needed to let Dom decide what he was or was not prepared to go through. I not only took his choice about it away from him, but I also took me away from him. If I hadn't seen Pierce today, I wouldn't have known just how much our separation was hurting Dom.

The thought scared me, but I realized I needed to do the right thing and give Dom the truth. What he decided to do with the information would be his choice and I'd have to trust that if he wanted to try to work things out between us that he would be doing it because he loved me and not because he felt obligated. I also had to be prepared for the fact that I could tell him the truth and he might not want to stick it out with me.

My day at work flew by and it wasn't long before I was walking out the front door to head to school. As I walked to my car, I pulled out my phone. I found Dom's name, tapped on the screen to call him, and waited as it rang. I ended up getting his voicemail.

"Hey Dom, it's me," I began. "Listen, I know we haven't spoken in a while, but I was hoping we could talk. I made a mistake and I just want the chance to apologize to you and explain myself. I don't know what will happen between us once I tell you the truth, but I'm prepared for whatever that is. I guess if you could give me a call when you get this, I'd really appreciate it. I'm leaving work now to go to school, but I was thinking maybe you could either stop over tonight or sometime this weekend so we can talk. I can come to you as well. I know there's that snowstorm coming later tonight, so I promise to be quick about it if you can make it tonight. Please just call me. I really want the chance to explain and I hope you'll be gracious enough to give that to me...even if I really don't deserve that from you right now. I'm sorry for—"

Before I had a chance to finish my sentence, my phone was pulled from my hand and an arm wrapped around my waist. I twisted my neck to look and see who was behind me, but the man's face was covered. The only thing I could see was his familiar eyes.

"George!" I shouted. "What are you doing?"

"He needs to know what it feels like," George seethed as he began pulling me away from my car.

"Who? George, please, let me go!"

I struggled against him, but even for an older man, he was too strong for me. I had no idea what was happening or with whom George was angry. All I knew was that he was not the sweet man that had been one of my regulars at the diner or the man who stopped into the library just to see my pretty face as he put it.

Despite my fight, George got me in the back of his car. I crawled across the seat and tried to get out the opposite side, but the door was locked. He must have put the child safety locks on because I couldn't get it open. Just as I turned my body to crawl up into the front so I could get out that way, I realized I wasn't alone in the car. Another man I didn't know sat in the front seat with a gun pointed at me. I immediately froze.

"Sit back and behave or I'll put a bullet in you," he threatened.

George got in the car and I sat there terrified, realizing that this was, by far, the worst bout of bad luck I'd ever had. Bad luck of epic proportions.

And while it might have been the oddest thing to think

about, all that was running through my mind was that I never got to tell Dom how much I loved him.

Dom

My brain felt so muddled over the last several days, I sometimes didn't know if I was coming or going. For starters, it was one day shy of three weeks since I'd seen or spoken to Ekko in person. I wanted, more than anything, to go after her and fight for us, but I still had no idea what battle I was fighting. Sadly, I couldn't even begin to figure that out either.

The case at work had taken on a life of its own. I still did not have the final piece of the puzzle and I had been spending my days recently trying to narrow down the homeowners. Most of them were either young families or elderly couples. Nothing stood out to me as odd and their names weren't familiar.

I knew that my tolerance for just about anything right now was lacking. Normally, a case like this would bother me, but the unresolved situation with Ekko made it worse.

I missed her so much. As each day passed and I didn't see her face or hear her voice, I became more and more agitated. The guys at work knew what was happening and they did their best not to get in my way. I hated that I'd become that guy and I knew that if something didn't give soon, I was going to lose my mind.

It was approaching the end of the normal business day on Friday and I was still no closer to having any answers. Realizing that I'd been spending countless hours on this case lately, I decided it might be a good idea for me to head out early and take a break from it for a few hours.

I went back to the break room, grabbed a bottle of water, and started walking back to my office to get my phone and my keys when I saw Levi walking toward me with Pierce. Levi was carrying an envelope.

We walked into Levi's office instead as he explained, "I was just about to head out and I found this outside on your truck."

I took the envelope from him and tore it open. When I pulled the final piece of the puzzle out, the back of it was facing me. There was an entire message on that single piece.

Now it's your turn to see what that feels like.

I flipped over the piece and my heart began racing. As I had suspected, my house was in the picture, but that wasn't the problem. This picture was of Ekko and me standing outside next to her car. The picture had to have been taken from sometime between her birthday and Thanksgiving. She had her arms around my waist and was smiling as she looked up at me.

"What does it say?" Pierce asked.

I handed the piece over to him and he read it as Levi looked on.

"The other pieces said, 'You took everything from me' and this says, 'Now it's your turn to see what that feels like.'"

"You've got to make sure she's alright," Levi suggested.

"I've got to go," I stated as I started walking out of his office.

"I saw her today," Pierce chimed in.

I stopped in my tracks and turned toward him. "What?"

He gave me a few nods before he explained, "I was on my way into the office this morning and I saw her walking by the diner. Turns out her battery died on her car and she was planning to walk to the bus stop so she could get to work."

"The bus stop is nearly two miles down the road from the diner!" I declared, even though Levi and Pierce already knew it. "Why wouldn't she call me? Was she okay?"

"Yeah. She was shivering when she first got in my truck, though. I made her sit in the truck to warm up while I took care of her car and jumped the battery."

I closed my eyes and dropped my head, trying to process the information that Pierce had just given me. What was going on with her? Ekko was in trouble and needed help and she never reached out to me. Instead, she risked her safety and thought that walking in below freezing temperatures was a better choice.

"Thank you for taking care of her."

Pierce shook his head and insisted, "It was no problem. Really."

"I've got to go check on her. Until I figure this case out, I'm going to see if I can convince her to move back in with me. Something tells me that it's not going to be easy."

"If you need anything, Dom, just let us know. And if moving into your place isn't an option for her, she's welcome to stay with Elle and me," Levi offered.

"Thanks. Hopefully it won't come to that."

I walked out of Levi's office and back into my own. I grabbed my keys and phone off my desk. The display on my phone lit up when my finger bumped it and I saw that I had a missed call and a voicemail.

Ekko had called me.

For three weeks, I'd been hoping she'd call. The moment she did, I missed it.

I tried to call her right back, but her phone went right to voicemail. She had school today and while it was still too early for class to start, maybe she shut the phone off ahead of time.

I decided not to leave a message. Instead, I went to my

voicemail to listen to the one she left. The second I heard her voice, my heart began racing. I felt alive again. Ekko wanted to get together with me and explain why she ended things. She made it sound like there was a possibility of reconciling. I was so caught up in the first part of her message that I nearly missed out on the second part of it.

"Please just call me. I really want the chance to explain and I hope you'll be gracious enough to give that to me...even if I really don't deserve that from you right now. I'm sorry for...George...What are you doing?"

My body was on alert as I listened to Ekko's voice get farther and farther away. I heard a man, who I assumed must have been George, say, "He needs to know what it feels like."

Then, just barely, I could make out words from her terrified voice.

"Who? George...please. Let me go."

I listened until the message ended and only heard Ekko's screams before the line went dead. I ran out of my office yelling for Pierce and Levi as I took off toward Trent's office. Thankfully, he hadn't left work yet.

"You've got to get me the camera footage for the Windsor Public Library now," I demanded. "Ekko's in trouble."

"What's going on Dom?" Levi asked.

"Someone named George has Ekko," I explained. "She left me a voicemail just a few minutes ago as she was leaving work."

I played the end of the message for them.

They looked at me in horror. "I'll grab De Luca and Locke since they're still here. We'll go through the files and see if we can find someone named George in them," Pierce announced.

"You've got to get that camera footage," I pleaded with Trent.

"I'm close, man. Just a few more seconds."

"Fuck, Levi. What am I going to do if he hurts her?" I asked as I began pacing in Trent's office feeling my rage build.

"She's a fighter, Dom. You know that better than anyone. We'll find her. She's going to be alright."

As I paced the room and waited for Trent to pull up the footage, I thought about Ekko's message. She said she made a mistake. I hoped it meant she wanted to try again. I needed to hear her voice again, so I held the phone to my ear and re-played the message hoping that it wasn't going to be the last time I ever heard her voice.

CHAPTER 24

Dom

"**I**'VE GOT IT," TRENT SHOUTED FROM BEHIND ONE OF HIS computer screens.

I raced over to the other side of his desk and saw it happen. Ekko walked out of the library, pulled out her phone, and called me. She was speaking until he came up behind her, grabbed the phone out of her hand, and pulled her over to his SUV. When he got in the car, he got in on the passenger side, which meant he wasn't working alone.

As much as I wanted to focus on just my girl because I hadn't seen her in so long, I couldn't. She needed me to find her before something even worse happened. Unfortunately, I couldn't stop replaying that scene in my head.

"Can we zoom in on the plate?" Levi asked, though it came out like an order.

Trent zoomed in and got us the full plate number. Then, he pulled up another database on another computer screen. He put the plate number in and instantly pulled up the owner information. The SUV was registered to a man named Johnathan Samuels.

Pierce walked back in the room and stated, "Locke and De Luca are working on pulling up all the cases that have anyone with the name George associated with them. Do we have any additional information? Have you checked out the footage?"

"We have a plate number for the SUV she was taken away in. It's registered to a Johnathan Samuels," Levi shared. "Let's scan our records for that name as well."

Pierce nodded and walked out of the room.

"What about the homes near yours?" Trent asked. "Were any of them owned by a George or even someone with the name Samuels."

I couldn't think. My mind was so consumed with worry for Ekko. I'd never, in all my years as a private investigator, experienced the inability to react and respond in high-stakes situations. Thankfully, Levi and Trent must have realized it because Levi came over to me and ordered, "Sit down."

I sat.

"Breathe and think, Dom. Michaels and I can go through all of the homeowner information you've already researched, but that's going to waste time. We need to get to Ekko, so you need to breathe and focus. Homeowners. George. Johnathan. Samuels. Do any of those names ring a bell?"

I took in two breaths and tried to recall the research. After a few minutes, I blurted, "Samuels. There was a Samuels. William and Maria, though."

"Great. Trent, search the county public records for homeowners on Dom's street. See if you can pull them up," Levi instructed. "Is there anything else you can remember about them, Dom?"

"Fuck," I bit out. "There were so many I went through. Everyone was either elderly couples or young families. I can't remember anything right now, Levi."

"Alright, I'm grabbing your files and giving these names to the boys. Sit tight and just keep breathing, Dom."

Levi walked out, and I sat there with my elbows on my thighs, my hands clasped tight against my forehead. I was trying to think, but all I could remember is the video of Ekko being manhandled and tossed into the SUV. She was a fighter, but she was so small. This guy, George, had already overpowered her. If there was a second guy, perhaps Johnathan Samuels, she'd stand no chance.

"We're going to find her," Trent insisted.

"We have to. This can't be her story. Nothing but constant disappointments. She probably thinks there's nobody looking for her."

Trent continued working at his computer, but retorted, "I'm sure she believes you're doing everything you can to find her."

I stood and began pacing again. "Fuck, Michaels. She thinks I didn't answer the phone on purpose. She actually believes that she doesn't deserve the opportunity to talk to me. Ekko's going to assume the worst in this situation. And if she does, what reason will she have to fight?"

Trent glanced up and looked at me, but had no reply. He understood what I was saying. If someone constantly felt like they were fighting an uphill battle, with very little progress, it was safe to assume that when things got really bad, many people would find it easier to simply give up instead of hope.

He looked back at his screen and said, "William and Maria are a young couple with two children, both boys. William's father is Jonathan Samuels."

"Okay. So how do these people relate to me and how did Ekko know this guy George?"

"I'm not sure, but their house has the perfect view of yours. My guess is that your photo puzzle picture was taken from inside that house."

At that moment, Levi walked back in with Pierce, Holden, and Lorenzo. The looks on their faces were enough to tell me they had figured it out.

And whatever it was that they figured out, one thing was for sure.

It wasn't good.

"What?" I asked as I braced myself for the worst news possible.

Pierce spoke two words. "Jennifer Samuels."

When I stood there struggling to make a connection, Lorenzo helped me out by clarifying, "Jenny Sam."

It instantly clicked, and my blood went cold.

Ekko

"You look so much like her."

I had no idea what was happening. I sat in the back of an SUV while we drove for what felt like hours. The clock on the dash indicated; however, that it had only been just over one. The biggest reason for the long drive was that we were driving slow because of the storm. It had started snowing and the roads were already covered with at least half an inch of snow. During the drive, I decided it was in my best interests to remain quiet. One man, who I now knew was called John, had a gun. He didn't seem to be even remotely bothered by using it, so I wasn't going to do anything to make it worse for myself. I needed to be smart.

It was dark outside, making it difficult to see exactly where we were, but I did my best to try and remember my surroundings. The only problem with this was that we reached a point where there was nothing to see. I had been taken deep into the woods up a mountain to a small cabin. I began to worry that even if I managed to get away from John and George, I'd have nowhere to go. Between the remote location and the storm, my options were limited.

We arrived at the cabin and I was ushered out of the car and inside.

There was almost nothing inside and the place wasn't much warmer inside than it was outside. I found myself longing to be back in the car, if only for the warmth.

"Who?" I asked.

"Jenny," he stated nonchalantly as though I knew who she was. "I'll never forget the first time I saw you at the diner. It was like I was seeing her."

"Who's Jenny?" I pressed. I figured it was better for me if I kept him talking.

"She *was* my daughter," George seethed as he stepped closer to me.

"George!" John called.

George stopped advancing and took a minute to collect himself. Once he calmed himself down, he looked at me with the slightest hint of remorse in his face. "I could have been content with just visiting you at the diner and then at the library. It didn't have to come to this."

"Why am I here, George? Is it because I look like Jenny?"

He shook his head. "He was going to take you away, too. I couldn't let him do that."

"Who?"

"Your boyfriend," he answered. "He's responsible for the death of my daughter."

I gasped.

Dom killed George's daughter?

"And now he needs to know what it feels like when the person you love is taken away from you," George went on.

Maybe my break up with Dom would help me out of this situation. "George, I'm no longer with Dom. We haven't been together for the last three weeks."

George was surprised by this news. "He left you?"

I shook my head and answered, "No. I left him."

"Why?"

I didn't know why I was telling him any of this. I couldn't even understand my own mental strength at the moment. I'd been used to being in bad situations, but this was another level of crazy. It was like something else had taken over inside me. In a way, I guess I believed that if George was talking to me, he couldn't hurt me.

"It just wasn't going to work out between us. I didn't want to prolong the inevitable."

"So the breakup wasn't his idea?" George confirmed.

I shook my head.

"Does he want to be with you?"

"Yes."

George's expression changed. He was grinning, but it wasn't one that made me feel good. That look on his face changed everything and made an already bad predicament feel far worse. "That wasn't the correct answer, Ekko. If he still wants to be with you, then he's got something to lose. I need to make sure he knows what that feels like."

Damn it.

I didn't know how I was going to get myself out of this.

Unfortunately, it didn't matter because George looked to John and advised, "It's getting worse out there. We should head down and get what we need before the roads become impassable."

John moved to the door and George followed. I started following behind them, thinking if they were going somewhere to get whatever they needed, I'd be exposed to people. As was my luck, though, George made it to the door, turned around, and explained, "You'll be staying here. We'll be back to deal with you."

He pulled the door closed before I could get through. I heard them doing something with the lock and, despite trying with all my might, couldn't get the door opened. They'd locked me in from the outside.

Turning around, I scanned the cabin. There was a couch, a small table with a couple chairs, a few cabinets on the wall, and a fireplace on the far wall opposite the door. There were no windows and only two small kerosene lamps lit the space. There was one door on the other side of the space. I walked to the door and found it was a small bathroom. It wasn't the nicest, but I wasn't exactly in a position to be picky.

After taking care of business, I decided I needed a plan. I had no idea how long I'd be there by myself, but I knew that I'd be ready whenever George and John got back. The fireplace had several large logs in it. I walked over and found one that was large enough to do some damage, but small enough for me to handle. I figured with the element of surprise, I could take at least one of them out. If I was lucky, which was almost never the case for me, I'd be able to disorient both of them long enough to get in the car and get down the mountain.

With the log by my side, I walked over to the cabinets hoping to find something to start a fire with. The cold had already settled around me. Thankfully, I had my jacket on still, but without any heat in this place, I couldn't imagine anyone would survive very long. Opening the cabinets, I found they were mostly bare. One cabinet had a container of pretzels in it.

I was hungry and prepared for attack when George and John returned, so I pulled a handful of pretzels out and ate.

If I were anyone else, I might have gone stir crazy. The silver lining of all those years of neglect from my mother was now evident. I could stand to be by myself with virtually nothing and I wouldn't lose my mind. It was easy, and almost relaxing, for me to be alone with my thoughts. So I sat there, eating pretzels, and listened for the sound of the SUV climbing back up the mountain. As I did that, I allowed my thoughts to drift to Dom and distracted myself from the fact that my entire body was shivering and I was exhausted.

I had no idea how long it had been when I finally heard the car outside, but I knew it had to have been at least two hours. I stood behind the door with the log in my hand, ready to attack.

Their voices were just outside the door and the sound of someone fumbling with the lock told me I only had a few more seconds left.

The door opened, and John walked in first. He never saw me as I swung the log at his head with all my might. Just as I had hoped, he dropped to the ground. I pulled back and tried to swing again at George, but he reached out and knocked the log out of my hands. I went after it, but he came after me. Losing my footing as he grabbed me, I fell on my side, my shoulder taking the brunt of the fall. I rolled to my back, pulled my legs back, and kicked George. He stumbled backward, knocking over and breaking the kerosene lamp.

With George down, I ignored the pain in my shoulder and used my good arm to push myself up off the floor. I needed to get out of the cabin and into that car.

Unfortunately, John's body was blocking the door and I still had to pass George. I managed to get by George and just as I was about to step over John, my body was jerked backward. George had grabbed me by the collar of my jacket and spun me around, sending me flying across the room.

"You lied!" he roared. "We got a call from John's son that your so-called ex-boyfriend and a bunch of his friends showed up at his house."

I gasped.

Dom was looking for me.

He knew I was in trouble.

I choked back a sob.

George advanced on me, backing me up toward the far wall.

"So now there's been a change of plans. I know he's going to find you here. Unfortunately for you, by the time he gets here all he'll know is that you died a slow, painful death. Your suffering will end relatively quickly. His will go on…just like mine has for the last seven years."

After speaking those words, George backhanded me so hard my head flew back and hit the wall. I fell to the floor instantly. I was so disoriented, but I knew I couldn't close my eyes and sleep. I had to get out before it was too late. Every time I tried to open my eyes or lift my head, I was dizzy.

Breathe, Ekko. Just breathe. Dom is coming for you. Just breathe and get out.

Slowly, and using the wall for support, I rose to a seated position. I gradually opened my eyes. John was no longer in the doorway and the smell of kerosene was overpowering the cabin. I realized why as soon as the flash caught my attention from the side of the room. Not even a second later, George ran out of the cabin.

Fire.

I was not going to burn.

As quickly as I could, I stood. I took about two seconds to make sure I was steady on my feet and I ran to the door.

Relief swept through me as I yanked on the handle and the door opened. The SUV was nowhere in sight, and I couldn't see much of anything. I just knew I needed to head down the mountain, so I started walking.

The snow was falling so hard and the wind was whipping

around me. After pulling my hood up to cover my head, I slid my scarf up to cover my mouth and nose. My eyes and forehead were the only exposed parts of my body after I shoved my ungloved hands in my pockets.

Since the mountain was so steep, the descent down the mountain was done at a fast pace. I wasn't trying to run, but momentum was carrying me quickly. I trudged on, pushing myself to keep going. I didn't know if I'd make it, but I knew I had to try.

Life couldn't be this cruel. I'd been kidnapped and nearly burned alive, but I fought back to save myself as I'd done throughout my whole life. Surviving this trek down the mountain would just be one more thing I'd need to conquer.

CHAPTER 25

Dom

JUST OVER FIVE HOURS HAD PASSED SINCE EKKO WAS TAKEN. I had never felt more helpless in my entire life.

After the guys told me how this case was connected to me, my stomach sank. Jennifer Samuels died tragically in the crossfire of a drug bust. She got involved with the wrong people, got hooked on drugs, moved in with her boyfriend who was a dealer, and ultimately paid the price. George was her father; Johnathan was her uncle.

The guys and I made calls to the rest of the Cunningham Security team members and they paid a visit to the home George and Johnathan shared. There were no signs of them and no indication that they'd even been there. While the residence the brothers shared was being checked out, I hopped in my truck with Trent and Pierce as Levi followed behind me with Lorenzo and Holden. We left the office and made the trip to William's house. William was Johnathan's son and the second he saw us, it was evident that he already knew why we were stopping by. Even still, his loyalty remained with his father and he played stupid.

My only concern was getting Ekko safe, so the second the guys noticed me getting agitated, they took over the situation. Trent worked from the road searching for any properties that any member of the Samuels family owned. Realizing we weren't going to get anywhere, I stormed off toward the truck, frustrated. Halfway between the house and the truck, Trent put his window down and yelled, "Let's go boys. I think I've found them!"

I took off running and the guys were right behind me. We piled in the trucks as Trent entered the location into the GPS.

"Where are we headed?" I asked as we started driving.

"There's a piece of property forty-seven miles from here. It's a ton of acreage. There isn't a house on the property, but there is a small cabin pretty high up on the mountain," Trent explained.

"Are you sure this is it?"

"No, but we've got nothing else yet. I'll keep searching."

While Pierce called one of the guys in Levi's truck to update them, I pushed the pedal to the floor and drove much faster than was reasonable or safe considering the state of the roads in the storm. I didn't care, though. I needed to find her.

When we finally got off the exit that put us on the road ten miles from where the cabin was supposed to be located, I saw them.

"That's them. That's the SUV they took her in," I shouted.

I made a U-turn and followed them. Glancing up in my rearview, I saw that Levi was right behind us. I sped up. There was no way I was letting that vehicle out of my sight.

Once we were close, whoever was driving the car must have realized that we were behind them and drove faster.

"Careful, Dom," Pierce warned. "If they lose control with her in that car…"

He'd just barely gotten those words out when the SUV skidded and began fishtailing from one side of the road to the other. I backed off, hoping that would help them regain control of the vehicle. If Ekko got hurt, I'd never forgive myself.

Unfortunately, a gust of wind unsettled the car even further and it rolled, sending it careening across the road and down the embankment. I threw my truck into park, hopped out, and raced across the two-lane road.

Levi pulled his truck up to where the SUV came to a stop and kept the lights on so we could see. I was the first one at the car and I yanked open the back door.

It was empty.

Moving to the front passenger's side door, I pulled it open and found that two men were in the front. The passenger was out cold. The driver groaned. I ran around to the other side, yanked open his door, grabbed him by his collar, and yelled, "Where is she?!"

The expression on his face changed. It was unnerving. Then he said only one word.

"Burning."

My eyes darted back and forth trying to understand what he meant. "Is she in the cabin still?"

"You'll be too late," he goaded me.

"Go, Dom," Levi ordered. "I'll deal with him and get the fire department and ambulance on the way. The rest of the guys are behind us."

I yanked him out of the car and didn't wait to see him fall to the ground. Pierce, Trent, and I took off running back to my truck.

We hopped in and I was swinging the truck around before I even had the door closed. I drove as fast as I could down the road in the opposite direction hoping I would make it to her on time.

"Shit," Trent muttered after we'd been driving for a few minutes.

I glanced to the side and asked, "What?"

He pointed out the windshield and said, "Up there."

Flames had lit up a patch at the top of the mountain. He lit the cabin on fire with her inside. She was burning as I watched.

"I'm going to be fucking sick," I warned them, driving faster.

"Breathe, brother," Pierce encouraged me as Trent opened the windows.

I did my best to breathe through the awful churning in my gut.

"The satellite image shows there's an opening in the tree line just another half mile ahead. It's a clear shot all the way up to the cabin."

I took in another breath and blew it out.

I'm coming, Ekko. Please hang on.

I turned off the main road and my truck slowly started climbing the hill. The snow had gotten so heavy and the hill was steep. It took some time, but we finally made it to the top about a hundred feet from the cabin. I jumped out and took off running.

"Dom!" I heard one of the guys yell out.

But I didn't stop. I was going to get to her and I didn't care if I was going to have to go through the fire to save her.

Pierce was right behind me and, as we got closer, we realized just how much of the structure had been burned. We could see right through most of the walls on one side and the smell of kerosene was overwhelming. I moved to one of the adjoining walls that was compromised, but not completely engulfed. I blasted the wood with the bottom of my foot and watched the wall crumble. Then, I ran inside to find Ekko.

Desperately searching the small space, I didn't see her anywhere.

"She's not in there!" I yelled when I moved back through the opening where I'd kicked down the wall.

"Dom!" Trent called from about halfway between the truck and the cabin.

When we looked at him, he held up the flashlights and said, "There are tracks in the snow here. We've got to move quickly before they get covered."

She got out. My fighter got out.

Pierce and I raced back to where Trent was standing and the three of us took off down the mountain on foot.

"Ekko!" I yelled out, even though my lungs were burning.

I was running as fast as I could without disturbing the footprints.

The guys and I continued to yell out her name and listen for a reply, but we got nothing. The footprints continued. I was thankful for them because seeing them meant that she was still alive.

"Ekko!"

Silence.

"Ekko!"

More silence.

"Dom, look," Trent said, pointing his flashlight away from me. "Just ahead, two o'clock."

I followed the light and saw it. Ekko's body was lifeless on the ground, her purple jacket standing out against the freshly fallen, white snow.

"Ekko!" I called as I ran toward her.

Seconds later, I knelt beside her, rolled her over, and moved the hair from her face. "Ekko, sugar, open your eyes," I pleaded with her as I put my hands to her neck to find her pulse. It was there, but it was weak. Her face and her hands were ice cold and her clothes were sopping.

The guys came over to help assess her. "We've got to get her to a hospital," I stated. The dread in my tone was clear.

Suddenly, we saw the lights.

"Levi's here," Pierce announced. I stood with Ekko in my arms and began moving toward the path. The guys followed behind me, lighting the way with the flashlights as they pushed back the tree branches.

We finally reached the clear path where Levi's truck was waiting, and Trent opened the back door. I climbed in the back with Lorenzo. Levi took one look at her and immediately began backing down the mountain. "There are a couple of blankets behind the seat," he noted as he kept his eyes focused on the road behind us.

Just as he made it to the road, the fire trucks arrived. There was no ambulance in sight. Lorenzo pulled the blankets out from behind the seat.

"De Luca, I need your help," I said. "We've got to take this wet stuff off her before we wrap her in that."

"You've got it," he replied as he started taking the shoes off her feet.

While he did that, I took my jacket off and started working on hers. I got it off and unwrapped the soaked scarf from around her neck.

"You want me to take off her pants?" Lorenzo asked.

I didn't, but we had no choice. "Do it," I ordered through gritted teeth.

As he struggled to remove her pants that were stuck to her legs, I got rid of her top. Once we'd removed everything and Ekko was there in just her bra and panties, I took off my sweatshirt and slipped it over her head before Lorenzo helped me wrap her up in the blankets.

Then, I held her tight to my body with my lips pressed to her freezing forehead.

Ten minutes into the drive to the hospital, Ekko moaned.

"Are you with me, Ekko? Can you open your eyes?" I asked as I ran my fingers through her hair.

"Sleep," she rasped.

"Okay, sugar. Keep your eyes closed, but talk to me."

"You found me," she whispered.

My throat tightened. Did she think I would ever stop looking for her?

"I did," I replied.

"I saw your truck..." She trailed off. She paused and took a few more breaths before she finished, "That's when I knew I could rest...I knew you'd find me."

She began squirming in my arms, attempting to remove the blanket. "You need to keep the blanket on. You aren't warm enough yet."

"Shoulder," she replied.

"What's wrong with your shoulder? Did you hurt yourself?"

She shook her head. "Fight."

"Did he hurt you?"

Her lips trembled, but she nodded.

My eyes cut to Lorenzo's. The look on his face, I'm certain, mirrored my own.

I readjusted her in my arms, careful not to jostle her too much.

"Is that better?" I asked.

She nodded.

A few minutes of silence passed. I sat there and simply watched Ekko as she slept and took short, slow breaths.

"I love you, Dom," she whispered. My body tensed at her admission. I thought she had fallen asleep because she remained quiet for so long afterward. Suddenly, she spoke again. "I can't give you babies, but I'll love you forever."

What?

"Ekko, sugar, what are you talking about?"

She didn't respond.

A few minutes later, we arrived at the hospital. I rushed her inside and then it was a whirlwind of events as the medical professionals took over all around me until one of the nurses ushered me out to the waiting room. The guys stayed with me while I waited for news.

Some time had passed, and I needed to distract myself, so I asked, "What happened with George and Johnathan?"

"We waited for the police to arrive," Levi began. "I gave them a quick rundown of what happened and told them I'd follow up with Detective Baines. Once they had the Samuels brothers covered, we hopped in the truck and came down to help you."

Great.

No distraction there.

I stood and paced the waiting room. Finally, I leaned up against the wall crossing my arms over my chest and my feet at my ankles.

I can't give you babies, but I'll love you forever.

Was that what she wanted to explain to me? Or had some mild delirium set in from her being in the cold for too long?

I thought back to the conversation Ekko and I had the day she told me she wanted to end things.

You deserve so much more than I can give you. You deserve someone who can give you everything you want.

The context certainly fit if that's what she was referring to. But Ekko and I had talked about having children sometime in the future and that didn't scare her off. Why, suddenly, would it have changed?

I had a million questions I wanted to ask her, but my first concern was making sure that she was okay and that she didn't suffer any permanent or serious damage from everything she'd been through over the last several hours.

Finally, after what felt like an eternity, the door to the

waiting room opened. I saw the doctor walk in. I walked over, and she asked, "Are you Ekko's family?"

"She's my girlfriend."

"I'm sorry, but I'll need to contact her family first before giving any medical information."

"She doesn't have any," I stated, deadpanned and frustrated. "I'm the closest thing to family she's got."

"Sir, I'm sorry, but I'll have to wait until Miss Rose wakes up and tells me that then. I can only release information about her to her family."

"*When* she wakes up?" I repeated her words. "All I need to know right now is that she's going to wake up again. We can deal with everything else later. Can I see her?"

The doctor hesitated a moment before she agreed, "Sure. Follow me."

I looked back at the guys who gave me encouraging looks. "We'll wait here," Lorenzo said.

I gave them a curt nod and followed the doctor to Ekko's room.

"I'll be back to check on her in a little while," the doctor said before excusing herself and leaving me alone with my beautiful girl.

Walking farther into the room, I made my way over to the bed. Ekko was completely covered in warm blankets. She was being administered oxygen and IV fluids. Otherwise, she looked as though she was just sleeping.

Leaning over her, I pressed my lips to her forehead. She was warm. I kissed her cheek before grabbing a chair and sliding it over next to the bed. After settling myself in the seat, I slipped my hand under the blankets and held hers.

Then, I watched her while she slept.

The next thing I knew, I was being woken up by Ekko's thumb stroking back and forth over my knuckles. I lifted my head and realized it was early morning. At some point, I must have fallen asleep.

I looked over at Ekko to see she was awake. She gave me a small smile and murmured, "Hey."

That one word from her smiling, happy face was all it took. My emotions got the best of me and I dropped my head a minute, trying to rein them in. As I took a few deep breaths, she promised, "I'm okay now, Dom."

I stood up, framed her face with my hands, and kissed her. When I pulled back to look at her, I lamented, "I'm sorry, Ekko. I've never been so scared before in all my life."

"Me too," she whispered.

"I'm so sorry this happened," I apologized again. "I had been working on the case for weeks, but I never thought it was going to come back to you. I swear I had no idea."

"George said you were responsible for his daughter's death."

"I didn't kill her, Ekko. I was undercover and part of the team that went in on a drug bust. It resulted in a shootout and she was caught in the crossfire. I'm not proud to admit that she died, but I didn't kill her."

Her face softened. "I never thought that you did."

We stared at each other in silence for a bit before I asked, "Can I ask you a question?"

"Sure."

"Last night, after we found you and I got you in the truck, you said something to me."

"Okay?"

"Ekko, you told me for the first time that you loved me," I started. Her eyes immediately rounded in surprise, but I went on, "You then told me that you couldn't give me babies."

Surprise turned to shock, which ultimately turned to disappointment. Tears spilled over and fell down her cheeks. I wiped them away and whispered, "Whatever it is, Ekko, we'll deal with it together. Just tell me."

"I went to the gynecologist for a checkup a few days before you came by my house when I ended things between us. I explained all of my symptoms. After she did an exam, she told me that I have endometriosis."

I had no idea what it was, but I didn't like the sound of it. "What does that mean?"

"Tissue similar to what grows inside a woman's uterus is actually found outside my uterus. There's more to it, but ultimately, it means I'll experience painful, heavy periods, fatigue, and possibly a bunch of other awful symptoms. The worst of them, though, is that it can lead to infertility. The doctor told me that it's not impossible to get pregnant, but that it can be very difficult."

"Okay? So, I don't understand why you broke things off?"

"You want children, Dom," she retorted.

"So do you," I challenged.

"Yeah, but my years of bad luck is an indication to me that I need to be realistic here. I can't expect you to give up your dream of having a big family when I may struggle to give you one."

My heart broke for her. It broke for the fact that she believed she wasn't enough. "I love you, sugar. You. Kids or no kids, I love you. And if we get to a point where we are ready for kids and it doesn't happen naturally for us, there are other ways for us to still be parents."

Her lips parted. "Really?"

"Of course. You walked away from us because your doctor told you it *could* be difficult for you to have babies?"

Ekko's eyes filled with tears again. "I want you to have everything. I don't want to ruin the dreams you have for your future."

"What have I told you about your future?" I asked.

"Mine? You tell me to keep my head up and my eyes pointed forward."

"Why?"

"Because if I do that and stay focused on what's in front of me, that's how I'll find my future."

I grinned at her and dug deeper. "Do you know what I've been telling myself about finding my future lately?"

She shook her head.

"To keep my eyes on you." My voice was low. "You're my future, Ekko. No matter what that brings, I'll be happy as long as I've got you."

After a few seconds of silence, she rasped, "You can kiss me now."

I gave her the biggest smile before I leaned in and pressed a kiss to her lips. What started as an innocent, gentle kiss quickly turned into something more until we were interrupted by a familiar voice declaring, "Well, that's one way to warm up."

I pulled back from Ekko and we both turned our attention to the door.

"Hi, Kendall," Ekko greeted her.

"You've got some color back in your cheeks since I first saw you this morning," Kendall remarked. "I came in to check your vitals and you were both out of it." Kendall's eyes cut to mine. "If I wasn't so happy for you right now, I'd be pissed at you."

"Why?"

"I work here, and you never called to tell me that Ekko was brought in last night. You know I would have been here for you and for her."

She would have; I had no doubts about that. "It was the middle of the night and I knew you'd be in early this morning. I didn't want to wake you."

"Don't ever do that again," she scolded me before turning her attention back to Ekko. "How are you feeling?"

"Tired," Ekko replied.

"That's to be expected given everything you went through last night."

"When can I go home?"

Kendall's expression was contemplative. "Unfortunately, that's not my call to make. I'm just here to draw blood. The doctor wants to have another round done so she can compare the results to the ones from when you came in. As long as no major organs are in jeopardy, she'll probably have you out of here in no time."

Ekko held out her arm and croaked, "Okay, let's get this over with then."

"I'm good with a needle, babe. I promise to be gentle," Kendall said softly as she began working at Ekko's arm. Then, she looked at me and ordered, "Hold her other hand and say nice things to make her feel better."

Ekko didn't wait for me. She gave me her hand and leaned her head back on the pillow. "You heard the lady," she teased. "Say nice things to me."

"I love you."

She was beaming when she proclaimed, "I love you, too."

I didn't care that Kendall was there. Ekko told me she loved me. I leaned in and kissed her again.

"Done!" Kendall boomed.

Ekko and I turned our heads toward my sister. She held up the tubes of blood and reminded us, "I told you I was good with a needle."

"You aren't kidding. I didn't feel a thing."

Kendall winked at her. "You did. It just wasn't this," she explained as she held up the syringe.

"Yeah. You're right," Ekko agreed. "Can I use the

bathroom? I've got to pee so bad."

"Yep. Just be careful getting in and out of bed. I'll unplug your IV from the wall, but make sure Dom plugs it back in once you're settled in the bed again."

"I will."

"I would help you myself, but I know he's not going to let me."

"Go, Kendall," I demanded. "I've got her."

At that, Kendall walked out. I helped Ekko out of bed and to the bathroom. When she finished, I helped her back to the bed and plugged in her IV. She scooted to one side of the bed and said, "Climb in."

"I'm too big for the bed."

"I miss you, baby. Please?"

Nope. I wasn't going to win this battle. I shook my head, bent down to remove my shoes, and climbed into the bed next to her. Careful of her IV, I pulled her close to me. She settled right in and, for the first time in weeks, I finally felt at peace.

CHAPTER 26

Ekko

I F I HADN'T SPENT MOST OF MY LIFE FIGHTING FOR MYSELF, I wasn't sure I'd currently be in a hospital bed curled up in the arms of the man I was madly in love with.

With the incessant bad luck and one negative blow after another, it would have been easy and understandable for me to just give up.

But I didn't.

And now I was here.

I was also realizing just how foolish I had been over the last few weeks. I never imagined nor expected that the moment I told Dom the truth behind why I pulled away from him that he'd prove to me that I was the only thing that mattered to him.

But he did.

And now we were together again.

I ran down that mountain last night to save my life. When I saw Dom's truck pull off the road and up the hill, I succumbed to the exhaustion. I don't remember much of what happened once I collapsed on the ground other than telling myself that if I made it out of that situation alive, I'd never waste another precious moment. I vowed to myself that I'd live my life to the fullest, doing what made me happy, and I wouldn't apologize for it.

I had been in some pretty bad situations throughout my life, but none that made me fear for my life. Not until last night. And an experience like that makes you reconsider how you'll live that life moving forward if you survive.

I was no longer going to focus on the bad things in my life. Instead, last night taught me that I needed to be grateful for what I had and proud of what I'd achieved. Just because I didn't reach some milestone that I believed I should have already accomplished by a certain point in my life didn't mean that I was unworthy. It only meant that I had more obstacles to overcome to get there. For that, I was just going to be stronger in the end.

There was a whole slew of questions that still needed answers, like what exactly was going to happen with John and George, but I didn't want to focus on any of that today. Nope. I knew they had been taken into custody and that was enough for me for the time being. My goal for today was to celebrate the fact that I was alive and in love.

Dom and I had both fallen asleep after Kendall left my room. I woke up a few minutes ago, but he hadn't budged.

"Dom?" I called gently.

He slowly opened his eyes and took me in while I admired his dimples. Before we had an opportunity to say a word to each other, the door to my room swung open. Kendall and three other hospital personnel came in, with one of them pushing a cart with a piece of medical equipment on it.

"What's going on?" Dom asked as he sat up in the bed.

"Your blood work came back, Ekko," Kendall stated.

Oh no. Here is where I'd get the bad news.

"We should speak privately," the doctor suggested, her eyes sliding to the side toward Dom.

Shaking my head, I declined. "No. I want him here. Please

just tell me what it is."

She nodded her understanding. "Please accept my apologies, Miss Rose. I hadn't noticed on the report that came back after your first round of bloodwork, but I noticed it on this second round."

I swallowed hard and tried to prepare myself.

"Your HCG levels were elevated on the original blood work we took when you came in and they're even higher now."

I shook my head, not understanding. "I'm sorry. My what is high?"

Kendall cut in. "Your HCG. It's the pregnancy hormone!"

I blinked in surprise. "I...what?"

"It would seem, Miss Rose, that you're pregnant."

My head snapped to Dom. He was in just as much shock as I was. "What? That's not possible. I was at the gynecologist a couple weeks ago and she told me I had endometriosis."

The doctor shrugged her shoulders and explained, "That doesn't mean you can't get pregnant."

"Are you serious? Am I really pregnant?"

Kendall and the doctor both nodded at me before she continued, "We've brought up the ultrasound machine. I've got an obstetrician on the way here, but we don't want to delay in getting an ultrasound done considering what you went through last night."

I couldn't believe what I was hearing. Mild hypothermia didn't kill me, but I was certain the shock of hearing the doctor tell me I was pregnant would.

"Ekko?" Kendall interrupted my ridiculous thoughts.

"Hm?"

"The levels indicate you'd be early in this pregnancy. We'd be doing a transvaginal ultrasound as a result. It's an internal exam. Are you alright with that?"

"Three weeks," I blurted.

"What?"

"Three weeks ago, today. That's when it happened. Am I three weeks pregnant?"

Kendall let out a laugh and answered, "That was really too much information for me considering my brother is standing in the room, but no, you wouldn't be three weeks. If you're saying you conceived three weeks ago, then you'd be five weeks pregnant now."

I sat up straighter. In a matter of seconds, my life had completely changed.

"Ekko?"

I looked up at Dom.

"The ultrasound. Are you up for it?"

I didn't take my eyes off him as I nodded. The next few minutes passed with Kendall and the ultrasound technician positioning and preparing me for the ultrasound. As Dom held my hand, the wand was inserted, and a fuzzy black and white image popped up on the computer screen. The technician gently moved the wand until two black circles were showing.

"Oh my god," Kendall cried.

"What?" I worried. "Is something wrong?"

Her tear-filled eyes came to meet mine. She held them a moment before she looked to Dom.

"Kendall, what's wrong?" Dom demanded an answer.

"You're having twins," she cried.

I turned my head to the side and repeated Kendall's words to Dom. "We're having twins."

I couldn't read the look on Dom's face. It seemed like a whole bunch of emotions all rolled into one. Shock. Contentment. Worry. Bliss.

"Do you see this?" the technician asked.

Dom and I turned our attention back to the screen where

the technician was pointing.

"This fluttering you see here is your baby's heartbeat."

Dom's hand squeezed mine as the tears leaked from my eyes. I couldn't find any words, but the man beside me did. His voice was filled with emotion when he asked, "Is the second baby okay?"

A moment of silence passed before Kendall pointed at the fluttering and said, "There it is."

The grip Dom had on my hand grew tighter and he let out an audible breath. My feelings were all over the place.

The technician printed out a few sonograms. She kept a few for the obstetrician but gave three of them to us.

After she left, Kendall walked over to Dom and hugged him. "Congratulations."

He didn't respond. His silence worried me.

She leaned over the side of the bed to give me a hug and congratulate me next. Before she walked out the door, Dom called out to her.

"Kendall?"

She turned around and waited for him to speak.

"Thanks for being here."

She smiled at him. "I wouldn't have wanted to miss this for anything else in the world. I'm so happy for you."

"I'm sure this goes without saying, but can you be discreet until Ekko and I have a chance to absorb this?"

Kendall brought her thumb and forefinger up to her mouth, where she made a motion of zipping her lips, locking them, and throwing away the key before she walked out of the room.

Once we were alone, I turned my attention to Dom.

"Two babies," he whispered.

"Two babies," I repeated.

"How do you feel about this?" he asked.

"I'm happy, Dom. I'm so happy about it and I really hope you feel the same."

Both of his hands were still holding one of mine. His lips were pressed against my knuckles as he looked at me. Finally, he spoke. "You are the most incredible woman I've ever known," he began. "From the day I met you, you've proven to me just how strong you are. Working hard, going after what you want, you always find a way to persevere. The depth of your strength was made clear to me when you told me why you pulled away from me. You were willing to give me up so that I could have children. I'd like to think that there's no greater sacrifice you could ever make than that, but I know I'm wrong. You fought for your life last night and you did it while keeping our babies safe inside you. I'm convinced there isn't anything you can't do."

"Baby," I wept.

Dom climbed back in the bed with me, carefully positioning himself next to me. He gently placed his hand on my belly. "I love you, Ekko. And I already love these two babies more than my whole life, so I hope that dispels any fears you have about whether I'm happy about this."

"I love you too, Dom," I said softly.

We stayed like that for a long time, the weight of our new situation settling around us.

A few hours later, after the obstetrician came in to check me out, Dom questioned me about my shoulder, which ultimately ended in him demanding that it get check out. Lastly, the final results of my bloodwork proved that I was no longer in any danger from the hypothermia, so I was allowed to go home.

Thankfully, the Cunningham Security team made sure Dom's truck was brought to the hospital. Apparently, they'd also arranged to have my car picked up from the library, but the battery was dead again. Dom told them to have it taken to a shop owned by Lexi's brother, Logan Townsend. At some point before we left the hospital, one of the guys dropped off my purse and keys so I'd be able to get into my apartment.

When we left, Dom drove us straight to my place. The moment I stepped through the front door, I let out a sigh of relief. I could feel Dom's body right behind mine, so I leaned back into him. He wrapped his arms around me and kissed the top of my head.

"I really want a shower," I sighed.

"I'm fine with waiting for you to do that, but if you can wait a little longer, you can take a shower back at our place."

"Our place?" I asked, tilting my head back to look up at him.

He nodded. "Yes, our place. Formerly known as my place. I want you to move in with me, Ekko."

"What?"

Dom turned me in his arms so we were standing front to front. "Do you want to be with me?"

"Yes."

He smiled. "After everything we've been through the last few weeks, especially over the last twenty-four hours or so, I don't want to be without you. And you're pregnant with our babies right now. I don't want to miss a moment of your pregnancy. I'd say we could stay here, but this place won't be big enough come October."

When he put it like that, I knew there was no way I was going to turn down his invitation. Even still, I said, "I just moved into this place, Dom."

"I don't care. If you want to hang on to it for a while just to be sure, you can do that. But I think it's ridiculous to pay for a place where you'll never be coming back to live."

"What if things don't work out with us?" I worried.

"Ekko."

He said nothing else, so I shot back, "Dom."

"Things are going to work out between us, sugar."

"Something bad could happen and they might not," I retorted.

He took in a deep breath and let it out before he pointed out, "You and I barely knew each other when I found you sleeping in your car at the library. I refused to let you live like that then. Do you really think I'd kick the mother of my children, whether while you're pregnant or not, out on the street with no place to go?"

The mother of my children.

I grinned at him. "I'm going to be a mother."

"Yep."

"And you're going to be a daddy."

Something changed in his face. He gave me a gentle squeeze as he pulled me closer to him. "Yeah, I am."

I gave him a minute to process those thoughts before I agreed, "Okay, we can pack some of my things up before we go to your house for a shower."

"Our house," he corrected me.

"Our house," I repeated.

The instant the words were out of my mouth, Dom moved us down the hall to my bedroom, where he insisted I sit down to relax while he took orders from me about what items I wanted to bring. I tried to do it myself, but he refused to let me help.

Dom worked quickly and the next thing I knew, we were on our way to his place.

Our place.

I knew that was going to take some getting used to.

When we arrived, he ordered me inside while he brought in all of my things. I immediately climbed the stairs and walked into the master bathroom to start the shower. Once the water had warmed up, I stripped out of the scrubs Kendall loaned me and got in.

I hadn't been in the shower more than two or three minutes when the bathroom door opened. Dom walked in with my toiletries.

"I'll head downstairs and make you something to eat," he offered after setting my bag down on the sink.

I looked out and reached for him. I held on to his forearm. "Stay with me," I suggested.

He wrestled with it for not more than a few seconds before he pulled his shirt off and dropped his pants. After he got in, I walked toward him, pressed my cheek to his chest, and wrapped my arms around his waist. I hadn't felt his skin against mine in so long and I had truly missed the feel of him.

Dom held me in his arms, one of his hands running through my hair.

"I'm sorry for pushing you away," I lamented.

His hand moved to my neck and he ran his knuckles along my jaw. "It's done now. We've moved on from that."

"I know, but it was wrong for me to not give you the chance to make a choice about what you wanted," I pushed. "I just thought that if I told you about the endo, you'd stay with me out of obligation. I didn't want to take away your chances of becoming a father to a large family."

The arm around my waist gave me a squeeze. "I understand why you did it, Ekko. It's the most selfless thing anyone has ever done for me. Lucky for the both of us, your diagnosis didn't hinder your ability to get pregnant. And if it does down the road when we're ready for more, we'll deal with it together."

I tilted my head back and looked up at him. "Kiss me, baby."

Dom gave me what I asked for. His kiss was soft and gentle as my hands ran up his abdomen and over his chest. His fingers were tickling the small of my back while his other hand had a solid grip on my hair. In between kisses, he whispered, "Missed you so much."

"Mmm," I agreed as our tongues collided.

Dom was hard between us and I couldn't help but to wrap my hand around him and stroke him.

He groaned in response. I loved hearing it.

His hands moved to the sides of my head before he tore his mouth from mine.

"Slow down, sugar," he warned. "We're not doing this in here."

I whimpered, and he chuckled against my mouth.

"Let's finish in here and get you fed. Then, we'll have the rest of the night to do whatever you want. I promise."

My shoulders slumped. I was in such disbelief that he had such restraint. "What's for dinner?" I asked.

He grinned. "We'll do something quick and easy."

I immediately picked up the bottle of shampoo and got to work on finishing my shower. Dom did the same.

Not quite an hour later, we'd finished eating our quick-and-easy dinner.

Dom stayed true to his promise by carrying me upstairs immediately afterward and giving me what I wanted. It was unlike any other time we had been together. He was slow and gentle. He whispered sweet words against my lips and my belly. Somewhere in the middle of it, I realized he was taking his time and making love to me. And in the end, it was easily the greatest experience of my life.

Afterward, I was lying there, curled into Dom's side.

"Do you feel alright?" he asked.

"Perfect. Tired, but perfect."

It was the truth. To know that he was prepared to stand by my side when there was a chance that a pregnancy would be difficult to achieve was overwhelming. I knew he was a good man and I never expected he would have been cruel about it, but knowing that us not being together wasn't an option for him solidified it.

"Becoming a librarian is going to be difficult now," I noted.

"There's no rush," he started. "You'll complete your undergraduate in a few months and can apply for the online classes for your master's whenever you feel ready. I'll support you all the way through."

"Two kids will be a lot of work, though. I don't think I'll have the time for work, school, and newborns. I think I'm going to wait until they're a little older before I start my master's."

"We'll have help. Between Kendall, Jojo, and my mom, we'd be covered. You add Colton, Memphis, and my dad into the mix and we won't have to worry about a thing. You could still take classes if you wanted."

I lifted my head and stressed, "No. I'm completely fine with your family showering these two babies with all the love in the world, but I want to raise them. My mother was never there for me and I won't do that to them."

Dom gave me a soft smile. "They are already so lucky to have you."

"Are you alright with that?"

"Am I alright with what?"

"Me remaining a library assistant for the time being," I answered. "I won't be bringing in nearly as much money as I would if I were a librarian and there will be two more mouths to feed. I want to get there and it's important to me that I contribute financially. It's just that it won't be as much as it could be."

Dom carefully shifted us on the bed, so I was on my back and he was up against my side, his head propped up in his hand. "If you decided not to go back to work ever again, I wouldn't care. I can take care of us, Ekko. There's plenty of money already in the bank and Levi pays me well. I don't need to because I've been smart with my money, but I'd work my ass off if I had to just to take care of us and give you every-thing you deserve."

I loved him so much.

I pressed my hand to his chest and said, "Let's work on getting me out of my lease. That apartment was just a place to live. Until now, I haven't ever had a place to call home. Your heart feels a lot like home. And I think I want to stay there a while."

"You're going to stay there forever, sugar."

I grinned at him. "Yeah, I am."

Dom gave me his dimples. Then, he kissed my cheek be-fore moving down and kissing my belly.

"Goodnight, babies," he whispered there. When his face was in front of mine, he kissed me on my lips. He pulled back an inch. His voice was low. "Good night, Ekko. I love you."

"I love you, too."

Dom turned out the light, rolled toward me again, and tucked me tight to his body, my back to his front. We fell asleep with his hand splayed over my abdomen, protecting our babies the only way he could.

EPILOGUE

Ekko

"**I**T LOOKS ADORABLE."

"Are you sure, Kate?"

"Positive. Now, let's get you out of here so you can knock him off his feet."

It was the first Saturday in May and I was nineteen weeks pregnant. I was also a bride. A week after Dom and I found out we were having twins, he proposed to me. Of course, I said yes.

I had assumed we would wait until after the babies were born, but Dom didn't want to wait. I didn't want to be a very pregnant bride, so we compromised with a quick wedding. When his family found out that we were planning to get married within less than three months, his mom went crazy.

"That's not enough time!" his mom panicked.

"It's quick, but we'll help," Kendall chimed in.

Jojo was bursting with excitement, "I'm always up for a reason to have a celebration. This will be so much fun."

Outnumbered, Dom's mother had no choice but to hop on the wagon and dive into the planning with us. To be honest, I didn't need the fancy wedding and I expressed that from the beginning. They respected my wishes, left the big decisions up to me, and took care of a lot of the small details. The problem for me was that I was trying to plan a wedding while I was still working every day and while I was in my first trimester. I was constantly tired and really sick most days.

About a week into my second trimester, I started feeling better, but that was only a month ago. So much of the work for the wedding had already been done. I did wait until that point to go in search of a dress and I took my bridesmaids with me.

I never thought I'd ever have women there to stand by my side if I ever got married. I would have been grateful to have one, but I was fortunate to have four. Elle, Kendall, and Jojo were my bridesmaids; Kate was my maid of honor. She was still with Brett and they, too, had gotten engaged. She wasn't planning to get married until next year, so there was still plenty of time.

When it came to the guys, Dom had so many people he could have asked to stand up for him, but in the end, it was Colton who was his best man while Memphis, Levi, and Lorenzo stood in as his groomsmen.

The day had arrived, and I was finally ready to go see Dom. I decided I wanted us to have an intimate moment together before the actual ceremony, so we arranged to have a 'first-look' done. After Elle enlisted the help of her friend and Lexi's sister-in-law, Nikki, to do my hair and makeup, the girls got me in my dress and were ready to whisk me away to see my groom.

My only concern was my bump. I had started showing a few weeks ago and what I once thought would be cute was now concerning me. The whole reason I wanted to have the wedding sooner rather than later was that I didn't want to be an overly pregnant bride.

I chose a draped satin gown, so while it was very comfortable, it showed every curve of my body. I loved the dress so much when I tried it on because it looked fantastic, but I now had a much larger bump.

I frowned at Kate. "I just think I should have purchased some shapewear or something."

She took me by the hand and gave me a pep talk. "Ekko, you are gorgeous. You've got the most amazing man waiting to see you in your spectacular wedding gown." She put her hand on my belly. "This right here is going to be one of the things he remembers most about this day. Seeing you in this dress, marrying him, while you're carrying the babies the two of you made inside you. That's nothing to be embarrassed about, babe. It's beautiful."

"She's right," Kendall added.

"You are one smokin' hot, mama. My brother is seriously the luckiest man in the world," Jojo chimed in.

"Let's not forget that shapewear is the worst!" Kendall advised. "You'd be so uncomfortable."

Elle came and stood beside me. She wrapped her arm around my waist and assured me, "It would be a mistake to try and hide this, love. And Dom would not like seeing you trying to hide your bump either."

"Okay, I guess we can go then," I agreed.

The girls and I left the bridal suite at the wedding venue and they walked with me down to where I was going to be meeting Dom before our outdoor ceremony.

Our photographer, Emme James Cunningham, would be there to capture the moment for us. During the planning of the wedding, Dom suggested Emme as the photographer. I hadn't known when I met her at Elle's wedding and she was pregnant with twins that it was her profession, but I didn't hesitate to agree to booking her.

Sure enough, I arrived and found that Emme already had Dom facing the opposite direction. The smile on her face grew as she said something to Dom. Emme waved at me to come forward so I kept my eyes on Dom and walked toward him. It was hard to not look at him. He was stunning in his tux, and I was only seeing him from the back.

The closer I got, Emme gave some instruction, but she eventually backed away and took photos from a distance as we had our moment.

I reached out and wrapped my hand around Dom's bicep. He turned around, took one look at me, and lost his composure. Seeing my big, strong, tough guy break down with just that single glance at me made me tear up.

He pulled me into his arms and hugged me tightly. "You look amazing," he whispered in my ear.

I laughed and assured him, "It wasn't this snug when I bought it."

Dom looked in my eyes and smiled at me. "You're beautiful and this dress looks perfect on you."

"Thank you, baby."

He gave me a sweet kiss on the lips before he knelt down in front of me and pressed a kiss to my belly. Every morning when we woke up and every night before we went to sleep, Dom would kiss our babies. He rested his forehead there for a moment and finally stood to take me in his arms again.

"You are the most stunning woman I've ever laid my eyes on."

With my arms around his neck, Dom had lifted me off the ground and spun me around. When he set me back down on my feet, he framed my face with his hands. "I love you so much, Ekko."

"I love you too, Dom."

Dom kissed me again before he urged, "Come on. Let's go get married."

I held on to his arm as he walked me back to where my

girls were waiting for me.

Hours later, I had officially had the best day of my entire life. I was married and happy. Dom and I had a beautiful wedding ceremony followed by a reception, where he truly was the life of the party.

My life was wonderful. It had turned out better than I imagined, better than in the books I'd read. And even though, I'd been kidnapped and nearly killed, I'd survived and came out stronger. I didn't have to worry about my safety either because George and Johnathan were both in prison after having a whole slew of charges thrown at them, the most notable being kidnapping, arson, and attempted murder.

As I sat down to take a break after most of the guests had left, I realized just how wonderful my life was. I'd endured so many tragic life experiences, but in the end, I got my happily-ever-after with the man of my dreams.

"Are you ready to go get our wedding night celebration started, Mrs. Moore?"

"I would love to, Mr. Moore, but my feet hurt."

Dom bent down and scooped me up in his arms. "Looks like I'll have to give you a massage first."

With that, Dom carried me to our room, where we continued to celebrate our love.

Two and a half months later, we bought a bigger home for our family.

At the beginning of October, our precious Hendrix and our darling Grace were born. And just like that, Hank and Gracie became the center of our lives.

ACKNOWLEDGEMENTS

Gosh! How is this my seventh book?!?!

Before releasing Desperate, I decided to make some changes. The Cunningham Security series needed a facelift, so I pulled out all the stops to make it happen. And I'm so honored that I was able to work with some incredibly gifted people to make it happen.

To S.H. - Even though I gave you *nothing* to work with because I have zero artistic ability, you knocked the covers out of the park. I literally cried when I saw them. You are amazingly talented and I'm so excited for many, many more.

To E.M. - You are a rock star! Your feedback on this book was priceless. That email you sent with praises made my year. I appreciate you working to get this in for me even when your schedule was already full. I promise to send lots of lip balm for all your troubles!

To S.B. - My books are so pretty now! :heart eyes: Thank you for doing what you do because I have zero patience (and talent) for it. Can't wait for more!

To J.E. - My husband, my lover. You are the very definition of hard work and perseverance. Even after you spend your days working long hours to support our family, you still put in a hundred percent at home. Thanks for making me breakfast every morning as well as lunch and dinner on the weekends. I'm so lucky that you rarely let me get hangry. I love you.

To J.E. & J.E. - My two beautiful boys. There are not enough words in the world for me to tell you the lengths I'd go to give you the very best life has to offer. I only hope I'm succeeding. I will love you both forever.

To M.B. - Even through a move from one coast to the other, you still managed to read Desperate and give me your input. When I needed to take this project in a different route, you supported me all the way and I know how rare it is to find that. Thank you for showing me that there are still some genuinely good people left in the world.

To N, KP, JC, and the rest of the Inkslinger team - Thank you!! If it were for everything you all do, day in and day out, this would hardly be possible. Thank you for allowing me to be part of such a wonderful family of authors.

To my ARC Team Members - I love you girls! I'm not sure I can tell you just how much your support means to me. And with each book I release, I find myself growing more and more attached to you. I can't wait to give you all the spotlight. It's coming!!

To the book bloggers - I haven't met most of you, but you still take the time to share my work. Saying 'thank you' hardly feels like enough when I know that if it weren't for you, my stories wouldn't reach nearly as many readers. Book bloggers could totally rule the world!

To my loyal readers - What is an author without readers? I am because you are. Thank you.

OTHER BOOKS BY A.K. EVANS

The Everything Series

Everything I Need

Everything I Have

Everything I Want

Everything I Love

The Cunningham Security Series

Obsessed

Overcome

Desperate

Solitude

Burned

Unworthy

Surrender (Coming November 2019)

Betrayed (Coming February 2020)

Revived (Coming June 2020)

Road Trip Romance Series

Tip the Scales (Coming October 2019)

Play the Part (Coming December 2019)

CONNECT WITH A.K. EVANS

To stay connected with A.K. Evans and receive all the first looks at upcoming releases, latest news, or to simply follow along on her journey, be sure to add or follow her on social media. You can also get the scoop by signing up for the website newsletter.

The newsletter is delivered once a month, sometimes twice, and includes a monthly giveaway. Be sure to sign up:on my website.

Website: www.authorakevans.com

Facebook: www.facebook.com/authorAKEvans

Facebook Reader Group: www.facebook.com/groups/1285069088272037

Instagram: www.instagram.com/authorakevans

Twitter: twitter.com/AuthorAKEvans

Goodreads Author Page: www.goodreads.com/user/show/64525877-a-k-evans

Subscribe on YouTube: bit.ly2w01yb7

ABOUT A.K. EVANS

A.K. Evans is a married mother of two boys residing in a small town in northeastern Pennsylvania. After graduating from Lafayette College in 2004 with two degrees (one in English and one in Economics & Business), she pursued a career in the insurance and financial services industry. Not long after, Evans realized the career was not for her. She went on to manage her husband's performance automotive business and drive the shop race cars for the next thirteen years. While the business afforded her freedoms she wouldn't necessarily have had in a typical 9-5 job, after eleven years she was no longer receiving personal fulfillment from her chosen career path. Following many discussions, lots of thought, and tons of encouragement, Andrea decided to pursue her dream of becoming a writer.

Between her day job, writing, and homeschooling her two boys, Evans is left with very little free time. When she finds scraps of spare time, Evans enjoys reading, doing yoga, watching NY Rangers hockey, dancing, and vacationing with her family. Andrea, her husband, and her children are currently working on taking road trips to visit all 50 states (though, Alaska and Hawaii might require flights).

Made in the USA
Columbia, SC
29 March 2021